D0559694

SHAMUS
IN THE GREEN ROOM

ALSO BY SUSAN KANDEL

Not a Girl Detective

I Dreamed I Married Perry Mason

SHAMUS
IN THE GREEN ROOM

SUSAN KANDEL

WILLIAM MORROW
An Imprint of HarperCollins*Publishers*

HICKSVILLE PUBLIC LIBRARY
169 JERUSALEM AVENUE
HICKSVILLE, NY 11801

This book is a work of fiction. The characters, incidents, and dialogue are drawn from the author's imagination and are not to be construed as real. Any resemblance to actual events or persons, living or dead, is entirely coincidental.

SHAMUS IN THE GREEN ROOM. Copyright © 2006 by Susan Kandel. All rights reserved. Printed in the United States of America. No part of this book may be used or reproduced in any manner whatsoever without written permission except in the case of brief quotations embodied in critical articles and reviews. For information address HarperCollins Publishers, 10 East 53rd Street, New York, NY 10022.

HarperCollins books may be purchased for educational, business, or sales promotional use. For information please write: Special Markets Department, HarperCollins Publishers, 10 East 53rd Street, New York, NY 10022.

FIRST EDITION

Designed by Jeffrey Pennington

Printed on acid-free paper

Library of Congress Cataloging-in-Publication Data

Kandel, Susan, 1961–
    Shamus in the Green Room: a Cece Caruso mystery / Susan Kandel.—1st ed.
        p. cm.
    ISBN-13: 978-0-06-058109-1
    ISBN-10: 0-06-058109-3 (alk. paper)
        1. Women biographers—Fiction.   2. Hollywood (Los Angeles, Calif.)—Fiction.   3. Motion picture industry—Fiction.   I. Title.

PS3611.A53S26 2006
813'.6—dc22   2005044383

06 07 08 09 10 WBC/QWF 10 9 8 7 6 5 4 3 2 1

HKASVILLE PUBLIC LIBRARY
1601 BERKSALEM AVENUE
HKASVILLE, NY 11801

To Peter

ACKNOWLEDGMENTS

Thanks, as always, to my sage editor, Carolyn Marino, and superlative agent, Sandy Dijkstra, as well as to the dedicated people in their offices, in particular Taryn Fagerness and Samantha Hagerbaumer.

Thanks are also due to Deborah Michel and Didi Dunphy for their support and plot-tuning expertise; Captain David Campbell of the Los Angeles Coroner's Office, who showed me around the place and indulged my many questions; Don Herron, whose Dashiell Hammett Walking Tour of San Francisco was as spellbinding as I'd always heard; and the impassioned William P. Arney, current resident of 891 Post, Sam Spade's apartment, recently designated a literary landmark.

There are many excellent resources on Hammett's life and work. Of particular use were Julian Symons's *Dashiell Hammett;* Jo Hammett's *Dashiell Hammett: A Daughter Remembers;*

Richard Layman's *Shadow Man: The Life of Dashiell Hammett;* and Diane Johnson's *Dashiell Hammett: A Life.*

I could never forget Lawrence Block.

Margaret Waite introduced me to Palos Verdes and to the real Maren, who shares nothing with her fictional counterpart.

My husband indoctrinated me into the cult of Hammett and got me up on a surfboard. This book is for him.

SHAMUS
IN THE GREEN ROOM

CHAPTER ONE

Playing it cool wasn't in my repertoire, but that didn't mean I couldn't fake it.

I leaned against my silver Camry, ran my fingers through my hair, and laughed insouciantly.

"You're kidding, right?" asked my best friend, Lael.

"Ooh," said my daughter, Annie. "You probably shouldn't have worn white."

I swatted at a bee while trying to remember the last time I'd gone to a car wash.

"Bees love perfume," yelled my second-best friend, Bridget, who was walking up the path toward my house. "And I can smell yours from here."

"Isn't this exciting?" asked my neighbor Lois, of no one in particular. "Don't lose your place in line, now," she chided her twin sister, Marlene, who was placing a can of cat food in the driveway for the local strays. The bees headed her way, favoring

savory salmon over spicy Oriental notes. "It isn't every day that
Cece has a gentleman caller."

My fiancé, Peter Gambino, glowered at her.

"For the last time, he's not a gentleman caller." I twisted
around to brush the dust off my fur-trimmed wool pencil skirt
(Pierre Balmain, 1959)—which was *ivory,* not white, and
hardly designed for such maneuvers. "It's business. He's hired
me for the week."

"We've seen *Pretty Woman,*" said Marlene in a hushed tone.

Oh, they were evil, my friends and family, of which there
suddenly seemed to be far too many. I lifted up my Jackie O
sunglasses and frowned at the lot of them, lined up so inno-
cently on the front lawn of my house. Not for the first time was
I struck by the morphological similarity between welcoming
committees and firing squads. Poor man didn't know what he
was in for.

"Cece needs a lint brush," said my son-in-law, Vincent.

Like they cared.

"Do I have time to change?" I wondered out loud.

Eight people consulted watches.

"It's one minute to ten," cautioned Hilda, my gardener
Javier's thirteen-year-old niece.

Five people hoisted cameras.

"Promptness is the politesse of kings," said Lois, bending
down to wipe some grime off her scuffed patent leather pump.
I'd have gone for the stain on her dressing gown, which looked
like motor oil.

Three people clutched autograph books.

"How about one of those cookies?" Bridget asked Lael, who
slapped her outstretched hand.

Two women wiped lipstick off their teeth.

One little boy burped.

"Good job," said Vincent, his father, at the very same moment that Rafe Simic, world-famous movie star, he of the rippling biceps and laid-back attitude, pulled up in front of the house and hit a fire hydrant, sending a torrent of L.A. municipal water high up into the air.

"Water," said Alexander, enraptured.

"Actors," said Gambino under his breath. "Get a real job."

The flashbulbs went off as Rafe stepped out of something shiny, green, and foreign. Hitching up his jeans, which were riding low on his slim hips, he ambled around to inspect the front fender. Not even a scratch. He strode toward me through a shimmering scrim of water, like the Southern California born-and-bred Neptune he was.

I met him halfway.

Nothing fazes Cece Caruso.

"I've been meaning to get a new hydrant," I said.

He brushed a strand of blond hair out of his depthless blue eyes, which I barely even noticed. The smile I did notice. It moved slowly, like molasses.

"Hold on, you got something there." He plucked some oleander out of my long, brown hair and handed it to me.

Nothing good happens when you refuse a gift from the gods.

"I'll take that," said Annie, who had been in love with Rafe Simic since we'd moved to L.A. when she was still a little kid.

"Your sister?" Rafe asked, looking at me.

"Her daughter," said Annie, overenunciating each syllable. She tucked the blossom into the pocket of her overalls.

"I was a child bride," I explained.

"And now the matriarch of the clan," said Gambino,

grabbing three-year-old Alexander from his father and wielding him as proof.

That wasn't aggressive. Not exactly.

"Peter Gambino," he said, tucking Alexander under his arm sideways and sticking out his hand. "LAPD."

That was aggressive.

Little Alexander freed himself and scrambled over to Annie. "Tummy hurts," he said, though it sounded like "twoots." He had a Jolly Rancher in his mouth.

"We're leaving, sweetheart," Annie replied. "Have a good time in San Francisco." She looked at me pointedly. "Oleander is poisonous, you know."

"Yes, dear," I responded, kissing her cheek.

Rafe posed for a picture with Annie before she left. From there, he worked his way down the line. He had a profound effect upon the womenfolk. Hilda's mouth was hanging so far open I could see the food stuck in her braces. My neighbors Lois and Marlene, former showgirls now in their dotage (and I do mean dotage), were openly salivating, having forgotten entirely about my virtue.

"I've been enjoying your biography of Dashiell Hammett," Rafe said to me once Lois released her death grip. "It's taking a while, though." He laughed self-consciously. "But there's lots of useful stuff."

"Useful is as useful does," said Marlene, who handed him her tattered autograph book. "I have Fanny Brice in there."

"Cool."

"When he was a Pinkerton detective," I interjected, "Hammett investigated Nicky Arnstein, Fanny Brice's husband. You know, from *Funny Girl*?"

Rafe looked at me blankly.

"I'm really glad we're starting in San Francisco," I continued, undeterred. "You'll enjoy seeing the places I talk about in my book. The offices where Hammett worked his cases, the restaurants Sam Spade liked to eat at."

"I've been working with a nutritionist," he interrupted. "Her name is Siri."

"Excuse me?"

"Well, Hammett was so thin."

"He suffered all his life from TB," I said.

"Oh. Maybe you don't know." Rafe wrinkled his brow. "I'm not a method actor. I know Hammett liked hash browns, but Siri recommends avoiding potatoes."

"Potatoes," said Lael, scoffing. "Boring. Sweets are the thing." She handed Rafe a freshly baked snickerdoodle.

"Lael is my dearest friend and a master pastry chef," I explained.

"Freelance," she said, fingering her baby-fine blond hair. "Available day or night."

"Incorrigible girl," I said. She had four kids by four different fathers, no mean feat. "What time's our plane again?"

"Noon," said Rafe, checking his watch. "We should go."

Gambino was at the end of the line. He swept me into his arms and kissed me like he really meant it.

"I love you, too," I said, amused.

"Don't leave your heart in San Francisco," Lois warned as we ducked under the canopy of still-spurting water.

"Tony Bennett," murmured her twin, a faraway look in her eyes. "What a beautiful man."

Looking directly at Gambino, Rafe called out, "Somebody better call the Department of Water and Power."

My fiancé gave the movie star a thin-lipped smile.

I AM THIRTY-NINE YEARS OLD, LIVE IN WEST Hollywood, California, and make my living, such as it is, writing biographies of dead mystery writers. How I segued from being the tallest Miss Asbury Park, New Jersey, on record to that particular line of work is a long and only sporadically uplifting story involving an unsophisticated girl with big hair and the double-dealing preppie who preyed upon her, got her pregnant, married her, put her to work supporting his lackluster academic career, and cheated on her until she wised up and left him—but that's for another day.

Today's story is a happier one, about how that girl (who would be me), a die-hard mystery fan since she discovered Nancy Drew at the age of eleven, wound up confounding her English professor ex by writing a book about the author Dashiell Hammett. Not just any book, but a book that was still in print ten years later (unlike a certain bloated tome about James Fenimore Cooper, published by a third-tier university press), a book that actually made money (ditto), a book that had been optioned for the movies. Which is where Rafe Simic comes in.

Eight years ago I received a generous check from his production company, In the Green Room. They loved my book. They had plans for it—big plans. They'd rechristened it *Dash!* Rangy writer as tough-guy hero! It had prestige project written all over it.

As it turned out, however, *Dash!* went straight into turnaround while Rafe got rich and famous playing a succession of skate punks, ski bums, spies, mystics, and stoners. Go figure.

What I didn't know then was that Hollywood has its own inscrutable logic, a calculus of inestimable precision. The planets must be in alignment. The agents and development people, too. It was never the right time. Not, that is, until last year, when Rafe didn't get so much as a Golden Globe nod for his critically acclaimed role as a gay hustler on the run.

It was time to get serious.

And this was the role—the dual role—of a lifetime: Dashiell Hammett and the iconic detective he created, Sam Spade.

There was only one problem: Rafe didn't like to read. Not even the newspaper. Reading gave him a headache. He preferred to meditate. To climb tall mountains. To scuba dive. To parasail. Maybe it was the attention-deficit hyperactivity disorder. Or growing up in Palos Verdes, where it was so pretty outdoors. Which made the prospect of his playing a tubercular autodidact whose only sport was drinking somewhat daunting.

Red Harvest, The Dain Curse, The Maltese Falcon, The Glass Key, The Thin Man—nope, Rafe hadn't tackled a single one of the five novels. He did skim one of the Continental Op stories, "Zigzags of Treachery" (1924), mostly because the title reminded him of his experiences surfing Waimea Bay. Once, fleeing paparazzi, he hid in a video store and came out with the DVD of John Huston's *The Maltese Falcon,* but in the end refused to watch it for fear of being influenced by Bogie's portrayal of Spade. He loved the *Thin Man* movies, like most everybody except Hammett himself, who loathed them. I suppose cable television was good for something: one rainy Sunday, his yoga class canceled, Rafe caught the second half of *Julia,* the Jane Fonda movie about playwright Lillian Hellman,

Hammett's longtime girlfriend, who stood by him when he was imprisoned as an uncooperative witness during the McCarthy era. And that, I'm afraid, was the sum total of this would-be Golden Globe–winning actor's research into his character.

I'd learned all this just a few days ago, after receiving a call from Will Levander, Rafe's longtime manager and business partner. Will was in a panic. Principal shooting for *Dash!* was to commence in exactly three weeks. The script was ambitious. The director, young and cocky. The prosthetic nose for Lillian Hellman, a marvel. And then there was Rafe, who seemed to think looking good in a snap-brim hat and trench coat was all that was required of him.

He thought Pinkertons were a breed of dog.

When all seemed lost, however, Will had had an inspiration: *I* was his inspiration. I could spend two weeks with Rafe. I could be his own personal talking cure.

"I'm not a therapist!" I protested.

"I'll compensate you as if you were," Will replied.

That shut me right up.

"Rafe's therapist gets a hundred and fifty an hour, and she's full of shit. How about I pay you ten thousand for two weeks' work?"

I gasped at that point.

"You're a tough negotiator. Twenty thousand."

No wonder it costs ten bucks to go to the movies these days. I thought it was the unions.

"Look," he went on, "all you need to do is talk to Rafe about the books, about Hammett, his shattered health, writer's block, the whole creative thing. The twenties and speakeasies.

McCarthyism, the fifties. It's no biggie. Just let him soak up your knowledge. Pick your brain."

Nice metaphors. No wonder I felt violated. But I guess that was Hollywood. Which is how I found myself cruising down the 405 toward LAX with a man who'd set box-office records on three continents.

I gave him a sidelong glance.

He was dressed down in an army jacket, faded T-shirt, and grubby sandals, but god had blessed him in ways no Birkenstock could conceal. I pretended to be adjusting my midnight-blue suede pumps and looked again. He caught my eye but didn't so much as flinch. I suppose he was used to gawkers. I wondered how long it'd been since he'd gone out to dinner and not had the person at the next table watch him eat. I hated it when people watched me eat. But nobody really wanted to watch me eat.

"Cece."

"Rafe."

"Talk to me. I'm getting bored here," he said.

"Do you know what a speakeasy is?"

"A what? I can't hear you with all this wind."

The key would be taking it slow.

A brunette in a Porsche convertible put on some speed and veered alarmingly close.

"Oh, no," he muttered.

"Rafe Simic!" she screamed, grabbing on to her pink cowboy hat, which was about to blow off her head. "I love you!"

"I love you, too," shouted a guy with a cancerous tan coming up on our other side. He drove a black Jeep, which had a license plate that read "RDY2RCK."

Rafe smiled, then merged into the diamond lane.

"Rough life," I said loudly.

"I can't complain," he shouted back.

"Do you have that effect on everyone?"

He said something I couldn't hear. "What?" I bellowed.

"YOU SHOULD TALK!"

Gambino had told me to change. But I loved the way the ivory skirt looked with my black sweater with the bat-wing sleeves. The effect was very Anouk Aimée (Bridget's idea, by the way; she owned On the Bias, L.A.'s top vintage-clothing shop, and counseled me on all my purchases). Still, this was business, like I kept telling people who didn't believe me.

We exited at La Tijera.

"Listen." I straightened up in my seat. "There'll be none of that nonsense." I sounded like my mother.

"Sorry," he said, not looking very. Probably didn't get much practice. "A pattern set in childhood."

"What, flirting?" He must get away with murder, this guy.

"Falling in love with my teachers. Miss Horton, seventh grade. She was older but wiser."

"I hate to break it to you," I said, "but I'm not older."

"You are wiser."

This was true.

There was a scar running down Rafe's right cheek. I'd never noticed it onscreen. Nobody ever noticed Joan Crawford's freckles either. It's amazing what they can do with makeup. Not that Rafe needed any, trust me. The scar only heightened his beauty. It was like when Native American basket weavers put in a mistake on purpose.

Oh, I was a fine one for self-righteousness.

We turned left on Airport, at the See's Candies sign, which

proclaimed that one-pound boxes were now available at every terminal. God bless America. There were plenty of spaces in the short-term lot. We parked the car and walked across the tunnel, straight down to the United Airlines first class check-in, where they were waiting for us. There were effusive greetings all around. After a delightful exchange with a Mr. Hess, we were whisked up to the second floor by a Mrs. Price, who tried in vain to maintain her poise. Interesting how nobody minded when she instructed us to cut to the front of the security line.

This town loves its celebrities.

Ensconced in the Red Carpet Club adjacent to gate 71B, we ordered champagne—well, he did and I followed suit, though what I probably needed was a cold shower.

"To the Golden Gate Bridge," said Rafe, knocking back half the glass.

"To Alcatraz," I said, feeling giddy against my will.

"To Fisherman's Wharf," he said.

"To City Lights bookstore."

"To . . ."

No, not everyone loves a challenge.

"Crusty sourdough!" he finally blurted out.

A phalanx of small, quiet men suddenly materialized, bearing a complimentary fruit-and-cheese plate. "We're warming the bread right now, sir," said the boldest.

"Whatever you want, whenever you want it," I said, shaking my head. "Is that really the way you live?"

They were calling our flight now.

He grabbed both our bags and grinned at me. "Don't say you wouldn't if you could."

Either I was transparent or he was one smart dumb blond.

CHAPTER TWO

The cabbie driving us into the city had a buzz cut and lines on the back of his neck that resembled a tic-tac-toe board. I knew what had generated the vertical axes. That would be chatting up his captives.

"Lots of conventions this weekend," he said, turning his head sharply to the right. "Gourmet foods, action figures, skiwear."

Rafe was unzipping his duffel bag.

The cabbie turned his head again. He had an unusual profile. "Hotels are pretty much booked up. Even in the Tenderloin, folks, and that ain't pretty."

"I hope I didn't forget my lucky cap," muttered Rafe, going through his things. "I think I left it at Siri's."

"Who?" I asked.

"My nutritionist. Remember?"

"You got your hookers, your druggies, your homeless population," the cabbie informed us.

"Found it." Rafe put on the lucky cap.

The guy jerked his head sideways. It was the juxtaposition of flat nose and prominent chin that was so unlikely. "That a Dodgers cap? This is Barry Bonds's town, buddy. Better be careful."

"Nasty dude," said Rafe. "I played golf with him once. Charity tournament."

We rode for a while in silence. The cabbie put on light jazz just before the off-ramp.

"You two are awfully quiet." This time, when he turned around, he bumped the cab directly in front of us.

"Watch it there, pal!" Rafe grabbed on to me so I wouldn't go flying into the plastic barrier designed to protect the cabbie from us, and how ironic that was.

"I know the guy," the cabbie said, nodding. "We got the same insurance provider."

"Oh, good," I said.

"So where you folks from?"

"Los Angeles," Rafe said.

"Honeymooners, right?"

"Right," Rafe answered, sliding close.

"Wrong." The vinyl squeaked as I pushed him away. Must be the new perfume. Too much musk.

"Trouble in paradise? You'll patch things up this weekend. San Francisco"—the cabbie kissed his fingers to his lips—"is all about romance."

A saxophone wailed on KKSF, its notes as sinuous as the fog blanketing the Golden Gate Bridge. I had to admit it was romantic.

Rafe checked his cell phone for messages.

"You still have those smog alerts there in Los Angeles? I

was visiting once in 1975, and we couldn't even leave the motel."

"Smog gets such a bad rap," I said to Rafe.

"Sorry, what were you saying?" he asked.

"If there was no smog, we wouldn't have those beautiful pink-and-orange sunsets. It has to do with the particulate matter in the sky."

Rafe put his phone back in his pocket. "I thought it had to do with auto emissions."

The cabbie guffawed unbecomingly.

I missed Gambino already. But this was a job. And I needed the money.

Last month, little Alexander's mother, Roxana (a flake), had split with her new husband, Dave (a Christian rocker), and basically abandoned Alexander to the care of his father (Vincent), and Vincent's wife (who would be my daughter, Annie). Roxana was moving to Bali to study the ancient art of healing. No comment. And Annie and Vincent, who hadn't even been informed of Alexander's existence until he was close to two, were convinced she was never coming back. Apparently, there was a Balinese boyfriend, poor fool.

Anyway, while Annie and Vincent were thrilled by the prospect of raising Alexander, whom they loved dearly, they were worried about making ends meet. They were creative types (Annie was a set decorator; Vincent, a comic-book artist) and their resources were limited, which is why I needed the money. Annie and Vincent didn't know it, but my Rafe Simic windfall was going directly to them. I'd already informed my accountant, Mr. Keshigian, who was delighted I'd be receiving the annual gift-tax exclusion, not to mention significantly reducing my taxable income for the year.

"We're here," said Rafe, interrupting my thoughts. "Let's dump these bags and I'll mike you."

"Mike me?" I said, stepping out of the cab. I handed him his keys, which dangled from a Playboy-bunny key ring. "You left these on the seat, by the way."

The valet looked like a bouncer at a nightclub. "Welcome to the Clift, Mr. Simic." He took the bags and handed Rafe a claim check. "Good afternoon to you, too, miss. These will be in your rooms when you're ready."

"Thank you." I turned back to Rafe. "What did you mean, 'mike me'?"

"Don't worry. There's a release form."

"What are you talking about?"

There was a sudden ruckus across the street.

"Oh, shit," Rafe said. "I was hoping we could avoid this." He yanked the cab door open. "Get back in. Now!"

We pulled away from the curb with a screeching of tires.

The cabbie put the meter back on with a flourish.

His head was whipping around now in full *Exorcist* mode. And I had no Advil.

THERE MAY HAVE BEEN MORE LEISURELY WAYS to see the sights of San Francisco. But given that we were being chased by three photographers hanging out of a Lincoln Navigator, speed was paramount.

"Try to lose them," said Rafe. "There's a hundred bucks in it for you."

Amazing he could say that with a straight face.

"Good car, the Navigator," the cabbie said as we tore past a fleet of tour buses parked along Union Square. "But nobody can put pedal to the medal like I can! Name's Declan Chan." He indicated his license. It was a flattering picture. "And yes, I'm Irish."

"But isn't this Chinatown?" asked Rafe, as we sped up Grant, through a pair of ornate red gates inscribed with the word "Chinatown."

"Sure is," he replied. "Look down Ross Alley, folks. Every day two little old ladies make twenty thousand fortune cookies by hand down there. The conveyor belt looks like it's made of miniature waffle irons! Oops!"

He slammed on the brakes and I fell into Rafe's lap. "Would you turn around, please!" I yelled. "You should be watching the road!"

"I've got eyes in the back of my head. Our pursuers are still behind us, but I got plans."

We zigzagged up and down the narrow streets, past street-lights sculpted to look like golden dragons, cages filled with lit-tle turtles and squawking chickens, and pseudo antiques shops stuffed with pseudo antiques.

I thought of Hammett's fat, bald detective, the Continental Op. He said somewhere that if he never had to visit China-town again, it would be soon enough.

"Look out!" cried Rafe, who was starting to enjoy himself.

We swerved to avoid a line of children following their teacher, who was waving a tissue-paper phoenix mounted on a tall stick.

"Just like the movies, folks. It's always Chinese New Year!"

"Sorry," Rafe said, leaning into me. "This kind of thing happens to me a lot. You sort of get used to it after a while. I hope you're not too freaked out."

"It's pedal to the *metal*," I said under my breath. "With a *t*."

"Excuse me?" Declan Chan speaking.

"I didn't say anything."

"We're going over to Lombard now," he said, pulling a quick right. "And I would say that's gonna do it."

We pulled to a stop at the top of a treacherous slope. Lombard was famous for being the steepest, crookedest street in the city.

"Why are we stopping?" I asked.

"Sun Tzu's *The Art of War*. 'We apprise the enemy of our move so that he may more thoroughly fear us.'"

I wheeled around in my seat just in time to see the Navigator take off in the other direction. One look at the bumper-to-bumper traffic going down the hill had done it. So the guy was some sort of sage after all.

"Congratulations," said Rafe, handing him a crisp one-hundred-dollar bill.

"Thank you, sir. At this point, if I may be so bold, I'd suggest you walk down to Leavenworth. It'll be twenty minutes in the cab otherwise, not that I'm not enjoying your company."

"Leavenworth!" I exclaimed. "Hammett lived on Leavenworth!" Now it was my turn to get excited. "The San Loretto Apartments. That's where he finished writing *The Maltese Falcon*. Then he took off for New York with his girlfriend Nell Martin. He dedicated *The Maltese Falcon* to his wife, Jose, but *The Glass Key* went to Nell."

"Stop right there," Rafe said. He slipped something around my neck as we got out of the cab. "You're good for ninety minutes. Start over. I want to get every word."

And thus, with a Sony mini-microphone, was I granted immortality.

CHAPTER THREE

It was alarming how easily I went into full-lecture mode. I suppose that's what comes of having lived with a professor. My ex could pontificate on any subject, any time of day or night, regardless of whether or not he knew a thing about it: James Fenimore Cooper—that goes without saying; the chemical properties of laundry detergent; the history of religious cults; the origins of flypaper. We met when he was a grad student at Princeton and I was a senior at Asbury Park High, waiting tables at D'Amico's Pizza, on the boardwalk. I dazzled him with my black Spandex pants. He dazzled me with his knowledge of pizza toppings around the globe. Which just goes to show—well, I guess that's pretty obvious.

In Australia, by the way, they prefer fried eggs to pepperoni.

Rafe and I spent the rest of the afternoon walking and talking. I started at the beginning, with Hammett's childhood in Baltimore, cut short when he left school in 1908, at fourteen, to help his struggling father. He was never to return. For the next six years, he held half a dozen odd jobs. He worked as a stevedore, a messenger, a freight clerk. He operated a nail machine in a box factory. And he screwed up every time, which was the part of the story Rafe seemed to relate to.

While we ate ham-and-cheese sandwiches on a bench outside the public library, he regaled me with his own tales of youthful ineptitude.

There was his stint as a junior lifeguard, when a five-year-old girl almost drowned on his watch; the time he worked as a stock boy at a hardware store and was fired for roughhousing; his experience working construction his junior year of high school. Things were going well with the construction job until he realized the foreman was a con artist in search of apprentices.

"Once he saw I was useless hauling bricks," Rafe said between bites, "he kept me in the office with him, you know, filing stuff. But I screwed up with that, too. Finally, he tried me on the phones and he liked my smooth manner, or something like that."

The first of many, I supposed.

"He taught me everything he knew," Rafe continued. "One of his favorite scams was account boosting. Ever heard of it?"

"No," I replied.

"Federal Express introduced overnight delivery in 1981. It was a red-letter day for crooks."

"I don't get it."

"You get a credit card, charge up some stuff, then overpay by overnight delivery with a stolen check. When the payment exceeds the balance, you boost the credit line. Under federal law, banks have to post card payments before checks clear and so they have no choice but to credit your account. The next day you go to a bank machine and withdraw the excess on the card. Later, of course, the check bounces, but you're out long before that." Rafe stopped to take a breath. His eyes were aglow.

"You played a con artist in one of your movies," I said. "*Blue Sky in the Dark,* right? I rented it. You were excellent. I thought you were a good guy up to the very end."

"You think I'm kidding," he said with a grin. "I'm insulted."

"Don't be. I don't take a lot of people seriously."

We packed up our trash and tossed it in the can.

"You're not getting off that easy," he said. "My honor is at stake. Follow me."

He dragged me across the street to a tire store, stuck his head into the office, then pulled me farther down the block.

"What exactly are we looking for?" I asked.

"This is it."

We stopped outside a beat-up little storefront.

"I guarantee nobody's gonna know me in here," he said gleefully.

"Why should that matter?" I asked, getting nervous.

The flickering neon sign in the window read: IKE'S WINES AND SPIRITS, CA. 1941.

"The art of the short change," Rafe announced as the bell on the door chimed.

There was a large woman working the register, her head buried in a book. It was the St. James Bible.

"Don't do this, Rafe," I whispered, tugging at his shirt. "Look at what she's reading."

"I'll take two Reese's peanut butter cups," he said, grabbing a couple of Halloween-size candies from the jar beside her.

The woman looked up. Her head was ornamented with half a dozen pink hair curlers. "Seventy-five cents, sir."

Rafe handed her a ten.

I faked flipping through magazines while she rang it up. *Redbook. Self. Glamour.* He wasn't going to win a Golden Globe, he was going to be making license plates.

"Twenty-five cents makes a dollar," the woman began.

Rafe pocketed the quarter and turned to go.

"No, no!" she said, stopping him. "I'm not done here."

Rafe walked back to the counter, where she started slapping ones at him.

"That's two, three, four, one is five, five is ten."

"Thanks." Rafe gave her one of his high-wattage smiles. Oblivious, she went back to her reading.

"Are we done now?" I asked, relieved.

"You know what?" Rafe said, abruptly turning on his heel. "I don't really want all these dollars. Could I trouble you, ma'am, for a ten for five and five ones?"

Shit.

He walked back to the register, keys jangling in his pocket. The woman handed him a ten and he handed her the five and the fistful of ones she'd just given him.

"Listen, can you count that, make sure I gave you the right change?" He chuckled. "I've never been great with math."

She rolled her eyes. "Sure, I can do that. It's not like I have anything better to do."

She counted the bills, then scratched her head, careful not to disturb the curlers. "There's only nine here. You owe me another dollar."

Shit, shit, shit.

Rafe looked at her from between narrowed lids. "You have nine there, right?"

"Uh-huh." Her lids, dusted with pale green eyeshadow, narrowed, too.

"Tell you what, let me give you eleven more," he said, digging into his pocket for another single, "and I'll take a twenty."

She took the bills he offered, then snatched a twenty from the drawer and put it into the palm of his outstretched hand.

"Have a nice day," she said with finality.

"You, too," he replied.

Once we were outside, I turned on him. "What is wrong with you, Rafe?"

"C'mon. It's not like she was particularly nice."

"You want one of those photographers to get a picture of you committing petty larceny? You just stole that woman's money!"

"Good eye," he noted. "You're not going to rat me out, are you?"

"We're finished," I said, peeling off the microphone. "I quit."

"You quit?"

"You heard me."

"Cece. Slow down." He took me by the arms. "I was just showing off. Jeez."

He led me back into Ike's, where he confessed his so-called error to the woman, who was restocking the beef jerky. Glaring openly at him now, she slammed down a canister of Slim Jims and walked back to her register to check out his story.

"Well, I'll be damned," she said, blinking a few times. "I suppose I should thank you for being honest. More than most people can manage."

Rafe the choirboy said, "It's the way I was raised."

"God bless the mothers," she intoned, closing the register drawer.

We headed down Larkin in silence. Finally, I said, " 'A little knowledge is a dangerous thing.' "

He turned to me. "Bacardi in a wineglass."

I raised an eyebrow. "Sam Spade's drink. You've been doing your homework."

"I'm not so bad, really. Can we just move on? Please?"

"I'm thinking about it."

"I shouldn't have done that back there." Contrite he did rather well.

"No, you shouldn't have." Holier-than-thou I did better.

"I apologize." He did sound sincere.

"Let's just get to Hammett and the Pinkertons," I said.

"Which are not dogs."

"Which are not dogs. Which are detectives. Keep going."

We were in the Tenderloin now, usually described as the worst part of the city. It didn't seem all that different from West Hollywood. Outside the Phoenix Hotel, which had a massive plaster Buddha mounted on its flat roof, a homeless man waved a sign in my face: THE END OF THE WORLD IS NIGH. A toothless guy hanging out in a doorway asked if he could take me with him to Chicago. The usual stuff. Local color.

" 'We Never Sleep' was the Pinkerton motto," Rafe said. "Their logo was a big, unblinking eye. They predated J. Edgar Hoover's FBI, and functioned as a private security agency operating across state lines to try and protect good people from bad ones. Their watchwords were 'anonymity, morality, and objectivity.' How am I doing so far?"

"Better than I would have guessed." I filled in the blanks. "Hammett answered a vaguely worded ad in a Baltimore paper in 1915 and spent the next seven years, off and on, traveling America as a Pinkerton operative. That experience is what made him unique among pulp writers. He was a real-life tough guy. He had a dent in his head from being hit by a brick when he bungled a tailing job. He had the broken-off tip of a knife embedded in the heel of his hand. He taught his daughters how to break a handhold by pinching back the little finger. And knife scars? He had them up and down his legs."

Scars.

My gaze went involuntarily to Rafe's cheek. His hand found the spot, as if he'd just been slapped.

"I'm sorry," I said. "God, I'm so rude."

"It's okay." There was an uncomfortable pause. "Surfing accident when I was a kid. Got knocked under, didn't know which way was up. I was lucky, I guess. Broke my arm, got scraped up on the rocks a little, that was it. I'm not exactly a tough guy." He smiled sheepishly. "But I play one in the movies."

You are here to dispense information, I said to myself, not the other way around. Not to swap life stories. Not to make friends. "The Pinkerton experience was vital for Hammett," I said too loudly. "Every one of his characters was based on someone he encountered while working as an operative. Except Sam Spade. Spade was an original."

"I thought Spade was Hammett," Rafe said.

"Hammett was a detective, but Spade was a dream detective. Smart, fearless, a little bit cruel." A blond Satan. That's how Hammett described him. All sharp edges. Even his hair came to a point on his forehead. Rafe was going to need some fancy barber. "We're here, by the way."

"Where's here?" Rafe asked.

"Post Street, 891."

We stopped outside a four-story redbrick building at the corner of Hyde and Post, built in the teens, pretty much nondescript, with a Chinese laundry on the ground floor.

"This," I said, gesturing dramatically, "is the place Hammett lived when he created Sam Spade. Before Nell Martin. He lived here with his family. Apartment 401." I pointed to the top, right-hand corner. "It's also Sam Spade's apartment in *The Maltese Falcon*. The novel provides all the clues."

"Cool."

"And we're going inside." I pushed as many of the forty-six buzzers as I could cover with my open hand.

Rafe looked at me admiringly.

"Now don't do that," I said. "This is a pedagogical exercise. I'm a professional here."

"Of course," he said slyly. "It's not like you're showing off or anything."

I tapped my foot. "Somebody's going to let us in."

"Yes?" said a female voice.

I smiled triumphantly. "Delivery."

The buzzer sounded.

The lobby was large and airy, with a couple of potted palms in one corner and an extraordinary pressed-tin ceiling, unfortunately painted glossy white. I pulled open the elevator's folding brass grill and we entered the tiny box.

"This is the original elevator," I said. "It's the last one in the city with a rope cable."

"Thanks for telling me," Rafe said as we started our ascent to the fourth floor.

"When we get up there, don't say anything. Just follow me. I know where we're going."

"Okay."

"Hammett was claustrophobic," I said.

"Really?"

"I can't imagine how he handled this elevator."

"Pretty tight quarters," Rafe said, nodding.

"Every single day."

"Maybe he took the stairs."

"He was too sick by that point," I said. "Are you hot? Because I'm really warm."

"I'm fine."

"This elevator is sure taking its time." Every day Hammett would shut himself up in this cage, the air being sucked out of his lungs, the walls closing in around him.

Rafe's phone started to ring.

"Hello?"

I wiped the sweat off my brow.

"Speaking."

The elevator lurched to a stop.

Rafe put up his finger for me to wait. Then he hung up.

"What is it?" I asked.

His hand was trembling as he pushed the button for the lobby. The elevator creaked back into motion.

"What are you doing?" I pushed the emergency stop.

He released it. "I have to go back to L.A."

"Now? Why? What's going on?" I asked.

"What?" He hadn't even heard me.

"Why do you have to go back to L.A.?" I repeated.

"Why don't you stop asking me so many questions?"

"You don't have to jump down my throat."

"Sorry." He lowered his voice. "It was the coroner's office."

The elevator stopped with a shudder. Rafe put on his lucky hat and said, "They want me to identify a dead body."

CHAPTER
FOUR

We made it on to a ten o'clock flight, but didn't arrive at 1104 North Mission Road until close to one o'clock in the morning. Rafe parked the car, turned off the motor, and sat there, staring straight ahead.

The building was the color of mud, unremarkable except for the flashing LED display out front. "Don't make the coroner your designated driver!" "Call a cab or call the coroner!" "Visit our gift shop, 'Skeletons in the Closet'!" It was like Vegas. Everything was like Vegas.

"I guess this is it," I said.

"Guess so," Rafe answered, still staring.

"Okay, then." I reached for the door.

He wasn't moving.

"Should we go inside?" I asked.

"Yeah." He slapped the wheel with both hands and turned

toward me. His beautiful smile looked like he'd pasted it on crooked.

Joyless didn't begin to describe the atmosphere in the waiting room. Someone had made a valiant effort. The olive-green linoleum was spotless. The acoustic-tile ceiling was in good repair. Pictures of the L.A. County supervisors were arranged in a neat row. But all you could see was the pay phone mounted high on the wall opposite.

So much bad news to deliver.

Rafe sat down next to me. "Lady said it'd be a few minutes. Thanks for coming with me."

"Sure."

"I realize it was a lot to ask."

I smiled. "You okay?"

"Fine."

He wasn't that good an actor.

Sitting across from us was an older couple being interviewed by a younger woman, half in Spanish, half in English.

"*Cicatrices?*" That meant scars. The older woman traced a line across her forehead. The younger woman wrote something down on her clipboard.

"Tattoos?" The man indicated his shoulder. His wife shook her head and touched his arm. The younger woman wrote this down, too.

Rafe's eyes were closed. He was trying not to watch.

What color hair?

Brown.

What color eyes?

Brown.

Rafe had barely spoken a word since we'd gotten on the plane. I suppose there was nothing to say.

"What color shirt?" the younger woman asked.

The couple looked at one another, uncomprehending.

"Camisa?" she offered.

"Ah, camisa. Rayada." The man ran his finger across his chest. Striped.

The older woman crossed and uncrossed her ankles. Her husband patted her hand. I watched their reflections on the linoleum.

"Mr. Simic?"

We leapt to our feet.

"I'm Captain Donaldson. It's a pleasure meeting you. I wish it were under better circumstances."

Captain Donaldson was squat and reassuring. He had on a white shirt and government-issue glasses he must've had since the fifties.

"Thank you. This is my friend Cece Caruso."

He nodded. "Sit down. Please. I want to make this as easy as possible. I realize this is not where you'd like to be right now. Can I get you anything? Some water? A soda?"

Rafe shook his head.

"Young lady?"

"No, thank you."

"Well, then." He opened the manila file on his lap and fumbled noisily with some papers. "Here's what's going to happen."

Rafe took my hand. His was wet.

"I'm going to show you a Polaroid. You're going to take a look at it and tell me if you recognize the person in it. Then we'll be done. Are you ready?"

Rafe nodded.

Captain Donaldson slid a small color photograph facedown

across the table. When it was directly in front of Rafe, he turned it faceup, pulled his hand back, and waited.

It was a woman. Her blond hair was wild, her brown eyes wide open, her mouth a twisted gash. I turned away, the nausea rising. Out of the corner of my eye, I saw the older woman standing at the pay phone, crying.

A minute passed. I turned back to Rafe. He was studying the picture without touching it. Two minutes. Three. His hands were clenched in his lap. His face was unreadable. Captain Donaldson waited. The older couple left. The room was silent now.

Rafe cleared his throat.

Captain Donaldson leaned forward.

"I'm . . . I'm not sure," Rafe said.

There was a commotion at the door.

"What the—" someone said.

"Ah, Detective Smarinsky has arrived."

A reedy fellow with a yarmulke and bags under his eyes shook his head at the coffee he'd just sloshed on his navy-blue jacket, which was at least a size too big. "Don't get up," he said. "Sorry I'm late, and such a putz. Keep doing what you're doing. And here you go." He handed us each a business card.

"We were just looking at the Polaroid," Captain Donaldson said, frowning. "I think Mr. Simic needs a little more time."

"Lemme show you what I got," Smarinsky said, tossing his coffee into the trash. "Time to get this show on the road." He sat down, reached across me, shoved the Polaroid aside, and placed something in front of Rafe. "Like I told you on the phone, we haven't been able to ID the body. No wallet, no keys, no pocketbook, no nothing. No missing persons matching the description. We ran the prints through the system but didn't get a single hit. Bupkes. Zip. This was in the pocket of her jeans. It's the sum total of what we've got. That's why we called your manager."

"Will?" Rafe held on to the name like it was a life raft.

"Yeah, Will." Smarinsky pulled out his notes and paged through them. "Here it is. Will Levander. I told him I needed to talk to you. He gave me your number. So take a look. See if it rings some bells."

Sitting on the table, next to the Polaroid, was another photograph, this one black and white. The paper was waterlogged and one edge was ragged, as if it had been torn down the middle. The part that was left showed a towheaded teenager. He was handsome, with sleepy eyes. Grinning like a fox. Unmistakably Rafe. He had his arm around a girl with long hair.

I saw something pass across Rafe's face.

Smarinsky turned the photo over and tapped it with his finger. "This is the good part," he said.

There was an inscription scrawled across the back, and even though the ink had run, you could still read it: "Rafe and Me, Summer 1979."

"Lucky break for us that you're famous. Couple of gals in the office are fans. They knew it was you right away."

Rafe chewed on his lip. Then he looked at Donaldson, who smiled encouragingly.

"Take your time."

Rafe swallowed. "I know her."

Donaldson and Smarinsky exchanged glances.

"I need a name," said Smarinsky, his voice tense.

"I want to see the body."

Donaldson looked unhappy. "We try to discourage that, Mr. Simic. If you can make a positive ID from the Polaroid, it would be better for all concerned."

Rafe stood up. "I need to see the body."

"Let the man see the body," said Smarinsky, turning up his palms.

"Very well," the captain replied, looking extremely unhappy now.

Everybody stood. Smarinsky yanked up his pants, which were also too big.

"Cece," said Rafe in an unmistakable tone.

Oh, no.

"Will you come with me?" he asked.

I am superstitious. I am afraid of ghosts. I believe in haunted houses.

"Please," he said, his voice quavering.

Stricken, I turned to Captain Donaldson. "That's against regulations, isn't it? I mean, it's not like I'm the next of kin or anything."

Donaldson started to say something, but Smarinsky interrupted. "What the hell, am I right, Donaldson? The more the merrier."

This was a nightmare, a horrible, terrible day.

Someone buzzed us in. Hand in hand, Rafe and I walked through a heavy wooden door with a small glass window at the top, down a long, sterile corridor with low ceilings, and to the elevator, whose doors closed abruptly, shutting us inside, so that all we could smell was a horrible smell, sweet and rank, which was the smell of dead bodies.

The doors opened with a pop.

"Service floor," the captain said. "This way, please."

We followed him down the hall. Smarinsky gestured toward a map of Los Angeles County covered with arrows and pushpins.

"Crime scenes. We found your girl over here." He pointed to someplace in the South Bay. A small red arrow in the big blue water. "She'd been in there for twenty-four hours, give or take a few."

Donaldson moved us along, nodding briskly at someone in a puffy blue hazmat suit.

"It protects them during autopsies," Smarinsky explained. "Don't know how you do it, Donaldson. The fumes, man."

The captain ignored him and stopped in front of a stainless-steel table. The body was loosely wrapped in white sheets. He put his hand on Rafe's shoulder.

"Shall we proceed, Mr. Simic?"

Rafe nodded, sticking his hands in his pockets.

The captain pulled back the sheets and stepped away.

I looked at Rafe, who looked at the dead woman. His whole body went rigid with the effort. Then, when I couldn't look at him anymore, I looked at her. All I remember seeing was white. Lips drained of color. Hair like wintry branches. An endless expanse of cold, milky, white flesh.

Someone had closed her eyes.

"Maren Levander," Rafe said, his voice cracking. "Shit. I've got to call Will."

"Will?" I asked.

"Maren is his sister. Will is—was—her brother."

"And you?" Smarinsky asked.

Insensitive prick.

"I was her friend." Rafe put his head in his hands.

"Thank you, Mr. Simic." The captain pulled the sheet back

up. "That pretty much does it, for now. If you'll step into my office for a moment, we can take care of the paperwork."

"I'll escort the young lady to the waiting area," Smarinsky volunteered.

My legs felt shaky as we walked back to the elevator. We passed a dangerously high stack of folding chairs, then an open door. Two men in white jackets were sitting inside, working.

"You know what those guys in there can do?" Smarinsky asked me. "Sometimes the body's so shriveled up they can't get a print, so they peel the skin off the hands and put it on, like a glove. They get a print that way. Gotta have an iron stomach, though."

The doors to the elevator closed. I'd planned to hold my breath until I was in the proximity of fresh air, but Smarinsky kept asking me questions.

"What do you do for a living?"

"Write books."

"You and the movie star an item?"

"No."

"You are a resident of?"

"West Hollywood."

I couldn't tell if he was interrogating me or just trying to keep me company.

It was six in the morning by the time Rafe was done. We stepped outside. The sun was blaring, but it wasn't as bright as the flashbulbs popping in our faces.

"Fucking vultures," Rafe said. "They never leave me alone."

"I'm so sorry."

"I used to love her."

"I figured."

"Fuck."

"Let's get out of here."

"Good idea."

"I'm driving," I said, taking the keys out of his hand. "You're buying."

CHAPTER
FIVE

Coffee still costs a nickel at Philippe's, home of the French-dip sandwich, invented in 1918 when the original Philippe, who was French, was preparing a sandwich for a policeman and accidentally dropped the sliced roll into the drippings of a roasting pan.

You couldn't argue with the prices, not to mention the clientele, which was the polar opposite of starstruck: Amtrak riders stopping off on their way to Union Station across the street; electricians; municipal-court judges; housepainters. I may have detected a glimmer of recognition from the counterwoman who took our order, but she was too efficient to indulge in that kind of speculation. Rafe insisted he wasn't hungry, but I ordered pancakes for him, a hot pink pickled egg for me, and a coffee for each of us.

We took our trays and walked to the back room, where we found an empty booth.

"I can't eat yet," he said after sitting down. "What the hell am I thinking? I have to call Will." He stood up. "I left my phone in the car. I'll call him from out there. Is that okay?"

"Of course. Take your time."

I watched him go. His T-shirt was hanging off his shoulders. It looked a size bigger than it had the night before. Or maybe it was Rafe who looked a size smaller.

When he was gone, I pulled out my phone and called Gambino at work. I knew he'd be there. He's a robbery/homicide detective who takes his job very seriously. Lately, this has caused some problems, but that's another story.

I started crying the minute I heard his voice. When I was done crying, I was incoherent. When I was done being incoherent, the story came out and it was so awful, I started crying again. Halfway through, Gambino announced that he was coming to get me, but I put my foot down. We'd had that particular discussion before. And I wasn't prepared to go—not yet. After the experience we'd just shared, Rafe needed me. And maybe I needed him, too. Gambino said he understood. I knew those weren't just words. He didn't say things he didn't mean. There was a moment of silence and then Gambino got a call. He had to take it. He said he'd see me later at my place and not to worry, he was cooking, which was a mixed blessing. He was an excellent cook but not exactly efficient in the kitchen. I'd be cleaning for days.

After we hung up, I walked across the sawdust-covered floor and studied the Dodger memorabilia on the wall. Then I sat back down, cut the pickled egg into quarters, then eighths, and tried to put the slices back together again. But I couldn't make the yolks work.

Rafe came back with red eyes. "Will took it well."

"I'm glad."

"I mean, as well as you could expect."

"Of course."

He sat down. "If you love Maren, you get used to surprises, good ones and bad ones. That's just the way it is. That's just what makes her Maren."

He was still using the present tense. "I suppose he'll want to talk to the police," I said.

"Yeah, he's calling Detective Smarinsky right now. I never even asked the cause of death."

"And he'll have to notify the rest of the family."

"They're dead. There is no other family. It's just Will now." He cut into his pancakes so hard the knife scraped against the plate. "Shit," he said in disgust.

"It's okay."

"It's not okay." He pushed his plate away and raked his fingers through his hair. "And this whole thing messes up our plans. It's not like we have extra time here. The movie starts shooting soon."

"You're going to be brilliant."

"Maybe we could take just a day off," he said, "and then get back to what we were doing."

"That's fine."

"I guess I need to get my head together or something."

"Tell me more about Maren," I said.

Rafe became very interested in my empty coffee cup. "Can I get you a refill? You look like you need a refill. It's good coffee."

My face got hot. "I don't know what's wrong with me. You don't have to say anything."

He shook his head. "It's just that I can't believe this. I can't fucking believe this." He slammed his fist on the table, hard. "Why the hell is this happening?"

I thought of Gambino, always after me to be sensible. "I think maybe we should go."

"No!"

I looked at him.

"I'm sorry. I didn't mean to raise my voice. Look, can we just sit here for a little while longer?" he asked.

"Okay."

Rafe twisted his lucky hat in his hands. He folded and unfolded his napkin. Finally, he said, "We were inseparable."

"You and Maren?"

He tore his napkin into neat strips and arranged them on the scarred wooden tabletop. "It was me and Maren at first, when we were just kids. Then it was Will and his girlfriend, Lisa, too. Of course, I haven't seen Maren in years and years. Will's barely seen her, either. We split up before I made my first movie. God, it was so long ago. Back then," he said, shaking his head, "back then, though, we were unstoppable. The four of us. Nobody could touch us."

I didn't quite get it.

He started to smile. "Do you know Maren was the one who taught me to surf?"

I smiled back. "Really?"

"She wasn't like other people. She'd be the only girl out there at Lunada Bay, every single day. That's on the peninsula, the Palos Verdes Peninsula, where we grew up. Beautiful half-moon cut out of limestone? You had to scale these high cliffs, and brave the rocks just to get there. And deal with the surf Nazis who thought they owned the place. Maren never so much as batted an eye at those guys. She'd be out there, every storm season, where the waves would be breaking big—four, five o'clock in the morning and still dark out—and nobody's watching the sunrise because they're all watching her. She liked to ride the waves that scared the shit out of everybody else."

"She sounds amazing."

He looked at me curiously, then got up and threw the remains of his napkin away. I followed him with both our trays and dumped the contents into the receptacle. We walked outside. It was still early morning, but the sky was already choked with smog.

"When you come right down to it," Rafe said, "I don't know how amazing Maren was. She used to drive with her eyes closed sometimes. I think she had a death wish."

It was a strange thing to say, given the circumstances.

CHAPTER
SIX

O h, honey, not my Norma Kamali coat from the eighties!" I screamed, grabbing the scissors out of little Alexander's hands.

Mondays are hard, even under the best of circumstances. And my nerves were more than a little frayed from the events of the previous day.

"Bad tiger," said Alexander. "Snip, snip."

"He's a leopard," I replied, hanging the coat back up in my closet. "A fake one." Not that a three-year-old cared about my conflicted position vis-à-vis fur.

"Let's not play with my clothes, okay?" This kid could decimate my wardrobe in no time if I let him. Distraction was the thing. I'd learned that over the four hours and counting we'd been together. You don't want to say no; you want to propose alternatives.

I looked at Buster, my teacup poodle, snoring peacefully in his little wicker bed. "I know! Let's put makeup on the dog!"

No, even at his advanced age, Buster wasn't going to fall for that one. Fresh air. That was what we needed. We'd been cooped up for too long. I took Alexander by the hand and led him out the back door, down the brick steps, and into the backyard.

"Look at the pretty butterfly!" I pointed out a large black specimen with tiny white polka dots.

"Birdie!" Alexander said, reaching out his arms.

Close enough. "What do you say I put you to work?"

He nodded shyly.

I turned on the hose, sending the usual tremors through the plumbing system of my 1932 Spanish-style house, which was hanging on by a thread. That was part of its charm. Would the toilet flush? Would the doorbell chime? Would the wrought-iron sconces send crackling volts of electricity through my veins when I changed the bulbs? It was all so exciting and unpredictable.

"Come over here and hold the watering can under the water," I said to Alexander.

"Water! I can swim! I grow tall!"

"So tall," I said, kissing the top of his head. "And you are going to help the garden grow, too. The plants are thirsty. Don't they look sad?"

Buster's overactive bladder had pretty much destroyed the grass. I'd tried to train him to use the dog run, but he'd considered that an infringement upon his rights as the man of the house.

"Now take your little can over to the cilantro," I said, pointing to a sorry clump of feathery leaves that had all but dried to a crisp.

"Dead," Alexander intoned mournfully. He was right. Year after year I was defeated by cilantro.

"Not too much water now," I cautioned. "Too much isn't good either."

"I don't want water. I don't wanna work. I want juice. I'm thirsty. I'm hungry, too." Alexander dropped the watering can and started to cry.

"There, there, sweetheart," I said, picking him up. "Don't cry." He cried harder. "Cece's going to make you a beautiful lunch right this very minute." He was wailing inconsolably now. Poor kid had been through so much lately. I had no idea how Annie and Vincent were going to explain the fact that his mother was gone for good. Maybe she'd come back. She hadn't absolutely closed the door on that possibility. Still, I wondered if at this point that would be a good or a bad thing.

As soon as we set foot on the service porch, Mimi the cat appeared.

"Shall we feed the pussycat first?" I asked.

Alexander wiped his eyes. "How 'bout a peanut butter samwich? We could share."

"Good idea. We'll just give her some turkey and giblets as an appetizer." I cracked open a can of Fancy Feast and dumped it into her ceramic dish. Nothing but the best for Mimi.

We walked into the kitchen and assembled the items we needed, sidestepping the destruction wrought by last night's eggplant parmigiana, which was delicious, by the way. While the bread was toasting, I went into Annie's old room, which I now used as a guest room, though I rarely had guests. Why subject innocent people to a toilet that might not flush? I opened the closet door and flipped the light switch. What a mess. Even after she and Vincent had bought their house in Topanga Canyon, which had maybe quadruple the amount of storage space I have, Annie still hadn't cleared out all her old stuff. The girl was a packrat. One good thing was, there were sure to be some books or toys in one of the boxes. Maybe something Alexander would like.

"Pop, pop, pop," Alexander sang out. "Toast time!"

"No! Don't touch anything!" All I needed was for him to get electrocuted. That'd be the last time they let me baby-sit.

Jammed into the corner of the closet was a picture book and a forlorn Barbie with no hair. I snatched up both and ran back into the kitchen. Alexander was sitting on the floor with the jar of peanut butter in his lap.

"Good boy," I said, trading bald Barbie for the peanut butter. "Did anybody tell you never, ever, to put a knife in the toaster? You can get a bad shock. It can make your hair go crazy."

"Like your hair," he said, pointing.

"Why don't you sit right here at the kitchen table," I said, "and look at this nice book while I finish the sandwich."

"My mommy puts bananas in," he said in a small voice, "because bananas are fruit."

Oh, god. "That's a wonderful idea. I'm going to put bananas in, too." I had one black banana sitting on the counter. Maybe he wouldn't notice if I sliced it really thin.

"Okay!" I said brightly. "All ready. How about some chips?" Kids love chips. Everybody loves chips. Instant party.

"No chips."

"Cece will eat the chips. And Mimi. Mimi loves chips."

I sat down next to him and picked up the book.

"Clifford the Big Red Dog," I read. Why was he so big and red? His mother and father and brothers and sisters were all normal. They never explained that. Maybe it was some kind of post-Chernobyl thing.

"I think we can do better than this," I said. "I'll be right back."

"Barbie wants a samwich, too."

"Okay." I sliced off a tiny corner of Alexander's sandwich and arranged it on a saucer, though everyone knows Barbie doesn't touch carbs. I shoved some chips in my mouth. At least I had hair.

I went back into Annie's closet and waded through the debris. A purple thermos fell on my head. I shoved a Care Bears helmet and assorted knee and elbow pads out of my way. Then I saw an old trunk I remembered helping Annie pack full of papers and books. I dragged it into the middle of the floor and opened it.

Curious George Goes to the Hospital. A classic, if depressing. *Bread and Jam for Frances.* Always made me hungry. Yearbooks. Autograph books. And here—oh, too funny—was Annie's onetime prized possession: her Rafe Simic scrapbook. I'd almost forgotten the thing existed. The cover alone was blackmail material. "RAFE + ANNIE." She'd cut the letters out of old magazines and collaged them onto the baby-blue padded surface. It was still in good shape. Only the "R," surrounded by cupids and red hearts, was peeling.

I flipped to the first page. Rafe with shoulder-length hair in his first big film, *Dead Ahead.* He played a follower of the Grateful Dead who inadvertently witnesses a gangland-style execution. Rafe in wraparound shades and heavy gold jewelry,

Hicksville Public Library

Hollywood's vision of a sadistic drug lord. Rafe in costume as a samurai warrior, wielding a sword. A young Rafe with a gold crown on his head. This wasn't from any movie I remembered. Aha. This was real life. I looked down at the caption: "Rafe Simic, Prom King, and"—Jesus—"Maren Levander, Prom Queen." Morbid to a fault, I wondered what Maren had looked like when she was young and not dead. I peered closely and had to laugh.

Apparently, it ran in the family.

Annie had decapitated Palos Verdes High's prom queen of 1979, and collaged her own face where Maren's should have been.

"All done," Alexander called out.

"Coming," I answered, grabbing the scrapbook and *Frances* and heading into the kitchen.

Just then the key turned in the lock of the front door.

"Annie!" screamed Alexander, careening into her outstretched arms.

"Hi, there," she said. "How's my sweetheart?"

"I have something to show you," I said in a singsong voice.

"Mom, what's that on your jeans?"

I looked down. "I don't see anything. Have a look at this." I handed her the scrapbook.

"No, on the back. Gross."

I twisted around to see. It was something mushy and blackish. I looked at Alexander.

"Icky banana. Mommy never uses icky bananas."

"I can't believe you found this thing. Look at how cheesy it is. Say sorry, Alexander," Annie instructed.

"Sorry, 'Xander."

"Not to worry, baby," I said. "Use a napkin next time."

"Okay, Grandma."

Annie looked at me and I looked at Annie.

"What?" asked Alexander.

He was so serious, just like his father. I bent down to stroke his hair. It was as soft and slippery as silk.

"Turns out Grandma likes Mondays," I said, "that's what."

CHAPTER SEVEN

Tuesday morning and Rafe and I were back at it again, but I'd put my foot down when, by way of greeting, he pulled the mini-microphone out of the pocket of his baggy cargo shorts.

"To be perfectly honest," I said as we sped off in his freshly washed car, "I feel uncomfortable with that thing hanging around my neck."

"Not to be rude," he started—"and by the way, which way are we headed?" He took a bite of out an Egg McMuffin. "You want a bite? I don't usually eat this shit, but whatever."

"No, thank you." I'd had my own nourishing breakfast of stale graham crackers and coffee. My half-and-half had gone sour, so I'd created a mixture of whipping cream and nonfat milk, which should have amounted to the same thing but didn't. "We're heading east."

He took a left on Melrose, then stuffed the rest of his breakfast back into the cheery McDonald's bag and shoved it onto the backseat. "Like I was saying, I don't want to be rude, but this is a job and the mike is one of the job requirements."

"C'mon, Rafe. You know perfectly well you're never going to listen to these tapes."

"Oh, yes, I am. We have a whole closet devoted to audiovisual equipment. In Will's office."

"You think you're going to listen to them, I believe you. That way you can tune me out when you feel like it."

"Whoa. I didn't know this was about you."

"It isn't," I said, reddening.

"And for the record," he said, just missing the green light at Fairfax, "I'm listening to every word you're saying. I'm listening to the words in between the words. I'm listening to you breathing."

"That isn't necessary."

The light changed and he shifted back into gear. "It's not like I can help it. How far are we going?"

"Down to Paramount Studios."

"Cool. Look, Cece," he said, fiddling with the stereo, "I'm an actor. We take cues. To take a cue you've got to be listening and you've got to be watching. You've got to feel the other person's rhythms. It isn't personal, really. So just do your job, okay?" He settled on a rap station and cranked the volume so high the car started to shake.

I have always been a bad employee. I believe in punctuality and hard work, but deferring to one's superior, well, that part has always stuck in my craw. Which is why writing has been my salvation. Just me and my Bondi-blue iMac in my converted garage office with the Lucite desk and apple-green walls and floors. I should never have accepted this gig. But I did accept it, and now I had to suck it up.

"I've reconsidered. I would be delighted to wear the mike." I had to shout over the music. "If you would be so kind as to hand it over."

"Cool." He tried not to look too satisfied, but he could've tried harder.

Traffic was slow between Fairfax and La Brea. This was prime shopping turf for suburban Goths and punks who wouldn't dream of parking their cars far from the stud, spike, and shroud shops. After three, when school let out, it was even worse.

We stopped to let a kid wearing enormous black shorts with silver chains hanging down to his ankles cross the street. His clothes were no big deal. The impressive part was his head, which was shaved except for two clumps he'd dyed red and sculpted into devil's horns. Rafe took one look at him and said, "Cool"—again—which was really starting to irk me. Why did he keep saying that? The way I saw it, things were the opposite of cool. Why were we chatting about nothing? Why had he not said a word about our visit to the coroner's? It was strange. Not a single word about his dead former girlfriend. Of course, it wasn't my place to bring her up. If he wanted to forget about her, that was fine with me.

"You haven't said a word about Maren." It slipped out.

Rafe turned off the music. "Oh. I'm glad you brought that up. I'm going to need to take tomorrow off, too. Maren's body was released to Will this morning, and her ashes are going to be scattered off the cliffs in Palos Verdes at around eleven. Will said that's what she would've wanted. They ruled her death a suicide, by the way."

"I'm sorry," I said, chastened.

He reached over to turn on my mike. "Paramount Studios, Cece."

We parked the car at a meter opposite the ornate, historic archway at the north end of Bronson Avenue. According to Hollywood lore, the wrought-iron filigree at the top was added after crazed female fans of Rudolph Valentino overwhelmed security and streamed in over the original gate.

Rafe got out of the car and stuck his cap on his head. "Did you know Charles Bronson took his new name from this gate?"

"Alfred A. Knopf wanted Hammett to change his name. He thought it was too hard for people to pronounce."

"They wanted me to change my name, too. Robert Simon was their idea of a good name."

"Sounds like a lawyer."

"Lee Majors, the star of *The Six Million Dollar Man,* was born Harvey Lee Yeary. I met him a long time ago in the green room, waiting to go on with Jay Leno. Man, I'd have changed that name, too."

"Jay Leno?"

"Harvey Lee Yeary."

We sat on the hood of his car, looking north. There were billboards as far as the eye could see. Spearmint Rhino, an upscale gentlemen's club. Citibank. A horror movie featuring a girl in a towel wielding a knife. California avocados. In the distance were the snowcapped San Gabriel Mountains. I wondered how different it'd looked here in 1930. That was the year Hammett had arrived in Hollywood, fresh from writing four best-selling novels. David O. Selznick decided Hammett would class up the joint—write screenplays, doctor scripts, finesse dialogue. What neither of them knew, of course, was that Hammett's best work was already behind him.

"While he was at Paramount," I said out loud, "Hammett finished *The Thin Man*. That was the last book he'd ever write."

It was the part of his life most people couldn't fathom. Hammett lived for almost thirty years after *The Thin Man* without ever finishing another book. Just before he died, he was visited by a reporter who asked him why he kept three Underwood typewriters. Still in his pajamas at noon, the tall, gaunt, by then toothless man answered by saying he wanted to remind himself that he used to be a writer.

"What went wrong?" asked Rafe.

"I don't know," I answered. "He lived fast. He spent money like it was water. He liked women and alcohol, and he went through a lot of both."

"Did Hollywood ruin him?" Interesting question coming from an actor.

"He was sick. He was a drunk. He felt like a hack and wanted to be taken seriously." I paused. "Maybe he was already ruined."

"I get it," said Rafe, in a way that made me wonder.

LATER THAT NIGHT I BROUGHT THE SCRAP-book into bed with me.

"Look at this," I said to Gambino.

"Do I have to? I saw the guy in person and wasn't very impressed. And I'm busy here." Ever the optimist, he was scraping up the crystallized remains of a quart of Häagen-Dazs coffee ice cream.

"Oh, c'mon. You liked his car at least."

" 'I'm an idiot with money to burn.' That's what that car says."

"So what would you have bought?" I took the carton out of his hand, lifted up his arm, and draped it across my shoulders. Gambino pulled me in close. He was so big he made me feel tiny. I am 5 feet 11 and 144 pounds. I like to feel tiny. Jayne Mansfield, with whom I am obsessed, said it best: "I'm a big girl and I have to have a big guy."

"So, what kind of car?" I repeated.

"I'm thinking here." He peeled off his wire-rimmed glasses and shut his eyes for a moment. "Well, I would've said a 1971 Hemi Cuda convertible, which is the greatest muscle car Detroit ever built."

"But?"

"Nash Bridges already took it."

"He's a TV cop," I murmured consolingly, "but you're the real thing."

"What did Annie say when you dug up this thing?" he asked, changing the subject.

"She was mortified."

"Lusting after total strangers. You can't lust after people you actually know when you're a kid. It's too scary."

"Don't tell me you had a crush on some movie star." He didn't seem like the type. He was solid as a rock, salt of the earth. A little defensive, sometimes, but who isn't?

"I had the poster of Farrah Fawcett in the red one-piece bathing suit," he admitted.

"You remember what color bathing suit she was wearing?"

"What planet do you live on, Cece? That poster united a generation of teenage boys."

I sat straight up.

"What?"

"I just realized we've never gone swimming together." Late at night, this sort of thing could easily assume massive proportions. Gambino knew me well enough to nip it in the bud. He took my chin in his hand.

"We've also never taken a plane together. We've never packed a suitcase together. We've never purchased a major appliance together. It's okay. It really is."

"We should buy a refrigerator. I have a terrible refrigerator."

"First thing in the morning." He pulled me under the covers.

"Wait a second." I got out of bed, wriggled out of my sweats, and opened my chest of drawers.

Farrah Fawcett was not the only woman to ever make good use of a red one-piece bathing suit.

One hour later Gambino was in dreamland, but I was wide awake, with something on my mind. I looked at the clock: 11:34 P.M. I picked up the phone and called Annie.

"Did I wake you?" I whispered. "Oh, how unfortunate," I said, leaning down to pick up the ice-cream carton. "The ants are back."

"I told you to try the organic stuff. It works better. It doesn't kill them. It relocates them." Annie loved animals (bugs included) and was committed to deluding herself on such matters. "So what's going on?"

"Where'd you put the picture of the prom queen?"

"The who?"

"In the Rafe Simic scrapbook. You cut out her face and stuck yours in instead."

"Check the pocket in the back. Sweet dreams, Mom."

I shoved a couple of pillows behind my neck, flipped to the back of the scrapbook, slid my hand into the pocket, and felt around.

There it was.

You could count on Annie to never throw anything away.

I pulled out the tiny scrap and peered at it.

The girl in the picture was beautiful, but not in an obvious sort of way. She had wide-spaced eyes, a broad, slightly cock-eyed smile, small, pointy teeth, and a nose that looked like maybe it had been broken once or twice. Dimples. A dark tan.

And no resemblance whatsoever to the dead woman wrapped up in sheets at 1104 North Mission Road.

CHAPTER
EIGHT

I called Rafe at nine the next morning. He picked up on the first ring, which caught me off guard since I'd been pretty much planning to hang up.

"It's Cece."

"Hey, Cece. I'm a little crazed right now."

He didn't sound crazed. Nor surprised when I asked if I could attend the scattering of Maren's ashes.

"Do you need directions," he asked, "or do you want to come with me and Will?"

I lied and said I had something to do in the area afterward, so I'd take my own car. But what exactly do you do in Palos Verdes after you've watched the wrong person's ashes being flung out to sea?

I went over to the dryer, furiously yanked out the tangle of towels, and started to fold them. End over frayed end. The pile grew tall, then taller, then so tall it toppled over, which was perfect.

It was time for coffee. The ritual had a calming effect on me. It's like smokers with their cigarettes. Or hyperactive children with their Ritalin. Like Rafe.

I poured the remains of yesterday's pot into the sink. I rinsed out the carafe. The gold filter was caked with saturated grounds. I shook them out, then measured out ten cups' worth of freshly ground beans, dumped them into the freshly washed filter, and hit the On switch. Immediately, the water started to hiss and gurgle. I sat down at the kitchen table. The sound was hypnotic. By the time I was on my third cup, I was able to see the situation more clearly.

In the immortal words of Detective Smarinsky, what I had was bupkes. Nothing to indicate the dead woman wasn't Maren. People who've been floating belly-up for twenty-four hours do not maintain their Coppertone tans. What's more, the picture I'd seen of Maren had been reprinted from a yearbook. It was tiny. You couldn't really see a thing. Not to mention, Maren was a teenager then. People changed. They got wrinkles. They dyed their hair. They gained weight. They lost weight. I'd changed. Maren had, too. Nobody's a prom queen forever.

The clock over the stove read 10:07 A.M. I had to get going if I didn't want to be late, not that I wanted to go anymore, but now I was obligated. Why was I always so quick to jump the gun? Obviously, I craved drama. This was not a good character trait. I dropped my terry-cloth robe into the hamper and went into the bathroom to turn on the shower, which took precisely three and a half minutes to warm up. Just enough time to ponder my wardrobe.

I have to admit I was stumped when it came to appropriate attire. My salt-and-pepper tweed suit with the peplum would provide excellent camouflage in case a sudden gust of wind blew the remains my way, but the thought was too morbid, even for me. My Halston black jersey disco dress with the fluttery sleeves would certainly do, but black was probably hyperbolic, considering I'd never even met the deceased. I settled on something in between, an antique black-and-cream lace wrapper over a pair of high-waisted gray trousers. I blotted my red lips on a tissue, threw on my red crystal beads, and ran out to the office to get my MapQuest directions. Good thing, because Buster was trapped in there. I must've shut the door with him inside earlier in the morning.

"Bad boy," I said, smelling pee. Buster trained his wet brown eyes upon me, convincingly woebegone. Oh, I suppose it wasn't his fault. I'd pamper him tonight with a long meander around the neighborhood.

West Hollywood was doggie nirvana. As per local ordinance, you can't "own" a dog in this town; you can only be a "guardian." Literally thousands of them (dogs, not guardians) were concentrated in the four-block radius around my house: fat ones, skinny ones, ones that looked like rodents or miniature lions. Between the hours of five and seven P.M., they were out in full force. You really had to watch where you stepped.

I studied my directions. I'd requested multiple options.

Zoom Out showed the Palos Verdes Peninsula as a bump along the coastline somewhere southwest of L.A. and north of Long Beach. That much I already knew.

Zoom In was somewhat more informative, though it did leave out the choice details—the fact that the area boasted one of the highest per capita incomes in the United States, for example, and that if you lived there, you didn't have to lock your door at night, because you were so isolated from the rest of the city.

One road in, one road out.

It looked like I'd be taking the 405, which was always bad news. Fifty-one minutes was the estimate, but I'd allotted two hours, and it was a good thing, too. Traffic was backed to the airport, and didn't ease up until I exited at Hawthorne Boulevard, which is not coterminous with the city of Hawthorne (ditto Artesia Boulevard and Artesia).

L.A. geography is notoriously tricky. It can take years to master. That is why the *Thomas Guide* exists. The *Thomas Guide* is a thick map book you purchase when you move to L.A. You buy it at the gas station and you must get a new one every few years because inevitably the page you need has gone missing. You keep it in your car at all times. It is especially useful when your MapQuest directions are counterintuitive. For instance, who would believe that Palos Verdes Drive North segues directly into Palos Verdes Drive West, no turns required?

You live, you learn.

One road in, one road out.

The hills, dotted with red-roofed Spanish-style houses, rose behind me as I wound my way down to Paseo del Mar, which offered dazzling views of the blue-green water of the Pacific. Times like these called for a convertible. The back window on my Camry's passenger side was stuck halfway, so I rolled down the other windows. It basically counted.

The air smelled nice. Briny. All you could hear was the screeching of the gulls and the low-pitched hum of multiple pool heaters, trilling in unison. A gang of little girls in helmets and pastel-colored Lacoste shirts whooshed past on their bikes. Then their brothers, tan and handsome. A million bucks in orthodontia. I felt like I was in another world. Big houses. Big smiles. No punks with devil horns.

Rafe had said they'd be where Paseo del Mar meets Via Arroyo. I found the parking area beyond a secluded church. It was empty except for a few cars, which made sense since it wasn't actually surfing weather. Rafe had explained it the other day. It was the northern swells that made the surf so special here at Lunada Bay. They rolled in unspoiled by bottom drag and then tumbled over the reefs. November to March. Those were the months. Storm season.

I cut the motor and got out of the car. I saw Rafe and the others gathered on a broad patch of dirt, just beyond a wire-mesh fence shooting up from an overgrown spill of ice plant.

"Cece," Rafe called. "Over here."

After a quick peck on the cheek, he introduced me around. There was Kat, Will's personal assistant, a blonde wearing tie-dyed capris; Kat's boyfriend, Riley, also in tie-dye; Rafe's personal assistant, Fredericka, an African-American woman in blue jeans; and Fredericka's girlfriend, Lana, the only one dressed for the occasion, at least by L.A. standards, in a black Juicy Couture sweat suit and a white tank top, no bra.

"There's Will," said Fredericka. I turned and watched him get out of a black Range Rover. We'd never met, Will and I, only spoken on the phone. His appearance surprised me. He was Rafe's age but moved like he was years older. He had the swollen build of the high school athlete gone to seed. His face was soft, too, all jowls and puffs and bags. But maybe that was today. I tried not to stare at the granite urn in his hands. It was smaller than I'd expected.

"Let's go down closer to the water. Come on," Rafe said, throwing an arm around Will's shoulders.

"I'm so sorry," I said. Will nodded in acknowledgment, then started down the steep hillside.

I cursed my heels as I tried not to slip on the loose dirt and tiny rocks strewn across the makeshift path. We stopped on a large outcropping just above the narrow, rocky shore. It was shielded from the road by a clump of foliage.

No one spoke.

Everyone watched Will for a sign.

After a few minutes, Rafe turned to him and whispered, "Shall we begin?"

Will looked up toward the road.

"Are you waiting for someone else?" Kat asked solicitously. "Because we can wait as long as you need."

"Guess not." He handed the urn to Rafe, who looked nonplussed. Will shook out his hands and flexed his thick fingers, then interlaced them. "Thank you all for coming today. Maren and I don't have any family left, so this means a lot. To Rafe, too. We both loved her so much." His voice started to break. "Sorry," he said, smiling. "I'm going to make this brief. Maren wouldn't have wanted us to waste a beautiful morning talking about somebody who was dead."

Fredericka and her girlfriend exchanged glances. Kat put her hair up in a ponytail. The wind was blowing like crazy.

"Life is for the living, that's what Maren would have said. Am I right, Rafe?"

Rafe nodded.

"She was spectacular, my sister. Full of surprises. You couldn't always see them coming. Sometimes they'd throw you for a loop. But she was more exciting, more alive, than anybody else you could ever know. That's the Maren I want to remember. I want to remember the girl who broke her arm surfing, and as soon as she got her cast off, broke *my* arm wrestling me to the ground because I'd borrowed her board without asking."

Everybody laughed.

"Anybody else want to say anything?" He looked at Rafe, who promptly handed me the urn. To my surprise, I realized it was plastic, not granite.

Rafe walked up to the front of the group and brushed some dried weeds out of the way with his shoe.

"I met Maren the day I started high school," he began. "I was new to the area, didn't know anybody. I was sitting by myself at lunch, feeling like I was the sorriest soul on the planet, when this girl sat down beside me. She was beautiful." He smiled, taking his time. "Long blond hair, impish grin, devil-may-care attitude—I could see that right away. 'Meet me by the bike rack after school,' she whispered in my ear. And then she was gone. You didn't say no to Maren, so I was there, as soon as the bell rang, waiting. I waited for an hour, cussing myself out the whole time, because, of course, she didn't show. So I went home."

I glanced over at Will, whose head was down. The others were spellbound.

"The next day," Rafe continued, "I saw her first thing in the morning, laughing with her friends on the auditorium steps, but I didn't dare go up to her. I didn't want her to know I could give a shit. But at lunch there she was again. 'Meet me in the bleachers after school,' she whispered in my ear, and before I could protest, she was gone. All day long I wrestled with it. Would I go? Should I go? Yes. No." His brow was furrowed, like it was that day all over again, like he was fourteen years old, and had no idea what to do, what to say, who to be. "Of course, I did go. This time, though, I only waited thirty minutes before riding my bike home. When I got to my front door, she was sitting there waiting for me. She said I'd passed the test. I never did get around to asking her exactly what the test had been. Had I proved how stupid I was? Or how loyal? Or how crazy about her I already was?"

A car alarm went off in the distance. Rafe stopped, distracted by the noise. When it was quiet again, he seemed to have lost his bearings. Fredericka smiled at him, encouraging him to go on.

"It didn't matter to me then," he said finally, "and it doesn't matter to me now."

He came over and took the urn out of my hands. He held it for a moment, then passed it to Will. Will removed the lid and walked close to the water's edge, so close the waves lapped at his brown dress shoes. He shook the ashes out over the surf. A gust of wind picked them up. They seemed to hover in the same spot for a few seconds. I held my breath. And then, just like that, they were gone.

People started to go back up the path, but I stood there for I don't know how long. I watched the waves roll in and out.

In and out.

In and out.

My father and I are at the Jersey shore. He's talking about the moon. The moon controls the tide, like the puppeteer controls the puppet. Gravitational attraction. Sir Isaac Newton. My eyes glaze over. My father gives up. I'm just a girl. I should do what girls do. I write my name in the wet sand. I hunt for seashells. I build a castle.

I gave a start as the car alarm went off again. It took me a moment to remember where I was. It was time to go. I was the only one left. But then I noticed a woman standing on the slope of the hillside, silhouetted against a lacy pepper tree. I smiled at her without really looking at her.

Then I looked at her.

Her blond hair was short and cut close to her head. No earrings. The years had taken their toll on her skin, but she was striking. She had on a narrow, sleeveless dress, black, with a cowl neckline. She took off her dark glasses and, squinting against the sun, walked toward me.

It couldn't be.

"I know what you're thinking," she said.

I backed away and felt the water slosh around my ankles.

Her voice was soft, liquid. "You think you're seeing a ghost."

My voice felt like brambles in my throat. "Ghosts are dead. You're alive."

"I'm not who you think I am."

"Maren?" I could barely say it.

"We used to look so much alike," she said. "Everybody got us mixed up."

I was confused until I remembered Rafe's comments of the other day.

Nobody could touch us. It was always the four of us.

I struggled for her name. "Lisa?"

"That's right, I'm Lisa. Lisa Lapelt. And you are?"

"Cece Caruso." I extended my hand. She had a strong handshake. "You're the Lisa? Will's girlfriend?"

She smiled. "A lifetime ago. I haven't seen Will or Rafe, or Maren for that matter, in years. We all went our separate ways after high school." She started to fiddle with a diamond ring on her left hand. "We were so close then. We shouldn't have drifted so far apart."

"People change."

"They do," she said, nodding. "Were you close to Maren?"

"Not really," I said. "But I was with Rafe when he identified her body, so—"

"I see," she said, closing her eyes. "It's so horrible." She gave a small shiver.

"Suicide is a terrible thing."

"Suicide?" Her eyes popped open. They were dark brown, so dark you couldn't see where the pupils began or ended. "What are you saying? Maren didn't kill herself."

"According to the coroner's office, she did."

"Maren was the last person on earth who'd ever kill herself! Not in a million years. People don't change that much."

"The coroner's office released her body to Will after ruling her death a suicide," I said, feeling defensive for god knows what reason.

She shook her head violently. "I'd know. I'd know if she'd been that desperate."

"But you said you hadn't spoken to her in years."

"We were connected," Lisa said, impatient with me now. "We looked alike, but that was just the start of it. We *were* alike." She pulled back the neckline of her dress, revealing a delicate tattoo of a green-and-red hourglass. The yellow grains of sand had almost run out.

"When we were seventeen years old, we got the same tattoo in the exact same spot. Young and stupid, right?"

I stared at Lisa's tattoo.

Green, and red, and yellow.

My mind was reeling now. I thought back to the body under the white sheets.

White, and white, and white.

All I'd seen that morning was white.

Who was this woman?

Who was *that* woman?

CHAPTER NINE

I sat in my car for a long time.

I'd woken up this morning convinced that the body I'd seen at the coroner's office wasn't Maren's. But I'd talked myself out of it. I'd been rational. I'd resisted my natural impulse to complicate matters when they were already complicated enough.

Tans fade, I'd said to myself.

But not tattoos.

Tattoos don't just fade away.

Of course, Maren could have had her tattoo removed. It was possible, happened every day. But it didn't seem likely. The process was painful and expensive. What's more, yellow and green were the most difficult colors to get rid of, virtually guaranteed to leave fragments of pigment, and probably scars. I knew because Bridget had considered having her ankle tattoo removed last year, but had ultimately decided against it.

A person, she'd said, should learn to live with her mistakes.

Maybe there had never been any matching tattoos. Who got matching tattoos, anyway? I'd never heard of such a thing. It was absurd, just like the woman's insistence that she'd have known if Maren were planning to kill herself. I believe two people can have a psychic bond, but why should I put stock in anything *she* had to say? A complete stranger? How did I even know she *was* Lisa? I hadn't seen her talking to Will or Rafe, or anyone else for that matter. She'd materialized out of thin air when everyone else had long gone. Like a figment of my imagination.

No.

She was real, flesh and blood.

Which meant someone was lying.

I just didn't want that person to be Rafe.

PALOS VERDES IS CLOSE TO SAN PEDRO.

San Pedro is a port town.

Sailors get tattoos.

If it were the late seventies, and you were a couple of surfer girls from the Peninsula trying not to get caught, San Pedro is where you'd go.

It was as logical as a mathematical proof. The fact that I'm bad at math didn't so much as cross my mind.

I devised a plan. The *Thomas Guide* was a crucial part of this plan. By some miracle, the pages I needed (822 to 823) weren't missing. I studied them closely, tracing my route, in pencil, of course: you sully your *Thomas Guide* at your peril.

Yes, according to my calculations, Palos Verdes Drive South would lead me pretty much straight into San Pedro.

I headed down the hill, but traffic slowed to a crawl before I'd made much progress. Then it stopped entirely. Maybe it was a sign. Go home. Mind your own business. People were leaning out of their windows and yelling at anybody who'd listen. I turned on the radio—classic rock—and cranked up the volume to drown out the honking horns.

The Eagles were singing about a girl in a doorway and the ringing of a mission bell, which to me sounded not the least bit like hell. But it did rhyme.

Hell, as everybody knew, was being stuck behind a big rig with no passing lane.

I drummed my fingers on the wheel.

Biggest big rig I'd ever seen.

I checked the glove compartment for candy, but no such luck.

I listened to Santana. Then Neil Young. Then ABBA came on, and my patience was shot.

I leaned out my window like everybody else and yelled up to the driver of the big rig, "What's going on?"

He turned his head and yelled back, "Accident just past the Wayfarer's Chapel."

The Wayfarer's Chapel. That was where Jayne Mansfield married bulging muscleman Mickey Hargitay in 1958. Talk about signs.

Twenty minutes later I pulled into the parking lot, which was nestled in a dense hillside. The traffic would probably be unsnarled by the time I left.

I'd read about this place for years, but had never quite realized where it was located. It was built in the forties by Lloyd

Wright (Frank's son) out of triangular segments of glass, framed by aged redwood timbers. Wright used thirty- and sixty-degree angles throughout because they occurred naturally in snowflakes, crystals, and tree branches. It was so poetic, that idea.

I swung open the heavy door.

The chapel was empty.

Not unusual for a Wednesday.

I was halfway down the aisle before I realized what I was doing. That would be *walking down the aisle*. By the time I stopped in front of the altar, my legs were feeling pretty shaky. I looked through the glass at those trees. Pine? Pepper? My knees started to give out. The branches seemed as if they were grabbing at me. I couldn't breathe. I'd been imprisoned inside a crystal. Was this what Lloyd Wright was going for? Or was this me? Jayne Mansfield had stood on this very spot. I wondered how she'd felt on her wedding day. She wore pink lace and Mickey's ten-carat diamond, but they still didn't make it till death do us part.

Gambino had wanted to buy me a diamond. But I'd had a diamond the first time around, and we all know how that worked out. So I chose an emerald instead. It was tiny but perfect. I looked down at my hand and my breathing started to return to normal. I even broke into a tiny smile. Then, a tourist in a visor and shorts with many pockets bounced over cheerfully, asking if I'd please move because happy as I seemed, I was standing in the way of his picture.

It was time to go anyway.

Back to the car.

The traffic had cleared.

Back down the hill.

In search of Maren and Lisa.

They would have gone this same way, I was sure of it. But where exactly? All I saw were cargo cranes dotting the skyline, a stream of 99¢ Only stores, a handful of taquerias, and finally, a sign reading: COME BACK TO SAN PEDRO.

I hung a U-turn at the next corner. A block later, I drove past a sign reading: WELCOME TO SAN PEDRO.

They say the second time's the charm.

In Hammett's day, San Pedro was a center of union activity. Today, not only was it the home of the biggest cargo terminal in the United States, it was also the port of Los Angeles's world-cruise center. At any given moment, thousands of retirees were plunking down their life's savings to sail on ships departing from one of its numerous berths, where they'd be stuffed full of rich food that would hasten their deaths, not to mention those small cabins with notoriously bad air circulation.

All this I learned from the woman manning the desk at Limo San Pedro. I didn't need a limo, of course, but their blinking neon sign ("Serving lax at reasonable prices") struck me at the time as amusing. Also, there was a parking space out front. At the mere mention of the word *tattoo,* the woman whipped off her pale blue cardigan, her "Hi, I'm Ruth" button clattering noisily to the floor, and showed me her fairy tattoo. It was large. After I'd admired it sufficiently, she directed me to the tattoo parlor on the corner of Mesa and Pacific, which she said had been there forever.

Tattu du Jour, however, was not the place I was looking for. It was run by a young man from Paris who'd made a typing mistake when applying for his Fulbright and had wound up at Cal State Long Beach instead of UCLA. Turned out he liked the sea air and cheap rents, and had always dreamed of having his own business. He kept saying, "Be calm," to me, which I thought was a little rude, but as it turned out he was telling me to go to Beacon Street. There were a couple of tattoo parlors there.

No luck at ACME Deluxe Tattoos. The owner was out and the help was surly. He looked at me like I was crazy when I asked how long they'd been in business and if they kept any kind of records.

The place next door didn't appear to have a name, although there was a sign over the register, handwritten in ornate, Gothic letters, which read: St. Sabrina in Purgatory. A Hell's Angels–type with a long, grizzled beard was sitting behind the counter.

"Is the owner here?" I asked him.

"Who wants to know?" he asked, stroking his beard.

"Cece Ribisi." Which is the actual name of one of my spinster aunts.

He pointed to the sign. "Saint Sabrina is in Purgatory."

Of course she is. I tried to slink out the door, but he let out a belly laugh and said, "Just kidding. I'm the owner. Name's Frank. How you doing, Ms. Ribisi? Lemme guess. You want a butterfly."

My aunt Cece would never pick a butterfly. A crucifix, maybe? A cannoli? She was extremely overweight. "I'm not actually shopping for a tattoo today," I said, "but if I wanted one, I'd absolutely want a butterfly, and this would absolutely be the place."

"Cut the shit. You a cop? I do everything by the book here. Send the health inspector if you want. Go right ahead, missy. You aren't going to find anything—"

"Hold on a minute," I interrupted. "I am not a cop. A cop!" I laughed. "Hardly."

He looked dubious.

"You can tell by my shoes."

He ambled out from behind the counter, belly first, and studied my water-stained silk sandals with the amber Lucite heels.

"Cops never get their shoes wet, am I right, Frank?"

He gave me a grudging nod and went back to his seat behind the counter. "What do you want, then?"

"I'm trying to figure out where two girls from Palos Verdes would go if they wanted to get a really unusual tattoo and it was the seventies."

"You asking hypothetically?"

"It's kind of a complicated story."

He clasped his hands, eager as a schoolboy. "I like stories."

"It's not pretty."

"Do I look like I shock easy?"

"My husband's been cheating on me—"

"No way," he interrupted.

"With two women."

"Come on."

I nodded. "The only thing I know about them is that they grew up in Palos Verdes, and when they were kids, they got matching hourglass tattoos. Really beautiful. Special. On their shoulders. Right around here." I pulled back my silk wrapper and revealed a glimpse of my turquoise lace bra strap. I thought this might incline Frank toward my cause.

He smiled, revealing some very creative dental work. "I've been here since 'seventy-five, and it don't ring any bells, Ms. Ribisi."

"Too bad," I said. "I'd really like these women's names."

"Sluts." He shook his head. "Well, if the place still exists, there are release forms. They'd tell you their names."

"Who's been in town for a while? Doing really unique work?"

When he didn't answer, I reached into my purse and took out one of my business cards, which I'd designed myself to resemble a Tiffany's box. I'd gotten a deal on a thousand of them, which just goes to show there are no deals.

"Would you call me, Frank, if anything comes to you?"

"And to think," he said, gold teeth glinting, "I thought you were going to slip me a twenty."

"Would that help?"

"Might."

I pulled one out and gave it to him. He pocketed it, then turned his attention to my card.

"Caruso? Thought you said it was Ribisi."

"I've gone back to my maiden name," I said, "on account of—"

"Makes sense." He clapped his hands. "I'm sending you to see the Mayor, Ms. Caruso."

That seemed extreme.

"The Mayor runs this town. Knows everybody and everything. You describe the tattoo, Mayor'll give you the who, what, when, and where." Frank looked at his watch. "It's five o'clock. Why don't you head on over to the Spot? Say Frank sent you."

The Spot turned out to be a bar located in a little cottage with a big satellite dish. The "S" of the sign had flamed out, so if you didn't know, you'd think you were heading to "The

Pot." The "O" was a bull's-eye, with an arrow shot through it. I hoped it was a good omen.

The Spot smelled the way certain bars do, a stomach-churning goulash of stale beer, sweat, and cheese. There was a basketball game playing on a big screen behind the pool table, but all eyes were instantly on me. Good thing there were only four of them. One pair belonged to the bartender, the other to a sixtyish woman channeling *Dynasty*-era Joan Collins in a spangly royal-blue turban and matching pants suit. She was seated at the far end of the bar, under the Corona banner, eating peanuts while doing a crossword puzzle.

"What can I do you for?" asked the bartender.

"I'll have a club soda."

"You got it."

"With lime," I added, going for broke.

He squirted the club soda into a dirty glass, stuck a slice of lime on the rim, and slid it toward me, along with a bowl of pretzels. Guess you had to be a regular to get the nuts.

"Thanks," I said.

He watched me not drink.

"Something else you need?"

"Actually, I'm looking for the Mayor."

Silence.

"Frank sent me." I sounded like a bad movie.

" 'Path of virtuous conduct, to some,' " the woman said out loud.

"Kosher!" shouted the bartender.

"Three letters. What about humble, also three letters?"

"Shy?" he offered.

"Pie," I said. And I should know.

"Ooh, yes," she said, erasing something furiously. When she was done, she smiled at me. "Hear you're looking for the Mayor." She wiped the lipstick from the corners of her mouth and came over. "That would be me. Duly elected, sworn in, and officiating twenty-four/seven. Always available for my constituents. Will you vouch for me, Andy?"

"You have to ask, Mayor?"

The Mayor looked like she might have been pretty once, movie-star pretty. Those women go one of two ways. Either they live in denial, with overreaching hairdos and makeup, or they give up the ghost. The Mayor was in denial. "How's Frank these days?" she asked me.

I squirmed a little. "About the same."

"I worry about that boy. He's too giving, I keep telling him. You gotta keep some things for yourself. So. What are you in the market for?"

"Information," I said quickly.

"Don't worry, honey. We only sell drugs to folks we know. Laugh, Andy!" she commanded. "Tell this lady I'm joking!"

"You're a real joker, Mayor."

"What kind of information are we talking about?" she asked, serious now.

I explained the situation to the Mayor, going into as much detail as I could. I'd only seen Lisa's tattoo for a split second. The hourglass was tipped on its side and swathed in something satiny. The glass was what had struck me as so amazing. It was translucent, yet seemed to distort the skin underneath, like sea glass does.

The Mayor rubbed her chin, her nose, her forehead. She shook her head and massaged her neck. Finally, she said she had a couple of ideas. Could she look into them and call me?

I handed her a card and told her how much I'd appreciate it. Then she led me off to the ladies' bathroom. I told her I didn't need to use the facilities, but she said she had something to show me. We crammed into the small space, then she shut the door and peeled off her jacket.

Turned out she wanted to show off her own tattoos.

Over her right breast was a sexy devil pinup, with yellow flames licking at a pair of trim ankles. On her left arm there was a Celtic cross stretching from shoulder to elbow. It shimmered, like a stained-glass window.

"The first Mayor did them," she said proudly. "My late husband."

"Beautiful," I murmured.

She wanted more.

"He must've loved you a lot," I said.

"Thanks, sweetie." She put her jacket back on and hugged me good-bye. Her face felt cool and papery.

I tried not to think on the ride home, just to focus on the road.

CHAPTER TEN

Detective Smarinsky wasn't available the first time I tried him that evening. Or the second. The third time the watch commander asked me if it was an emergency. I didn't know how to answer that.

Around nine-thirty, I crawled into bed, exhausted. But once the lights were out, I was wide awake. I decided to go out to my office, where I regularly drifted into unconsciousness without trying.

It was almost one in the morning when Smarinsky called back. Sleep had continued to elude me. I was going through all my old Hammett books and papers for no particular reason.

"Hey, Ms. Caruso," he said. "Sorry about the hour. What's going on?"

Another question I didn't know how to answer.

"Good to hear from you, Detective. Busy day?"

No response.

"Me, too," I continued. "Busy, busy, busy."

"Ms. Caruso—"

I didn't let him finish. "I went to the scattering of Maren Levander's ashes."

He paused. "And why did you do that?"

Because I wasn't sure those were Maren's ashes. "Because I thought it was the decent thing to do," I said.

"And I need to know that because . . . ?"

"It's your case, isn't it?" I asked.

"Case closed. Suicide. Pity. End of story."

"That's what I'm curious about," I said. "How exactly did you make that determination?"

"I'm not running an all-night forensics seminar, Ms. Caruso. Ow!"

"What is it?"

"Nothing," he yelled. "Stupid table. No, I'm okay!" he bellowed. "My wife is concerned here."

"I'm sorry to disturb you, really I am, but you told me to call you if I had any questions."

"I'm officially rescinding the offer. And you don't seem to have any questions. Do you have any questions?" I thought I could hear his blood pressure rising.

"What about tattoos?"

"What about them?" One-sixty over eighty. One-eighty over ninety. I could kill him like this.

"Scars, tattoos, distinguishing marks? You ask about all those things when you ID a body," I said. "That's what you do, right?"

"Maren Levander had no distinguishing marks. You saw for yourself."

That was the problem. "Forget it. The whole thing was just so upsetting. I'm obviously crazy."

"Is there anything more?"

"No. Nothing." Coward.

"Good night then, Ms. Caruso."

I was turning off the computer when the phone rang again. Detective Smarinsky.

"I'm sorry I called you so many times," I said, feeling something like dread in the pit of my stomach.

"Come down to the station house tomorrow," he said.

You don't fool around with the police. My dad was a cop, my brothers are cops, I'm engaged to a cop. What was wrong with me?

"I'm fine," I said. "Really. I need a therapist, that's all. I have to learn to deal with death. Can you recommend somebody?"

"I'm not asking, Ms. Caruso."

I got that part.

"Let's make it noon," he said.

"Do I need a lawyer?"

"You watch too much TV."

"We're just chatting?" I asked hopefully.

"Just chatting."

Right.

THE PHONE RANG AGAIN. ANYONE BUT SMARIN-sky, I thought, still half asleep. I looked at the clock: 8:06 in the morning.

"Up and at 'em, honey," someone shouted in my ear. It was Bridget, sounding unnaturally chipper.

"What'd you do to the real Bridget?" I grumbled.

"Andrew and I went clubbing!" Andrew was last summer's
On the Bias intern: young, handsome, and the only one ever
who hadn't been gay. The two of them were in love, which I
think was a first for Bridget. Her natural ferocity held most
suitors at bay. "We were dancing all night!"

"Good for you." I picked my gray sweatshirt up off the
floor and tugged it over my head. I'd left the windows open last
night and it was cold. "Just don't give away your Schiaparelli
capelet today." I'd consulted the price tag the other day: 1,099
big ones. It was a beauty, but out of my league.

"I don't need sleep when I'm happy, as you know," Bridget said.

"I forgot."

"It's Thursday, Cece."

I waited a beat.

"The new magazines are out."

She was speaking of our mutual fetishes: *US Weekly, Star,
People,* and *In Touch.* It was pathetic, but most hobbies are.
"And?"

"And have you been to the newsstand yet?"

"Obviously not," I said.

"Better get over there." She hung up abruptly.

I stared at the phone, then shook my head. Gambino,
who'd come over around three, got up to take a shower.

"You must be exhausted," I said.

"Who was that?"

"Bridget." I hauled my uncooperative body out of bed.
Maybe I could tell Smarinsky I had the flu.

Gambino turned on the hot water and came out to look for

his clothes. He gathered up his pants and shirt from the floor, and retrieved his gun and holster from the hall closet.

"Do you have time to go out to breakfast with me?" I asked, wrapping my arms around his waist and nuzzling the back of his neck.

"Yeah. I don't have to be downtown until noon."

Me, neither. Of course, I wasn't telling him that. He had enough on his mind. He was due in court today, giving testimony in a murder case. A Colombian dealer had killed one of the department's longtime informants. Everybody knew the guy was guilty, but the case wasn't exactly airtight. Gambino and his partner, Tico, had been somewhat hasty. There was a question about the timing on their executing a warrant. Gambino's boss was looking for a scapegoat. There'd been a three-hour meeting with the D.A.'s office earlier in the week, and there were more to come. Tensions were high. The Colombian had fired his original counsel and hired a high-profile lawyer from out of town who had a reputation as a cop hater.

Gambino went back into the bathroom. I flung open the door to my closet and rooted around for something unimpeachable. Something pastel. Maybe with a Peter Pan collar. "What do you think about cheese Danishes at Canter's?" I called out.

"No complaints from me."

While Gambino was in the shower, his cell phone rang. I picked it up, but when I said hello, the caller hung up.

Twenty minutes later we pulled into the loading zone in front of Centerfold Newsstand on Fairfax.

"What's this?" Gambino asked.

"Pit stop."

He said he'd wait in the car.

"And there she is," crowed Antwon from his perch behind the counter. He put down the issue of *Maxim* he was perusing. He didn't look like the *Maxim* type, but you never can tell. Anyway, it's good to know your merchandise.

"So," Antwon asked, nibbling delicately on a pinkie nail, "how you doing, mystery woman?" When I looked puzzled, he leapt up from his seat, then walked me over to the rack directly opposite. There was an evil glint in his eye. "Voilà! And to think I knew you way back when!"

My gaze swept across the covers of the tabloids.

Oh, no.

"You take a good picture, woman!" Antwon's dreads were bouncing in glee. "Look at her," he said, dragging over a small woman holding an issue of *Soap Opera Digest* in her hand. "The buxom brunette beauty! One of my regulars!"

"Who Is She?" screamed *US Weekly* in bright red letters.

"Rafe in Love!" proclaimed *Star*.

"Buxom Brunette Beauty Steals Rafe's Heart!" elaborated *In Touch*.

People, at least, had taken the high road, with a shot of a former Olympic champion fighting Lou Gehrig's disease.

A horn honked outside. That would be my fiancé.

I hadn't counted on this particular development, though god knows why not. It was actually kind of funny, when you looked at it a certain way.

"You could buy 'em all out," offered Antwon. "That's what Liz Taylor did whenever she was on the covers. She'd send that husband of hers with the mullet cut."

"Larry Fortensky?"

"That's right. He'd come with his mullet cut, his tight

stonewashed jeans, and his big ol' minivan every morning for a week, loading 'em all into the back. Sweet Larry Fortensky!"

"Honey, what's taking so long?" Gambino had appeared.

I threw myself across the magazines, a despairing odalisque.

"What are you doing?" he asked.

"Resting," I said with a tight smile.

The *Soap Opera Digest* woman made herself scarce.

"Get up, Cece," Gambino said.

I got up and stood next to Antwon, who was twitching with excitement. Gambino picked up the top copy of *US Weekly*. The photograph on the cover had been taken as Rafe and I were exiting the coroner's office. Rafe had his arm around me protectively. The worst part was how awful I looked in that bat-wing-sleeve sweater. I was getting a breast reduction immediately.

Gambino looked at it for a minute or two, then tossed it nonchalantly back into the pile. "What, you think I'm some kind of Neanderthal?"

Antwon was about to answer when I kicked him.

"Garbage in, garbage out. Next week they'll have a new victim. Let's go."

Antwon gave me a little wave.

Canter's cheese Danishes might have made everything better, but unfortunately, they were closed for a film shoot.

Hooray, as they say, for Hollywood.

CHAPTER
ELEVEN

The one saving grace of the morning was Smarinsky canceling our meeting. Something more important had come up, and he'd decided to cut me loose. A simple call would've saved me the trip, but I had a suspicion this was his way of punishing me. It was fine. I wasn't due at Rafe's until later in the afternoon, and I had no idea what I was supposed to say to him. I wasn't at the point where I could accuse him of anything. Not yet, at least. But there were still avenues to explore. Since I was downtown already, I thought I'd take a chance and see if Captain Donaldson was in. He was a far more pleasant character than his colleague. Maybe I could pump him more successfully.

Donaldson was busy on the service floor, but would be free in half an hour, if I could wait. In the meantime, I asked the receptionist to point me in the direction of the gift shop.

Shopping is an outstanding way to kill time. And assuming

you aren't averse to debt, it's an excellent stress reducer, as well. All those colors and textures get the blood flowing, wash out the toxins. Of course, retail establishments run the gamut and, sad to say, Skeletons in the Closet lacked mightily in the ambience department. The goods weren't much to speak of either. I have no idea what kind of person would clamor for a pair of Undertaker boxers, with a pattern of dead-body logos, or a Foot with Toe Tag T, though I do find it curious that there were no smalls in the pile. Lots of XXLs, though.

"Careful! That's a breakable!" The shrill voice came from behind a stack of glossy black gift bags imprinted with the ever-popular dead-body logo. A woman appeared, wielding a Kit Kat bar like it was a grenade. I put down the skull paperweight/business card holder I'd picked up—with fine anatomical detail, spring-mounted jaw, and snap-off top—and looked at my watch. I had to go, anyway.

Captain Donaldson was waiting in the lobby. He smiled at me as if we were old friends. It was disarming, which was probably the point. He hadn't gotten where he was by getting people to clam up. That was Detective Smarinsky's specialty.

"I finished up more quickly than I expected," he said.

Doing what, I didn't want to know. He reeked of formaldehyde.

"Shall we go somewhere more private, Ms. Caruso?"

"Yes, thank you."

His office was a muddle of papers, the walls lined with thick, leather-bound books on intriguing subjects like statistical genetics, perinatal autopsies, forensic entomology, disposition of toxic drugs and chemicals, practical aspects of ballistics, medicolegal investigations. Intriguing to some of us, at least. He offered me a seat. The chair felt sticky.

"So what can I do for you today?" He faced me across a jumble of rainbow-hued file folders.

I didn't answer immediately.

"Your experience here must have been most upsetting. I can only imagine. Something like that isn't easily forgotten. It can churn up all sorts of confused feelings."

Father McGarrigle. That's who he reminded me of. Our parish priest back in Asbury Park. My mother desperately wanted me to marry his nephew, Taylor, who was gay. Last I heard, he was in Miami, running an Asian-fusion restaurant. Taylor, I mean.

"I appreciate your sensitivity, Captain, but I'm actually not here about Maren Levander."

"Oh, no?" He plucked a yellow file out of the stack and started running his fingers across the tab.

"I write books about crime fiction," I said. "I don't know if you knew that."

"I did not," he replied. "How fascinating. Fiction, of course, is the operative word. I don't mean to be insulting, but even best-selling writers get it wrong. I could write my own book about that!"

"That's exactly why I'm here, Captain Donaldson. I want to get it right."

He launched in. "One-third of all deaths are reported to the coroner. Sixty-five thousand people die each year in L.A. County, so that makes about twenty thousand deaths we have to contend with. These include all nonnatural deaths: accidents, homicides, suicides—"

"Let me stop you right there," I interrupted. "What I'm interested in is how those rulings are made. Let's take suicide."

"All right."

"How do you know that a person, say, swallowed pills on purpose? How do you know they didn't accidentally overdose, or that someone didn't force them to ingest a whole bottle of Valium or whatever, maybe at gunpoint?"

"What colorful scenarios. Your books must be very exciting."

"I don't write mysteries per se. I write *about* them. Actually, I write about the people who write them—the dead ones. Dead mystery writers." Well said, Cece.

"Ah. Fascinating. A species of critic. Well, you keep after them. Standards are so important."

I nodded in agreement, though biographers don't exactly toe the line as far as standards go. We're the vultures, the ones who swoop down on the dead. We rifle through their drawers, read their letters, air their dirty laundry.

"As for your query," he went on, "we wrestle with questions of truth every day."

"How can you ever be certain you're right?"

"The truth is always there in front of you, Ms. Caruso. You just have to be ready to confront it." The captain put down the file and coughed into his hands. "Excuse me." He pounded on his chest. "Too many years of smoking. Back to your example, though. Let's take another one, shall we?"

"All right."

"Let's say that a person's body is found near a cliff. An unidentified person. Did that person jump, or was she—he or she, I should say—pushed, or did he or she merely slip and fall?"

Father McGarrigle could do that, too. See right through you.

"If it was an accident," he continued, "we'd expect to find certain conditions in place. Unsteady terrain, loose rocks, slippery mud." Which was not the case in Lunada Bay. Not in September, at least.

"And if it was a homicide?"

"If the person was pushed, we would expect to find bruising consistent with that particular activity. If this person was found on his or her back, we'd look for such bruising on the chest. If this person was found facedown, we'd look for bruising on the back. We would also look for signs of multiple footprints."

"And suicide?" My heart was pounding now.

"We'd try to ascertain state of mind. We'd be talking to friends, family." He stopped and looked directly at me. "Of course, if there was a note, and its authenticity was undisputed, well, that would be that. Barring any complicating factors, the ruling would be made immediately."

"And the body would be released."

"The body would be released. The matter would be closed." He took the file and put it in his top drawer. Then he closed the drawer and stood.

"I'm afraid I have a meeting right now. Perhaps we can continue this at a later date."

I unstuck myself from the chair and followed him to the door.

"One last thing." Captain Donaldson placed an avuncular hand on my shoulder. "I am available if you need to talk about anything. Please feel free to call me or drop by like you did today." He gestured around his office. "These are your tax dollars at work, after all."

As I walked down the corridor and through the heavy wooden door, I felt more confused than ever. Worse yet, it was starting to feel like normal.

ON THE WAY TO RAFE'S, I CALLED IN FOR MY messages. There was one from my daughter, Annie, who said she didn't want to say I told you so, but did anyway; one from Bridget, whose grandmother had seen me on the cover of *In Touch* at the hairdresser's and was wondering if she bought her own copy, would I sign it?; one from Lael, who wanted to borrow the bat-wing-sleeve sweater for a date tomorrow night; one from Gambino, calling from the hallway outside the courtroom for moral support; and one from the Mayor, who said she had news.

I returned Gambino's call first, but didn't get an answer. I called the Mayor next and got Andy at the Spot, who said the Mayor hadn't been in all day, but she'd instructed him to tell me to get in touch with Barker, who was expecting to hear from me. He said this like I knew who Barker was. Then he gave me a number with an 818 area code, which I did know was the San Fernando Valley, on the other side of the hill.

I needed to pull over. I found a shady spot on Pico in front of a belly-dancing studio whose front entrance was flanked by a pair of headless mannequins wearing dusty old harem pants, silver-coin belts, and cropped gauzy tops. A genre of vintage I had yet to plumb.

I got Barker's wife, Helene. She told me I could reach her husband at Jumbo's Clown Room. Must be she and Barker had some sort of understanding because Helene sounded way too blasé about her husband's bar of choice, which I knew from as-siduous reading of the tabloids, as opposed to personal experi-ence, to be a strip joint in Hollywood where Courtney Love had once danced.

"Jumbo's Clown Room!"

I asked for Barker.

"Barker who?" the guy on the other end of the phone asked.

Good question.

"Is there a Barker here?" I heard him yelling over the music.

There was noise, like maybe the phone had fallen onto the floor, some fumbling, then a voice said, "This is Barker."

I still didn't know if it was his first or last name.

"Hello. This is Cece Caruso. I got your name from the Mayor."

"Yeah, sorry about the a-hole who answered the phone. He's new."

"I understand."

"So you were asking about some hourglass tattoos. Two girls."

"That's right," I said, keeping my voice steady.

"Heard those girls are screwing your husband."

"Yes, well, I think so. I'm not a hundred percent sure. Still, I'm very upset."

"You wanted their names," he said.

"Yes."

"Listen, I gotta tell you something right off the bat. I don't care what the Mayor might have told you, I'm not getting involved in any murder-for-hire shit, nothing like that. I'm clean as a whistle and staying that way."

"You're kidding, right? Hello? Mr. Barker?"

"Name's Barker."

"Barker. I'm sorry if the Mayor gave you that impression. I don't want to hurt them. Not at all. That's the furthest thing from my mind." I laughed nervously. "Oh, my god."

"Good to hear. Hey, can you call me back on my cell? This prick here is giving me shit about tying up his line."

"Sure." Sure I will. Sure I'll call back my new friend, Barker, a tattoo artist at a strip bar worried I think he's a hit man.

He answered on the third ring. Taking his time. A man of leisure.

"No new identities," Barker said right off the bat, "no fake passports, no funny prescriptions. You talk to the Mayor about that shit, okay? That's her turf."

"Okay."

"Damn straight."

"So those girls," I prompted.

"Yeah."

"Yeah?"

"I remember 'em," he finally said. "Long time ago. Must've been more than twenty years by now. I did 'em. I don't mean I fornicated with them, because they were underage, of course, with fake IDs they must have done themselves they were so pathetic. A blind person could've spotted them a mile away. But I was drinking then, and couldn't give a shit, and the statute of limitations is up on that particular infraction, anyways."

Someone honked at me. "You leaving?" A guy in a BMW looking for a parking space. I shook my head, annoyed.

"Sorry," I said, turning my attention back to Barker. "I'd like to be totally clear here. You said you did them. That means you gave them matching tattoos?"

"Good work, wasn't it?"

Well, that was that.

If he'd tattooed both of them, then the woman I'd seen, the woman with the unmarked white skin, couldn't have been Maren.

"They were spoiled brats," Barker said. "Sexy as hell, though. Had that rich-bitch vibe going. Said their boyfriends were Bay Boys."

"What's that, a rock band?"

"Surf punks. Local badasses. Still around, still going strong all these years later. But I didn't believe 'em for a second. No girls who hung with Bay Boys would be stupid enough to offer to blow me for the price of a couple of tattoos."

Okay.

"The weird thing was, they had a kid with them. That's what was so fucked up. She didn't look happy to be there. It wasn't any place for a kid."

Proof. I needed proof. Something, anything, to bring to Smarinsky and Donaldson. "Are there records? Release forms?"

"Not anymore. That shit is long gone. I sold the place. It's a Payless shoe store now."

I took my last shot. "You're absolutely sure? The tattoos were located on these girls' shoulders, both of them?"

"On their shoulders. Supposed to be exactly the same. I cheated a little, though. The hourglasses weren't exactly the same. One of them, don't remember who was who, that girl had less time than the other one."

I'll say.

I TOOK OVERLAND TO WASHINGTON, WASHINGton to Ocean, and Ocean to Venice Beach.

The same refrain kept playing over and over again in my head.

Rafe is a liar.

Rafe is a liar.

Rafe is a liar.

I should have known when I saw him in action at Ike's liquor store. I should have walked away then, like I should be walking away now. But I couldn't, somehow. I couldn't just walk away.

"I know what you did," I sputtered, red faced, when he opened the thick, plate-glass door of his canal-front house. Strange that a person so enamored of privacy would live some-place transparent to the outside. Maybe he liked the illusion that he had nothing to hide.

He didn't answer me right away. He turned around. At first, I thought maybe there was someone else there. Maybe Will—Will, who could fix anything, except this.

But Rafe was alone. It was quiet. All I could hear was the quacking of the ducks, who wanted somebody to toss them a crust of bread. Ducks don't have it so easy.

Rafe turned back to me.

"Let's take a walk. I owe you an explanation." He shut the glass door behind him—carefully, as if it were the first time, or the last.

CHAPTER
TWELVE

It didn't occur to me to be scared. What I felt was punch-drunk, as if I were going through the motions without really inhabiting my body.

I followed Rafe down the cracked sidewalk, house after anonymous house. Some had small rowboats tied to the weathered wooden docks. Here and there, thickets of palm trees cast shadows on the glassy water. We stopped at a bridge wrapped with tiny Christmas lights and watched a couple in a red boat float by. The woman's laughter skipped along the surface of the water, like stones. It was absurdly pastoral.

Venice, California, was established around 1900. It was going to be a simulacrum of the original, with classical arcades, Moorish accents, and twenty miles of waterways. But these were mostly paved over by the end of the twenties to make room for cars. For decades afterward, the few remaining canals languished, swampy and mosquito infested. An urban-renewal project in the eighties made them desirable again, and so expensive only the very rich could afford to live nearby.

Rafe was very rich. He could have whatever he wanted.

"They tried to kill all the ducks a few years back," he said, breaking the silence. "Muscovy ducks. They had some awful disease, and they were afraid it would spread to the wild flocks. A bunch of people from the neighborhood gathered them up in the middle of the night and took them to secret locations to save their lives."

"Is there a reason you're telling me this now?" I asked.

"People do strange things in the name of love."

"Not good enough," I snapped.

"Dude," Rafe said, waving at a tall man in a Rolling Stones T-shirt crossing the next bridge over. "Sam the man. How you doin'? We going to see you Saturday?"

"Wouldn't miss it." The man walked on, then turned around. "Give my best to Will."

"My neighbor." Rafe stuck his hands in his pockets and looked out at the water. "Guy used to have a rowboat, but it was stolen last year."

"Stop it, Rafe," I ordered. "I'm not leaving until you talk to me."

"What is it that you think you know?"

"Aren't you going to mike me?" I demanded.

"I deserved that. I said I'd explain everything. But not here."

"Yes, here." I noticed some gang graffiti carved onto the bridge's wooden post. Nobody's immune.

"Back at my house," he said. "C'mon."

That's when it occurred to me to be scared. "I'm not going

with you to your house." I wanted to stay exactly where I was, where everybody could see us.

"Have it your way," Rafe said, shrugging. "What do I care anymore?"

"Stop with the melodrama."

Rafe ran his fingers through his blond hair. It was still wet from the shower. "I got a letter from Maren around three weeks ago."

"Go on."

"Hadn't heard from her in years. It was short. She said she was in big fucking trouble."

"Why should you care?" I demanded. "You just said you hadn't heard from her in years."

"We had a past. We had a bond."

Another bond.

"She said she wasn't going to see me again," he went on, "that she needed to disappear. And that I should prepare myself for anything. That I shouldn't be sad. I shouldn't worry. I should be happy." He lowered his voice. "She was saying goodbye. I thought it was a suicide note. I told Will. He thought so, too. But we didn't know where she was, how to find her, how to stop her."

"Did you show it to Captain Donaldson?"

He nodded. "Him and Smarinsky."

"And they agreed?"

He nodded again.

"But it wasn't a suicide note," I said. "Because that wasn't Maren we saw, was it?"

He was silent.

"Answer me, Rafe. That wasn't Maren, was it?"

He was barely audible. "No."

I exploded. "Do you realize what you've done? That you've committed a crime? That you've lied to everyone—to the police, for god's sake—and that you've implicated me? How dare you?" Just then, something occurred to me. "Oh, my god. Does Will know?"

He shook his head.

"Will never saw the body?"

"He said he couldn't face it."

I felt sick all over. "He trusted you! And now he thinks his sister is dead! How could you do this to him?"

"For all I know, she *is* dead by now. It's complicated, Cece."

"That's an understatement."

He turned to go, but I grabbed his arm. "I'm not finished here. You haven't explained why you did it."

He pulled away from me. "You don't understand. Maren had a way of getting in over her head. She's always been attracted to danger. She hung out with some really bad people."

"So?"

"So I read between the lines. I had to help her."

"I don't know what that means."

"I'm an actor. Like I explained to you before, I know what people are saying even when they're not saying it."

"What are you talking about?" I asked, exasperated.

"She needed to run away. Not to exist."

"I don't understand."

"Maren Levander had to die."

Slowly, irrefutably, it hit me. "Are you saying you helped Maren stage her own death?"

He looked at me, his defenses down. "You can't say no to Maren."

"Jesus, so you killed some innocent woman so you could pretend she was Maren?"

"No, no," he said, shaking his head fervently. "Of course not. I can't believe you'd think something like that of me. Jesus. But when I got to the coroner's office and they showed me the picture they'd found in her pocket, that picture of me and Maren from the old days, I understood what I was supposed to do."

"You were supposed to identify the woman as Maren."

"Yes."

It was as if she'd put a spell on him.

Like Elvira, the dangerous redhead in Hammett's Op stories. The price of loving her was death.

In "The House on Turk Street," she seduces a bank messenger into stealing $100,000 for her, then blithely gets him killed; in "The Girl with the Silver Eyes," she gets an informant named Porky Grunt to stand in front of the Op's car and empty his gun at him in a lunatic attempt to save her. The Op was the only man able to resist her. Only the Op was as cold and hard as she was. But Rafe was no Op.

I chose my words carefully. "Your loyalty to Maren is misplaced, Rafe. You need to do the right thing here."

"Haven't you ever done the wrong thing for the right reason, Cece?"

"That isn't the point. Did you ever stop and ask yourself who she was?"

"Who?"

I closed my eyes. "The dead woman. Or how she happened to appear just when Maren needed her? Can you possibly be that naive?"

"You can stop right there. Maren had nothing to do with

that woman's death." He looked as if he truly believed what he was saying. But that's what he got paid for.

"Rafe. Think about it for a minute. What other possible explanation can there be?"

He took my hands. "I don't know, but I know Maren. I know her better than anybody. She's been involved in some shady stuff, I'll admit that. She got mixed up with the wrong people, maybe even broke a few laws. But she isn't a killer. I know that to the bottom of my soul. I'm asking you to trust me."

"Like Will trusted you?"

"You have to let it go, Cece."

"Let it go?" I asked incredulously. "How can I—"

But he wouldn't let me interrupt.

"I'm hoping Maren made it out alive. I'm praying she did. If she did, what I did, the lie I told, was worth it. Whoever the other woman was, whatever happened to her, we can't help her now. It's too late."

Maybe I couldn't help the other woman, but I also couldn't forget about her, as if she'd never existed. How could I just forget about her?

Who was she?

How had she died?

Then it hit me, like a ton of bricks.

Maren.

Maren could tell me.

CHAPTER THIRTEEN

K nock, knock."

   "Who's there?"

"Cece."

"Cece who?"

"Open the door or you're dead."

Lael's teenage son, Tommy, opened the door, stepping quickly out of the way so as not to be trampled by his younger half sisters, Nina and Zoe, who were obviously intent on ambushing me before I could get as far as the living room. Not that the entry hall wasn't a destination in and of itself. In its current incarnation, it resembled a homeless encampment, the walls lined with ripped cardboard boxes, the floor covered with threadbare quilts. Tommy was sleeping there while his mother fixed up his bedroom. Fixing up rooms was Lael's passion, if not her talent. Her ramshackle Beachwood Canyon compound (I use that word advisedly) was testament to that fact.

"Since when did you people get so serious about security?" I asked, hugging the girls, who smelled like candy apples.

"We were robbed last night!" Zoe squealed. "Mommy bought us new lip gloss!"

"Get off Cece now," Nina ordered her younger sister.

"Your mother didn't mention a word about it to me."

"I'm in the kitchen," Lael called out. "Come see the Snow Queen!"

Lael was poised in front of what looked like a ziggurat of yellow sponges.

"It's taken me all day to figure out how to construct the sleigh. The Snow Queen's going to be reclining, pulled by four swans, all wrapped up in blankets. The party's in Malibu at six-thirty." She looked up at the clock anxiously. "Once I get the buttercream right, I'm home free. But for some reason, batch after batch tastes like pumpkin."

"You were robbed?"

"It was nothing. The birds are done. Want to see them?"

"They have blue eyes," Nina said proudly.

Lael opened the refrigerator to show me four exquisitely sculpted sugar-paste swans lying on a paper plate. "I used a toothpick," she said.

"I can't believe you're so calm, Lael. Were you home when they broke in?"

"We were at Tommy's baseball practice. But then the baby started fussing, so we left. Tommy was going to catch a ride home with some friends. Did I tell you he has a girlfriend now?"

"Christine," Zoe said, bursting into giggles.

"Anyway, when we walked inside, I knew something wasn't right."

Given the usual mess, I wondered how anybody could tell, but I kept my mouth shut.

"I put the kids in the car and locked the door, then went back inside. The stereo was gone, and the big TV, and that was it. They left my jewelry, not that it's worth anything."

"What did the cops say?" I asked.

"That I could pretty much forget about getting my stuff back," she said. "And that I should change the locks, which I did this morning. That's that, I suppose."

"Very philosophical." I gave her a hug of condolence, then produced the bat-wing-sleeve sweater. "Who's the big date with?"

She blushed. "The cop. He knows Gambino. He was adorable."

It should be noted that Lael never met a man she didn't consider adorable, and vice versa. She had long, straight blond hair, Marilyn Monroe's body, and no use whatsoever for clothes, although she did bow to convention by wearing them. She loved perfume, scented bath oils, and knitting long scarves. She was invariably disheveled. This, however, had proved to be no impediment whatsoever to her bustling love life.

"Do you have a minute, Lael?"

She shooed the children out and closed the door behind them.

"What's going on?" she asked.

I shrugged.

"Let me guess. More trouble with the movie star?"

She knew the story up until the coroner's office. I filled her in on the Mayor, and Barker, and this afternoon's conversation with Rafe.

She whipped off her cat's-eye glasses and shook them at me. "It seems to me I've doled out this particular bit of advice before. But for the sake of clarity, I'll reiterate."

I tapped my foot.

"Don't do it, Cece. Don't do what you always do. Talk to Gambino. The police have to be informed. I realize Rafe Simic is gorgeous, but come on."

"It isn't that, and you know it. What if he's right? That's what I'm worried about. What if he's done the one thing he could do to save Maren's life, and my going to the police winds up getting her killed?"

"I can't answer that."

"You know how cops are," I said. "They show up, make a lot of noise, ask a lot of questions, and suddenly everybody knows Maren's not really dead. So the bad guys kill her."

"Oh, come on. What bad guys?"

"I don't know," I admitted. "Some people she got involved with."

"What about the real dead woman?"

"Yeah, well, that's the other problem."

"Someone out there must be looking for her," Lael protested. "It isn't right."

"There's nothing left of her. I don't know how on earth she could ever be identified now. And nobody matching her description was reported missing."

"That was days ago. Maybe the situation's changed." Lael paced a little bit, then licked something off her fingers. "Can't you ask Gambino?"

"I don't think that's going to go over very well. And I can't bother him now. There's a situation at work. He's having problems." I didn't want to say more. Not until I'd spoken to him. Lael knew not to push it.

"Maybe I could ask Officer Murray," she said coyly.

"No way. I know you want to help, but it's bad enough one of us is in over her head."

"Honey, you know I like the feeling."

One of the many reasons we were kindred spirits.

THE MALTESE FALCON. CHAPTER SEVEN. THAT was what I'd been looking for the other night when I couldn't sleep. It came to me as I drove home.

In the seventh chapter of *The Maltese Falcon,* the hardboiled P.I. Sam Spade tells the duplicitous Brigid O'Shaughnessy a long and involved story about a man named Flitcraft.

Flitcraft, a husband and father of two, works in real estate in Tacoma. One day, he leaves his office to go to lunch, and he never returns.

Like a fist, Spade says, when you open your hand. Nothing left. Gone.

What happened was this: going to lunch Flitcraft approached a construction site, and just as he passed by, a beam fell ten stories down, smacking the sidewalk in front of him. The beam didn't touch him, but a piece of sidewalk chipped off and hit his cheek, taking off a piece of skin. This near-miss experience changed everything. In an instant, Flitcraft understood that life was governed by blind chance, that a sudden, random event could shatter even the most carefully laid plans. So he decided to get in sync with that randomness by simply walking away from his life.

The thing was, when Spade caught up with Flitcraft, it was several years later. He'd settled in Spokane and he'd married. His second wife didn't look much like the first, but they were more alike than different. Spade explained it by saying that Flitcraft adjusted himself to beams falling, and then no more of them fell, so he adjusted himself to them not falling.

It was a good story. But its meaning still eluded me, all these years later.

Are we all chameleons, able to turn on a dime? Or creatures of habit, doomed to repeat past mistakes? Are chameleons the consummate creatures of habit?

I didn't know. It was a mystery. And Maren had somehow become part of it. I didn't understand the woman—not yet, at least. But this much I suspected: a beam had fallen near her, and she had adjusted herself accordingly.

CHAPTER
FOURTEEN

I was still thinking about Flitcraft later that evening.

"Literary analysis," I explained to Buster, "is complex."

He wasn't listening. He had his nose down to the ground. Sniffing enthralled him as I never could.

"Stories," I pressed on, "can have multiple, even contradictory meanings. Like people."

The Doberman from around the corner approached Buster respectfully. The big ones have manners. The little ones get all up in your face.

"How about you?" I asked, turning to Gambino. "Are you listening to me?"

"No," he answered, shoving his cell phone into his pocket. "I was checking for messages."

"Are you expecting someone?"

"Tico," he said quickly. "He hasn't called back."

I glanced at Gambino's watch. Ten-thirty was too late to be

walking the dog, but we'd needed to go to the market anyway. There was nothing in the house for breakfast. "He probably went straight to sleep. It's been a long day."

"Probably helped the kids with their homework, then watched the fight on HBO."

"That's what I've been saying. People are who they are." I took his arm. "You and Tico are good cops. You did everything right. He's a scumbag who's done everything wrong."

"I know that and you know that," Gambino said. "Everybody knows that, but I guess it isn't the point."

At approximately eight in the morning on May 17, Gambino and Tico executed a search warrant for cocaine and drug paraphernalia at Julio Gonzalez's small, two-bedroom Westwood apartment. The warrant was based on information, corroborated by a controlled buy, that Gonzalez was selling cocaine out of his home. Gambino and Tico positioned themselves at the front door, then knocked and announced themselves. After waiting approximately twenty seconds and getting no response, they forcibly entered the apartment, where they discovered Gonzalez in the altogether, having just emerged from the shower.

Their search of the premises yielded a number of loaded weapons, a bulletproof vest, rock and crack cocaine, and four scales. Gonzalez was charged with possession of a controlled substance with intent to distribute, possession of firearms as an unlawful drug user, and, when one of those firearms was identified as the weapon used to kill police informant Bram Moscone two weeks earlier, murder in the first degree.

The question was whether the officers had failed to wait a reasonable amount of time before entering the apartment, thereby violating Gonzalez's Fourth Amendment rights. If the search was deemed illegal, there'd be no more case. Nothing taken out of the apartment could be used. Fruit of the poisoned tree. Nobody knew what was going to happen.

We tied Buster up to the *New York Times* box. I used to sneak him into the market inside my purse, but that was before the incident at the seafood counter.

"I'll get the eggs," Gambino volunteered.

"Organic," I reminded him.

"In Buffalo, you can buy a house for what those cost a dozen."

Gambino was from Buffalo. This explained many things about him. His workaholism, for example. People from Buffalo work very hard so they don't have to return to Buffalo.

"What's the average temperature in western New York ten months of the year?" I asked.

"Below zero."

"What's the average age of the members of the Friar's Club?" We liked to play this game.

"Dead."

I kissed him on the cheek. "You get the eggs, I'll get the mangos."

In the produce section, I ran into my neighbor Butch, who had embarked upon a major landscaping project. He was currently having huge boulders and small cast-iron statues of Indian goddesses positioned in front of his house, in and around the multicolored ivy. For the hundredth time, he offered me the use of his back garden for my wedding. He'd done it up last year in a kind of English-country idiom, with four overflowing wheelbarrows and an artful array of dried-fruit wreaths and straw picture hats bolted to the garage wall. I reminded him that we hadn't even set a date.

"Why the hell not?" he asked. "Don't you want to make an honest woman of Cece?" He directed the last question to Gambino, who was just then walking our way, one hand holding the phone to his ear, the other holding a red plastic basket piled high with stuff we didn't need.

"What?" Gambino asked distractedly, shoving his phone back in his pocket.

"Your wedding!" Butch slapped him on the back, hard.

Helpless, I watched half a dozen organic eggs topple out of the red basket and onto the floor.

"There goes my retirement," Gambino muttered.

"Honey," I said.

"Wet spill on aisle six," went out over the loudspeaker.

"At least you *can* get married," Butch said, sighing.

GAMBINO LEFT THE NEXT MORNING AFTER BE-ing fortified with huevos rancheros and mango *con limón*. We'd lived in L.A. long enough that it felt about as exotic as cornflakes.

I poured myself another cup of coffee and opened the front page. Then I closed it and picked up the phone.

"What city and listing?"

"Palos Verdes. Lisa Lapelt." She'd told me her last name the day we'd met, down by the water. "It's a residence."

A human being got on the line. "Can you spell that, please?"

I did my best.

"I'm sorry. We have nothing listed."

"Any Lapelt, anywhere in the South Bay?" I pleaded.

"One moment, please."

Maren was going to lead me to the dead woman. But first I had to get to Maren.

"I'm sorry. We have nothing listed."

Was Lapelt her married name? Her maiden name? Not that it mattered. Lapelt was the name she was using. "How about a business?" I tried.

"I have a Lapelt Industries in Long Beach."

"I'll take that."

I pressed one to be connected.

Another recording.

I didn't know the extension of the party I wished to speak to, so I waited for the menu. Press one for institutional investors. Press two for sales. Press three for research and development. Press four for career opportunities. Impatient, I pressed zero for I have no idea whatsoever.

"How may I direct your call?"

"Lisa Lapelt, please," I said.

"One moment."

"What kind of company is this, by the way?"

"I'll put you through to public relations, if you'd like."

"No," I said quickly, "that won't be necessary."

Another voice, brisk and efficient: "Office of the president."

First the Mayor, now the president. "Is she in?"

"She who?"

"The president," I said. "Lisa Lapelt."

"Do you mean Mr. Lapelt's daughter?"

Ah. "Yes."

"Let me connect you to her husband's secretary. One moment, please."

Another voice, this one more brusque: "Sales floor."

The plot thickens.

"I'm trying to get in touch with Lisa Lapelt," I said. "I understand this is her husband's number."

"Would you like to speak to Mr. Scofield?"

"No, I don't want to bother Richard while he's working."

"Stephen."

That was too easy. "Actually, I'm a friend of a friend of Stephen's wife, Lisa, from high school. The one I was actually hoping to speak to was her. Do you think I could get their home phone number?"

It was a simple request. All she could do was hang up on me.

She hung up on me.

Damn.

The phone rang. I snatched it up.

"Hello?"

It was Rafe, wondering if I'd happened to find his keys. He'd lost them again. But luckily he had two sets. He also wanted to know if I'd given any thought to our last conversation. I told him I had. Then he said something I couldn't make out.

"Where are you?" I asked. "I'm losing you."

"Sorry," he said, his voice cracking. "I'm on a soundstage. We're doing pickup shots. Listen, I've gotta go. They're calling me. Wardrobe. Can we keep working together, Cece? I'd really like to finish what we started."

Keep your friends close and your enemies closer. Which one was he?

I told him I wasn't feeling well. It was that time of year. Tomorrow would be better. I'd take a double dose of Claritin. He recommended a visit to his nutritionist, Siri, which I promised to take him up on if the pharmaceuticals failed, which in my experience they rarely do.

We set up a date for eleven A.M. the following day at the Beverly Wilshire Hotel in Beverly Hills. During the thirties, while under contract to MGM, Hammett had lived there, off and on, in a six-bedroom penthouse that rented back then for two thousand bucks a month. He rode around in limousines, usually leased, and kept a chauffeur companion. There was much to discuss.

I sneezed a couple more times for emphasis before hanging up. Then I called information again. This time I asked for the Stephen Scofield residence, anywhere in Los Angeles or Orange County. And an address, too, if available.

Within seconds, I had an address in Redondo Beach and had been connected.

No answer. No machine.

I cracked open the breakfast-room window. I could hear the birds chirping and the local strays meowing. A pair of chipmunks was playing tag in my next-door neighbor's lemon tree. The sky was blue and the air felt cool and dry. Which didn't bother me in the slightest because I didn't have allergies, of course. What I did have was a case of wanderlust.

A drive to Redondo Beach would certainly remedy that.

CHAPTER
FIFTEEN

Lisa Lapelt Scofield lived in a modest Cape Cod–style house, with green clapboard siding and red and white impatiens lining the brick path up to the door.

There were two cars parked in the driveway.

One was a green Honda Odyssey.

The other was Rafe Simic's convertible.

Stunned, I swerved toward the curb, almost plowing into a hulking Lou's Fireplaces van parked across the street from the house.

I turned off the engine and tried to catch my breath.

Some soundstage. Well, I already knew the man was a liar. Maybe Lisa was a liar, too. Poor Stephen Scofield. What would he say if he knew that while he was hard at work selling god knows what, his wife was home entertaining men? Sexy, rich, famous men (one, at least) who could do a lot more than buy her a chubby minivan with fifteen cup holders, enough for seven passengers to double up, plus a bottle for the baby (Lael had recited the stats to me more than once; she was dying for someone to buy her a Honda Odyssey).

It could be perfectly innocent. Two old friends comforting each other. Suicide devastates the survivors. Only, Lisa seemed to know very well that Maren hadn't killed herself. Maybe she knew a lot more than that. Maybe she knew everything.

Suddenly, I slumped in my seat. Not getting caught was a priority here. There wasn't any good way to explain my current whereabouts. Researching post–WWII housing tracts was hardly plausible.

Then my cell phone rang. I practically jumped out of my skin. I fished it out of my purse and looked at the glowing display. Annie.

"Hi, honey," I whispered. "I'm kind of in the middle of something. Can I call you later?" I started up the car and turned at the corner.

"It's Alexander, Mom. He was up all last night again."

"Is he sick?" I parked in the shade of a massive oak tree. There was no way they could see me all the way over here, but I had a perfect view of the front door.

"It's nightmares. He keeps seeing his mom, he says, and she's caught in a terrible fire and he wants to save her, but he can't. I don't know what to do for him."

"I could kill that woman," I said. "Have you heard anything from her?"

"Not a word. Vincent says she's spacey."

"That's letting her off pretty easy, don't you think?"

"I know."

My voice softened. "Try warm milk with cinnamon and nutmeg."

"Okay. What's new with you?"

I didn't want to involve Annie in this. "The usual."

"How's Rafe?" she asked.

"More complicated than I would've guessed."

"Who isn't? I can't even begin to understand Roxana. I knew she was a flake, but this is insane. The ex-wife from hell. And they were never even married. Can you believe I have to deal with this, Mom?"

The front door opened and Rafe emerged. Lisa was right behind him, wearing very short shorts. Her legs were good. He pulled his lucky hat low over his eyes.

"Annie," I said quickly, "I've got to go."

"Maybe all ex-wives are crazy," Annie mused.

"I'm an ex-wife and I'm not crazy."

She didn't touch that, which goes to show how well I raised her. "Rafe's ex-wife was crazy. She spent time at Silver Hill, in Connecticut. It's where famous people go."

"Rafe was married?" I asked incredulously.

Lisa walked Rafe to his car and hugged him good-bye. He stroked her short blond hair, then put both hands on the sides of her face and kissed the top of her head. Weren't they worried about the neighbors? This is suburbia, folks. Everybody peeps through the curtains. Still, that kiss was hard to read. It didn't have the feel of romance. It had the feel of good-bye.

"I can't believe you didn't know that, Mom. There's a picture of her in the scrapbook."

"Who is she?"

Rafe pulled out, and Lisa hopped into the minivan and pulled out right behind him. He went left, toward the freeway; she went right. Shit. Which one of them was I supposed to follow?

"Her name is Myrrh," Annie said. "They were young and it was brief. She's some kind of artist."

Left or right? Left or right? I whacked the wheel in frustration. Oh, what was the point? I was no Declan Chan. I'd barely even heard of *The Art of War*. And they were both gone, anyway. I'd blown it.

"Myrrh recently opened a shop right near you, in fact," Annie continued. "Handmade, unique gifts, that sort of thing."

She had my full attention now. "Right near me?"

"On Third, by Crescent Heights."

I turned the key in the ignition.

STUCK IN TRAFFIC, I GOT TO THINKING ABOUT the ex–Mrs. Flitcraft. She probably could've used a Silver Hill break, too. Her husband has a near-death experience and gets to go on an existential quest, while she's left behind to deal with the kids and a mortgage. It just didn't seem fair.

Dashiell Hammett's relationship with his ex-wife, Josephine Dolan (known as Jose), the mother of his two daughters, struck me as more of the same. The rationale for his living apart from his family, at least in the beginning, was his illness. The little girls needed to be protected from infection. But the truth of the matter was that on top of his physical frailty, the drinking, womanizing, writing, and, later, the political activism depleted him. Sucked him dry. There was nothing left over for his family. I guess it's not all that remarkable. Just sad.

Myrrh Simic. What a name.

Her shop was located on a stretch of Third Street where the mom-and-pop merchants were battling it out with the newcomers, hustling curried chickpeas for $18 a pound, Day of the Dead figurines for hipsters too busy to make the trek downtown to Olvera Street, and imported tuberose candles. I saw a For Rent sign up in front of a watch-repair shop I'd gone into once, years before. The locksmith was still next door, holding on for dear life.

Madame Irina, the tarot-card reader, another old-timer, was open for consultations at 1168. Barbara, of Barbara's BodyWorks—an arriviste, clearly—was offering shiatsu massages at 1172. But the glossy red door at 1170, ornamented by a half-moon of iridescent blue tiles, was closed, the stoop littered with half a dozen delivery menus.

I knocked anyway.

The door was opened by a trim, middle-aged man with a shaved head. He hit the lights and beckoned me inside.

My initial response: beguiling, if schizophrenic.

The back wall was covered by a black-and-white mural of an Egyptian pharaoh in a horse-drawn chariot. The opposite wall was painted fuchsia, and plastered with little gold-star stickers. There was a streamlined, velvet Deco sofa, with a hand-painted Moroccan tea table on either side. Only the Sparklett's water dispenser broke the mood.

"I love that you can walk in those," the man said, appraising my four-inch, canary-yellow, ankle-strap sandals.

"What makes you think that?" I only wore them because they looked so nice with my blue cotton circle skirt, flowered georgette top, and fraying wicker handbag, which I'd bought on consignment when I was twenty-one. "I would show you my blisters, but we've only just met."

He reached behind the sofa and pulled out an old record album. "Edith Piaf?"

I visualized a dark-haired woman with a beret. "Great."

He took the record out of its sleeve and put it on.

"Ah," he murmured. " 'La Vie en Rose.' "

I had a good time browsing. The merchandise tended toward the eccentric: tiny, papier-mâché animals; baskets woven out of gum wrappers; rugs made out of tire tread; chocolates shaped like babies' heads. One corner of the room was given over to period costumes. Idly, I picked up a Marie Antoinette wig.

"Try it on," he said.

"That's okay," I said, laughing. "I have enough trouble with the crazy hair I was born with." I stopped short.

"It's okay." He stroked his head. "You can talk about hair around me. This was a choice."

"Is Myrrh here today?" I asked before I could embarrass myself further.

"Are you a friend?"

"I'd like to be."

"That is so sweet. Let me get her."

He flipped the record over, then went into the back. I put the wig back where it belonged and sat down on an easy chair made of corrugated cardboard. Immediately, I felt something give. I sprang to my feet guiltily. No more eggplant parmigiana for me. I made my way over to the chocolates—only to sniff. Rosemary. Maybe they were soaps.

A compact woman chattering into a cell phone walked into the room. She was swathed in a pleated bronze caftan, her hair piled high on her head. She reminded me somehow of a peanut, like she'd been pulled from the earth.

"Big kiss," she said, smacking the phone. Then, to me: "So it *is* you! Byron's never wrong."

Byron, the bald man, looked pleased.

"I don't think we've actually met," I said.

"Oh, we know who you are, mystery woman," she said, winking conspiratorially. "The buxom brunette beauty! Rafe's new girlfriend! Now don't look so glum. It isn't all bad, take it from me."

I started to protest but couldn't get a word in edgewise.

"If I'd known then half of what I know now, I'd have enjoyed it a lot more. But no," she said. "I was so nervous about everything. Didn't like people going through our trash, trying to figure out what brand of toothpaste we used. Didn't like the pretty girls in my face all the time. Didn't like the whole entourage thing. I wound up taking it out on Rafe. You're here for advice, right?"

This time I got as far as opening my mouth.

"He's a sweet guy," she said. "The sex is good."

Byron tittered.

"Great, actually. So go for it! Just don't expect it to last forever." She appraised my wicker bag with a shopkeeper's practiced eye. "You're going to blow it eventually."

Well. Even Bridget approved of that bag. "Are you speaking from experience?"

"Honey, listen. I mean no disrespect. A guy like Rafe can have anything he wants. Nothing personal—I really mean it—but are you so perfect that you can be anything he wants all the time, forever and always?"

"I suppose not," I conceded.

"I, for example, got fat."

"You're not fat," said the loyal Byron.

She walked over to the cardboard chairs and with a determined thrust fixed the one I'd thought I'd broken. "So. Does Rafe still keep Will around?"

She made him sound like a lapdog. "Will's still around. But I've only met him once in the flesh. His sister died recently." I suppose I expected a reaction, but not the one I got.

Myrrh started to cry—first quietly, then in heaving sobs. Even Byron was at a loss.

"Sweetie, oh, god. Please. Let me get you something. Oh, dear." Byron led her over to the sofa and started plumping pillows. I'd never seen such frantic plumping. By now Myrrh was crying so hard she couldn't see straight. Her hands were flying in all directions.

"What is it?" Byron asked, looking like he might faint himself. "Iced tea, something stronger, bourbon, maybe? Sweetheart, just tell me what you need."

She shook her head. "Get me a Kleenex, would you?"

He ran to the back and came back with a box.

"Here, doll." He sat down right next to her, so close I thought he was going to blow her nose for her. "They're moisturized."

"Maren must have meant a lot to you," I said.

Myrrh wiped her eyes and smoothed down her caftan. Then she took a deep breath. "Forgive me. I get really emotional." She shook her head. "Poor Will. He adored her."

"And Rafe. They were so close."

"Oh, Rafe." Myrrh waved her hand dismissively. "Will was the one she was close to. Rafe was always jealous of what they had. He could never compete with that kind of love. It was a little weird, actually." She blew her nose and Byron put out his hand for the tissue.

"What do you mean, 'weird'?" I asked.

"Will would do anything for Maren."

"He was her brother."

Myrrh was unconvinced. "I'm talking if she had a parking ticket on her windshield, he'd snatch it off and pay it before she even saw it. If she got a bad fortune in her fortune cookie, he'd immediately give her his."

"I guess Will has always been service oriented."

"You don't know the half of it. Oh, Will. What will he do now? Poor soul. Can you imagine giving up your own life so you can focus on cleaning up other people's shit?"

"Not easy," I said.

"Not with Maren around, it wasn't. I admired the girl, don't get me wrong, she was a firecracker, but she took advantage of her brother."

"Like Rafe does?"

"No comment," Myrrh said quietly.

"Do you talk to Rafe much?" I asked.

Byron looked at her expectantly.

"Here's another Maren and Will story for you," she said, avoiding the question. "Maren was a big doper when they were kids. But Will wouldn't let her keep her pot anywhere near her room. He hid it for her in his surfing bag, so if anybody got caught, it'd be him. He took all her lickings for her. I'm not kidding. And she let him."

"Don't say you wouldn't if you could." That's what Rafe had said to me the day we'd met.

Myrrh's voice was steady. "I wouldn't even if I could."

"Come on. It's hard to say no to that kind of devotion. What I'm wondering is how you earn it."

Myrrh tucked a loose strand of hair behind her ear. "That's the thing, honey. You don't earn it. You assume it as your birthright."

"Do you have kids' costumes?" I asked suddenly.

Byron looked up from the wigs and responded with a nod. "Firemen?"

He walked over to a French provincial armoire and threw it open. "Peter Pan. Go-go dancer. Luke Skywalker. Pumpkin, isn't that cute, for a baby? Fairy princess. Renaissance princess. Fireman." He handed me a tiny red suit, with a plastic helmet, hose, and badge.

"Do you have a little boy?" Myrrh asked with a smile.

"A grandson."

"You're so young," said Byron admiringly.

"Rafe never wanted kids," Myrrh said. Her eyes looked sad. "Is your grandson getting ready for Halloween already?"

I shook my head. "He's been having nightmares. I thought he could keep this stuff by the side of his bed. He needs to put out some fires."

Myrrh put her head on Byron's shoulder. "Oh, honey, don't we all?"

CHAPTER
SIXTEEN

spent the evening at Annie's.

The distance between our houses was insignificant by L.A. standards (twenty miles), but after work on Fridays, when westbound traffic was particularly heavy, instances of road rage were not uncommon.

I cursed through the entirety of the evening news on NPR, for example, plus a special report on the dangers of eating farmed salmon. But once I turned off Pacific Coast Highway and headed into Topanga Canyon, I started to feel better. It was that good . . . that good hippie mojo. They pumped it into the air up there.

Myrrh was not the woman I would've expected Rafe to marry.

Annie was gardening when I arrived. She was always so hopeful. But her succulents didn't look good. Vincent and Alexander were out, buying a new collar for Pandora, their hairless chihuahua. They came home around seven and we had dinner, something stewlike that I'm guessing involved tofu, tamari, and most assuredly yeast. I'd made the mistake of asking in the past. It was better not to know.

Maybe, after Maren, Rafe was looking for someone more down-to-earth. I wasn't surprised to hear he didn't want a child. Why would he want a child? He *was* a child.

Alexander wore his fireman's costume to dinner. After we'd cleared the table, he decided he wanted to show their neighbors, the Ellises. Annie shoveled the leftovers into a Tupperware container for them. They were going to be thrilled. The Ellises were the source of the yeast fixation. They even put yeast in guacamole.

After everybody left, I checked my messages. There were two. My mother called from New Jersey, wanting to know how I could have cheated on my wonderful fiancé. Nice to know she was keeping up on the literature. The curveball came from Lisa Lapelt: Call me instantly, she said.

Lisa picked up on the first ring and let me have it. Apparently, I'd alarmed her husband's secretary, who, thanks to the wonder that is caller ID, had made a note of my number. She'd described me as a crazy woman and considered calling the police, which struck me as overkill to say the least, but in the spirit of cooperation I forced myself to apologize, explaining to Lisa that if I'd overstepped, it was only because I'd been desperate to speak with her. This begged an obvious question.

"Why?" she asked.

Why? How was I supposed to know why? I had no idea why.

"Because," I started feebly, "well, because—you do know I'm employed by Rafe, don't you? Did he mention that?"

"No, he didn't mention it." She continued in the feeble vein

I'd opened up. "Because we haven't really spoken, I mean. Just at the funeral, in the parking lot. We talked for a minute, maybe two minutes, before I left." Lisa put her hand over the receiver for a second, then came back. "I have to put you on hold, okay?" There was a click. She was working hard, I had to give her that. Meanwhile, I had a minute to think strategy. I had no strategy.

"I'm back," she said.

"Everything okay?" I asked.

"Yes."

"Not for poor Rafe," I said.

"Why is that?"

"Like I was saying before, Rafe hired me—actually, Will hired me, to prep Rafe for his upcoming role. Maybe you've read about it? *Dash!* is the movie's name. It's about the writer Dashiell Hammett."

"That must be interesting work."

"It's very stressful. Shooting starts soon. And the thing is, Rafe is so consumed with what happened to Maren I can't really get him to focus."

"I'm not sure what I can do," she said.

"Well, you knew him so well, and Maren, too, I thought maybe you'd have a handle on how to deal with this. I really want to help him."

"Someone we loved is dead," she snapped. "There's no good way to deal with it. It's a problem for everyone."

"What do you mean?"

"I don't know. Look." She took a deep breath. "Maren is a hard one to get over. It's going to take all of us a long time."

"What was she like back in high school?"

"Maren? She was funny and smart. A great athlete. A

champion debater. Organized the blood drive. Was president of the film society. Prom queen. Of course Rafe loved her. Everyone did. She was a golden girl."

Talk about hard work. On a scale of one to ten, Lisa got a ten. I coughed in response.

"What's *that* supposed to mean?" she asked, a nasty edge to her voice.

"Nothing. It's just interesting to hear you say that."

"And why would that be?"

"Because that's not exactly how you described her the other day. 'Young and stupid,' I think that's what you said."

"I was upset," she retorted. "Don't hold me to anything I said that day."

"It's just that I heard Maren used to hang out with these scary surf punks—you know what I mean, hang out *hang out*? I only mention it because I'm wondering if, well, maybe in the end, it's those memories that are getting Rafe down."

She didn't answer right away.

"Hello? Lisa?"

No fool, she chose her words carefully. "From the moment she saw him, Maren was utterly devoted to Rafe."

"You would know better than me," I said.

"That's right, I would. Look, I don't know who you got your information from, but if you're talking about the Bay Boys, Maren wouldn't give any of them the time of day, and that's the truth. It's laughable! She hated them, and they hated her. They slashed her tires when she went surfing at Lunada. More than once, I might add. They were hoodlums."

"That must've made her mad. Or did she get even?"

She let out a breath. "Now I get it. You've been doing some reading."

"Actually, I—"

"Just do me a favor and don't believe everything you read."

"I don't."

"Of course you don't," she continued. "You more than anyone know exactly what I'm talking about. I just saw your picture at the market checkout stand. Rafe's new girlfriend. Ha!"

I heard the front door open. Pandora the hairless dog raced in, hopped up on the bed, and ran around in circles before curling up into a tiny ball. My family was back.

"Listen, Lisa, I've got to run. I think I know what to do now. You've been really helpful."

Silence.

"I'll send Rafe your regards," I said.

She hung up without saying good-bye.

Alexander came in wearing a beatific grin.

"Mom, where are you?" Annie called from the kitchen. "We brought cookies from the Ellises. No dairy, no oil, no sugar!"

Alexander handed me something small, dark, and oozing. It reminded me of the slime the saber-toothed tigers and woolly mammoths got stuck in at the La Brea Tar Pits.

"Eat it," he demanded.

I looked at Pandora, bald as a billiard ball, and inspiration struck. "I'm going to take it home for Barbie."

Alexander nodded his approval. "Barbie's very hungry."

I GOT HOME AROUND TEN. I TOOK CARE OF the pets, changed into sweats, and checked the mail. Bills and junk, as usual. Then I whipped out the old George Foreman grill, which I'd repurposed as a panini maker.

A person needed dinner after dinner at Annie's.

I had half a bottle of Chianti. I had fontina, still in decent shape. And I'd saved the last of the prosciutto, even though it was graying unbecomingly around the edges. The staples of the Mediterranean diet. I ate lustily, thinking of Sophia Loren. When I was finished, I went out to my office, turned on the computer, and learned that there are five surf meccas to avoid: Pakistan, Java, Morocco, the Maldives, and Lunada Bay.

The reasons to avoid Pakistan, Java, Morocco, and the Maldives are pretty obvious.

The reason to avoid Lunada is the Bay Boys.

The Bay Boys were all over the Internet.

For thirty years and counting, they'd practiced gang-style intimidation to guard the waves in Palos Verdes from being surfed by nonlocals.

You can tell a nonlocal because he's the one wearing his wet suit down the cliffs. You can tell a Bay Boy because he's the one in his old soccer cleats slashing the other guy's tires, smashing his windows, crippling his engine, and throwing rocks at him as he makes his way down the trail. And god forbid the guy tries to paddle out on his nonlocal board to take a place in the lineup.

The Bay Boys describe themselves as a brotherhood, with no written rules, dues, or officers. Instead, there are codes, pacts, and taboos. Their number holds at around fifty, ranging in age from the midteens to the sixties. They're rich and white and the cops won't touch them. Why should they? The folks in P.V. seemed to be pretty happy with things the way they were. No outsiders means no petty crime, no tacky surfmobiles, no riffraff tossing beer bottles or peeing on the lawns of their multimillion-dollar homes.

I learned the following from *Surfer* magazine, May 1998: Matt Cavenaugh, a champion longboarder from Torrance, was surfing alone when four locals paddled out and told him he had to leave or there'd be hell to pay. When he reached his car, Cavenaugh used his cell phone to call police, who arrived on the scene only to cite him for expired plates.

And this, from the archives of www.surfline.com: Tobias Stevens of Hermosa Beach got both kneecaps shattered and a two-inch laceration on the side of the head when he and his teenage son decided to surf Lunada. The cops later described Stevens as "aggressive," and arrested his son, who had inflicted a bruise on the upper thigh of one of his father's six attackers—all of whom were let go without so much as a warning.

This from the *O.C. Weekly,* November 11, 1999: Jim Barron, a visitor from Cleveland, Ohio, lost four teeth and four tires when he wandered down to photograph the surf break and encountered four members of the Bay Boys. After talking with the cops for two hours, Barron suddenly decided not to press charges.

And that wasn't even the good part.

The good part was buried in "I Was a Fucking Bay Boy," a twenty-page memoir of the seventies, posted anonymously, and I quote:

It's 1978. Reverend Jim Jones has fed 900 of his followers cyanide-laced Kool-Aid. "Dust in the Wind" is playing on the car stereo. And my good buddy, Oscar Nichols, a fellow Bay Boy, a legendary board shaper at the age of twenty, gets arrested for rape. The victim is a sixteen-year-old girl, another surfer. Pretty. Popular. A local. The community is in an uproar. The charges, however, are dropped two weeks later. The chief of police apologizes. Turns out the girl took back her story. Claimed she was confused. Sex is complicated when you're young and innocent. Young and innocent. Yeah, right.

This is what Lisa was talking about when she told me not to believe everything I read.

Maren.

The pretty, popular surfer was Maren.

After the incident, Oscar Nichols left town for a while. He later said he thought he was a smart guy, but he wasn't used to being played.

At the tender age of sixteen, however, Maren was obviously used to being a player.

CHAPTER SEVENTEEN

I t was five in the morning when I awoke to the sound of glass breaking.

There was no mistaking that sound.

I bolted upright in bed. My heart started to race, my hands started to sweat, and every hysterical thought I've ever entertained flooded into my brain simultaneously: this is what you get for living alone in a big city; don't look strangers in the eye; why aren't you married by now?; if you were murdered in your bed it would be days before anyone noticed; they're going to boil your pets alive; there's anthrax in your mailbox; never open the door to men selling magazine subscriptions; use your car keys as a weapon when walking through an underground parking lot.

I fumbled around on the night table. Where was the phone? Not here, of course. Should I turn on the light? No. Why not? No idea. My knee brushed against something unfamiliar, something hard under the covers on the other side of the bed. Gambino's new phone, a not-cheap Samsung flip top. I cupped it in my sweaty palm. He must've forgotten it here yesterday. Thank god.

I studied the display. Damn. Low battery. Gambino always forgot to charge his phone. Just as I was about to dial 911, it started to ring. The sound was deafening. Frantically, I switched it to vibrate. The vibrations felt like jackhammers. Sweet Jesus, I almost threw the thing across the room.

"Hello?" My lips were moving, but I wasn't sure if I was making a sound.

No answer. And it was too late for 911. The indicator had faded to black.

Power out.

I put the phone down, wrapped myself up in my sheets, crept out of bed, and crouched down next to my armoire. Was I being robbed? I didn't have anything worth stealing. But the burglar didn't know that. I could push the armoire over on top of him if he came in here. I could make a break for the front door. I could sneak out the French doors and hide in my office. But where had the sound come from? I'd been sleeping. I didn't know. The living room? The kitchen? I didn't exactly want to bump into him. But maybe there was no one there. Maybe it wasn't a break-in. Maybe it was just the wind. I took several deep breaths and listened to the silence.

One, two, three, four, five.

Nothing.

I tiptoed toward the closed door of my bedroom and slowly turned the knob.

Six, seven, eight, nine—all of a sudden, I felt something touch me, and I let out a piercing scream.

To my chagrin, I realized that what had touched me was Buster, who seemed to think this was a good time for an early-morning stroll. I scooped him up and moved cautiously down the hall.

Still no sound.

I glanced into the bathroom. The usual mess.

Into Annie's old room. Ditto.

Into the kitchen. Ditto. I reached into the drawer and pulled out a corkscrew. I would've gotten the butcher knife, but it was in the sink, with bits of fontina cheese stuck on it.

Fight or flight?

I'm from Jersey. Please.

"Who's here?" I called out. Then, again, in a louder voice, "Get the hell out of my house!"

There was no response.

"I have nothing!" I screamed at the top of my lungs. "Not even a big-screen TV!"

Still no answer.

Whoever had been here was gone. That was something, at least.

Corkscrew still in hand, I walked into the dining room, which faced the street. And right away I saw it, in one of the windows.

Lines radiating out in all directions, like the filaments of a spider's web. At the center, a small hole, maybe a third of an inch in diameter.

A hole the size of a bullet.

I brought my hand up to my mouth. The corkscrew slipped to the floor. I looked down, dazed. Tiny bits of glass glittered, like diamonds.

Now Buster started barking.

"You're a little late, boy," I breathed in his ear. He wriggled out of my grip and ran in the other direction.

But it didn't make sense. Burglars don't shoot into houses and then just go away.

Then, with a shiver, I remembered the bad guys.

The bad guys Maren was involved with.

The bad guys she was running from.

Maybe they knew I was asking about Maren. Maybe they knew she wasn't dead. Maybe they thought I knew where she was. But that was absurd. How could they know any of it? I didn't even know if they existed.

I peered out the dining room window. The sun was starting to come up. A Laura Scudder's potato chip truck thundered down the street. The sky was filled with gray clouds. It was going to rain. I sidestepped the glass, walked over to the front door, and cautiously, taking my time, opened it and looked outside.

It didn't look like the end of the world. It looked, in fact, like a perfectly ordinary day. Butch was walking his terrier. Marlene was roaming the street in her ancient dressing gown, carrying two cans of cat food. The trash containers were out front, waiting for the early-morning pickup. The *L.A. Times* was right where it belonged, on my welcome mat. And there was the *New York Times,* in its blue plastic wrap, just under the broken window.

Oh, shit.

Of course it wasn't a bullet hole.

Me and my taste for drama.

It was the paper guy: he'd hit the window with the *New York Times,* and broken it.

I laughed out loud.

Man, oh, man—he could've at least had the courtesy to ring the bell and let me know. I picked up the papers, brought them inside, and put on a pot of coffee. I'd sweep everything up after coffee. I had masking tape somewhere. I'd cover the hole until I could get the glass company over here.

The delivery guy missed.

That was all.

I spent the rest of the day thinking it was so.

CHAPTER
EIGHTEEN

In all the commotion I wound up missing breakfast, which
was a good thing because when I finally found Rafe in the
lounge just off the rear entrance of the Beverly Wilshire Hotel,
he forced me to ingest a lobster corn dog with sweet-and-spicy
mustard, a mini ahi-tuna burger with onion marmalade and
apple-smoked bacon, and a smoked-salmon pizzelle with shallot-
chive crème fraîche and caviar, which only in Beverly Hills con-
stituted bar food.

"The management sent them over," Rafe said, tipping his
cap in the direction of the hostess, who was on the phone, no
doubt alerting sundry friends and relations that Rafe Simic was
in the house. "Siri would kill me if I ate shit like that."

"Do I look like a trash can?" I asked, licking my fingers.
"Don't answer that."

Rafe signaled for the waiter, who came over accompanied
by a busboy holding a sheet of hotel stationery and a pen.

"Can you sign this for my aunt?" he asked shyly. "She loves your movies."

"No problem," said Rafe. "What's her name?"

"Angelica."

"Did you need something else, sir?" the waiter asked.

Rafe handed the autograph to the busboy with a smile. "Two Beverly Hills iced teas." The waiter bowed his head as they left.

A couple in matching warm-up suits clutching Niketown bags appeared in their wake. "Can we get a picture with you two?" The wife had a New Jersey accent. It made me homesick. I still owed my mother a call. But I was hanging up if she uttered so much as a word about the bat-wing-sleeve sweater. My mother disapproves of my passion for vintage clothing. Actually, she disapproves of me in general.

"Earth to Cece," said Rafe. He pulled me close while the husband drafted the hostess into taking the shot. They had brand-new camera equipment, so we all had a short tutorial.

Following their departure, the waiter appeared with our drinks. They were impressive. Mint leaves, umbrellas, and cherries were involved. I consulted the menu. A Beverly Hills iced tea consisted of Bombay Sapphire gin, Ketel One vodka, Cointreau, and lime juice, topped off with Veuve Cliquot. Just the thing for an eleven A.M. business meeting, if that's what this in fact was.

I took a sip and studied Rafe doing the same. Siri was really doing a number on him. He was looking awfully thin—a lot, in fact, like Hammett on the original dust jacket for *The Thin Man,* except for the slouchy tweeds, hat, and cane part. That was the point, of course. Siri was getting paid what was no doubt a serious wage. And the movie started shooting in exactly nine days.

That photo of Hammett was famous. It played off of Knopf's promotional material, in which the author's charm figured as much as the book's racy content. It also made the case that Hammett had based the suave drunk, Nick Charles, on himself. But Nick was not, in fact, the thin man. The thin man wasn't the hero of the piece. The thin man was the victim, the murdered inventor, Clyde Wynant.

Nobody sees him come, nobody sees him go.

Rafe rubbed his upper lip distractedly.

"Is that a mustache you're growing?" Hammett was famous for his mustache.

"It's an experiment," Rafe answered. "What do you think of your iced tea?"

I took another sip. "Good. But I think we should get started. Did you see the vitrine in the corridor?"

"The one with the *Pretty Woman* script in it?"

Pretty Woman had been filmed at the Beverly Wilshire, which was Hollywood's vision of Old World luxe. Back in the thirties, when Hammett lived here, it must've been something, but the Four Seasons chain, which had bought it recently, put way too much stock in marble and crystal, if you asked me.

"No, of course not," I answered. "I meant the one with the Hammett memorabilia."

"I was supposed to do a movie with Julia Roberts last year, but the financing fell through." Rafe's phone rang. "Excuse me."

Movie people liked to talk about other movie people. Also, herbs and dietary restrictions. That about summed it up.

Now my phone was ringing. Actually, it was Gambino's.

I'd charged it up and taken it with me, because mine was unfindable, as usual.

"Hello?"

They hung up.

"Wrong number?" Rafe asked. "Sorry, I'm on hold. It'll be just a minute." He pulled out his wallet and started rearranging his credit cards.

"They have a three-page manuscript in that vitrine," I said, apparently for my own benefit exclusively, "with a page of handwritten notes, from Hammett's last, unpublished story, 'Something, Somewhere Else.'"

Rafe indicated his cell. "I hate when they play elevator music."

"In those notes," I persisted, "it looked like Hammett was working through names: Abe (Swede) Grundquist, Lee Branch, Paulie Horris. You can see the list he made out. He was a genius at names: Tin-Star Joplin, Bunny Keough, the Whosis Kid." I paused, waiting for a sign of life. I was getting tired of fighting for this man's attention.

"Rafe? Hello? Calling Rafe Simic!" I shouted the words into my mini-microphone. "Nine days until D-day!"

"I don't have earphones on, Cece," he said coolly. "What are you doing?"

My phone started ringing again.

"Who is this?" I snapped.

"It's me," Gambino said. "Look, just turn off my phone, okay? Then you won't be bothered. Any calls will go straight to the machine."

"Love you," I said grimly, hanging up.

Rafe hung up, as well.

"Let's get another round," he said, starting to signal the

waiter. "You do remember the party tonight, right? My place, around nine. Bring whoever."

I pushed my drink away and slammed my napkin onto the table. "Are you feeling prepared, Rafe? Are you ready to play Dashiell Hammett? Do you understand what made him tick? Have you ever even heard of the House Un-American Committee? Do you realize Hammett was grilled by Roy Cohn, that he went to jail rather than betray his friends? Do you know about the whole Lillian Hellman thing? How she commandeered his legacy? I'm asking because I'm getting the sense that you're pretty much done with my services. And if that's the case, that's fine, really it is. Because the last thing I want to do is bore you."

I stood up, shaking with rage. I knew it was misdirected, at least partially. I was still upset about what'd happened in the morning. But I was also angry. Angry at myself for what I hadn't done. Angry at Rafe for what he had done. The things I knew about, and the things I didn't.

Rafe looked surprised. "Cece, c'mon. You knew from the beginning that I wasn't exactly a model student." His laughter rang hollow. "Seriously, this has been kind of intense for me, this whole thing. But you're off the hook, believe me. You've done a good job."

"Spare me, please."

"I didn't tell you, but I finally finished your book. It wasn't easy, but I did it." He started fiddling with his key ring, then stuck it in his pocket. "So I get it. I get the left-wing politics. I get what led up to it—that part I *really* get. I get that Hammett fucked up in Hollywood. I know about all the money he owed the hotel, the parties, the hookers he brought up to the penthouse. How he infuriated the studio by not attending meetings, blowing off his responsibilities. How he nursed this fantasy of writing a real novel while shoveling shit for MGM. Things got kind of out of hand. He was making a hundred thousand a year during the Depression. It's hard to handle all that money, and even harder to live with people's expectations."

He stared into space for a minute, then pulled out his key ring and started playing with it again.

I blinked hard, then sat down.

"People count on you," Rafe went on in a quiet voice, "for whatever they need. You give them what they need, they're happy. The machine keeps on humming. You let them down, it comes grinding to a halt. That's how it works. The pressure sucks. It can get so bad that you just want to escape. Into booze, sex, whatever. Because you know you're not good enough. You'll never be good enough. You fooled them for a while, but they'll figure you out soon enough. And then what do you have? You get by on luck, but what good are you if your luck's gone?"

He almost had me, until he got to that last line.

It was stolen directly from *The Glass Key*.

I looked him in the eye, and he gave me a wicked smile.

At that moment, he looked exactly like a blond Satan.

CHAPTER NINETEEN

Another round of Beverly Hills iced teas later, we went our separate ways.

Rafe went to pick up the alcohol for his party.

I went to see the man Maren Levander had accused of rape.

Oscar Nichols. A legendary board shaper at the age of twenty. He was a shaman, a maker of magic. Those types don't stray far from home.

I found him no more than fifteen miles from Lunada Bay.

Sunset Beach, California (population: 1,288; elevation: 5 feet), didn't look like much at first, a nondescript stretch of coast highway, the kind of place people invariably describe in terms of the more interesting places it falls between. Oscar Nichols's surf shop, Rocket Fish, seemed to follow the same general pattern.

On one side was Taste of Napa, with its kinky, wine-themed mural (testicular grapes bulging on the vine); on the other was

Captain Jack's, whose massive wooden sign featured a necrotic
fisherman in a long, gray raincoat. In between them was an
undistinguished, split-level wooden building with an exterior
staircase and a bad paint job (medium blue and peeling). If you
weren't looking for it, you'd definitely miss it. The two spaces
out front were occupied by a brown van and a VW bus on life
support, so I parked at the 7-Eleven two doors down.

Upon entering, I was assaulted by ska and the smell of
pot. I realized right away I wasn't the target demographic.
Everything in there was alien to me: surf wax; leashes; rash
guards; wraparound sunglasses; high-performance watches; silvery board bags; sneakers. And surfboards, dozens and dozens
of them, propped against the wall like long licks of candy, slot-
ted onto plywood shelves, hanging from the air-conditioning
vents.

I'd had to duck a little coming in.

"Hey," said the kid behind the counter, noticing me. He
took a not-ungraceful slug of his Mountain Dew Baja Blast.

"Hey. How's it going?"

He mulled that one over. "Cool," he said, nodding.

"Can we help you?" asked a girl wearing a striped wool cap,
pulled down low over her eyes. She stopped folding sweatshirts
and glared at the kid, who looked down at the huge number of
Jack in the Box wrappers, slick with grease, arrayed before him.

"Man, sorry about the mess." He quickly crumpled them
up and tossed them in a garbage can already brimming with
Jack in the Box wrappers. Not exactly thinking outside the bun.

"Rabbit. Go find Hog's Ping-Pong balls." She was taking
charge. He came out from behind the counter, his cords hanging so low I could see the boxer shorts clinging to his bony
frame, and retreated meekly to the back.

"Please, don't get up," I said to the girl, feeling a little meek myself. "I'm just looking." I fished a quarter out of the bottom of my purse and got some Hot Tamales from the gumball machine. I popped a couple in my mouth. Then I sniffed. The smell of pot had been overtaken by the smell of dog. I found him around the corner, a white German shepherd sleeping in his bed, just under the Volcom display. I bent down to stroke his glossy fur. He let out a powerful snore, then rolled over.

Brand loyalty was a big concept here. Everything was organized by label: Dakine, Hurley, Reef, Lost, Billabong, RVCA. That went for the surf wax, too: Mrs. Palmer's Sex Wax people were not to be confused with Mr. Zog's Original Sex Wax people. After much deliberation, I decided I liked the O'Neill logo best, an elegant, curling wave. I touched one of their full-body wet suits. It looked slimy, but felt like velvet.

"That's the Psycho Two," said a guy with long, dirty hair holding a cup of Starbucks coffee. "It's hell to get on, but the wrist and ankle seals are awesome. You surf?"

"No," I answered.

"You look like you've got good upper-body strength. You'd be a natural."

"I told you, man," said the original kid, Rabbit, who'd reappeared to feed the fish in the aquarium, "no hitting on the customers. Queenie's gonna skin your ass."

"I'm trembling." They had a good laugh over that one.

"So," I asked, "Oscar around today?"

They exchanged gleeful glances.

"He's in the shaping bay." The dirty-haired kid, whose T-shirt said he loved soccer moms, pointed to the open back door. "Just through there. Next door to the garage with the sunflower painted on it. If you ever want a lesson, remember, I'm available. Ask for Hog."

He and Rabbit slapped each other on the butts and made low, growling noises, like bear cubs. This woke up the dog, who sauntered over. Rabbit pulled a biscuit out of his pocket and made the dog sit for it.

The back door opened onto a narrow street that cut through a grassy median strip and dead-ended in a tangle of ice plant and beach trash. After that, there was a sparkling expanse of sand, then the ocean. It was a beautiful day. A dozen white sails were silhouetted against the sky. This was what people saw in their California dreams. They edited out the trash.

The garage with the sunflower on it belonged to one of the few beach shacks left. It was charming, with weathered shingles, a rainbow flag, and an old-fashioned mailbox. A short man wearing a Rasta hat was carrying a bag of groceries inside. The rest of the houses fronting the ocean were overscaled redos, some good, some bad. The Swiss chalet was very bad. Oscar's place was better. It occupied the garage of a two-story nautical number called "The Sea Spray," and yes, there was an anchor. Through the open doors, I could see somebody inside, wearing a mask that made me think of mustard gas. He was poised over a surfboard resting on what looked like an upside-down picnic table, with soft blue booties on the ends of each leg. In his hand was a sander making a tremendous racket.

"Hello?"

He looked up.

"Oscar Nichols?"

He turned off the sander and removed the mask.

He had close-cropped graying hair, a craggy face, and a

beer gut hanging over one truly god-awful pair of board
shorts: zebra striped, with orange slashes down the sides. But
Oscar Nichols had the look. Gets you every time. He ran his
eyes up and down my body, then slowly wiped his hands on
a rag.

"You don't look like a local." He had a smoker's voice, low,
with gravel in it.

My hand flew up to my floppy felt hat. Then I glanced
down at my clingy jersey dress, hip-slung silver belt, and brown
suede boots. I'd been going for Ali MacGraw at the airport,
circa 1971, mostly for Rafe's benefit, but I probably should've
changed before heading to the beach.

"Suppose not."

"Let me guess." He circled around me, taking his time. "I
got it. You represent a consortium of Japanese businessmen
who want to invest in Rocket Fish."

"No."

He scratched his head. "You want me to endorse your new
line of ladies' surf wear."

"No."

He smiled absently. "Bet you didn't know that every board
has a sweet spot. It can take a while to find it, but when you do,
ooh, baby, it's poetry in motion."

"I'm not here about a board, Mr. Nichols."

"Your loss," he said, rising to the challenge.

"I'm here about Maren Levander," I said.

Funny how her name sent people right into a tailspin. He
crouched down and shook his head.

"That bitch."

Succinct.

"I don't have anything to say to you." He stood up, businesslike now. "You should go."

"Just listen to me. I think she's at it again. Lying. Screwing with people's heads. Maybe worse."

"What are you talking about? She's dead."

"Maybe."

He laughed. "Oh, that's perfect. Of course she's not dead. Vampires don't die. They suck the life out of you, but they don't die. Sorry," he said, shaking his head, "I can't help you."

"Yes, you can. You can tell me about her. You can help me understand her. Then maybe there'll be a chance."

"A chance for what?" he asked.

"I don't know." I thought about it for a minute. "Justice."

He shook his head again, then just left. He knew how to leave. He'd done it once before.

"Wait. Please wait." I hurried after him, along the road for half a block, then down toward the water.

So much for my boots.

He was angry. His steps cut like knives into the sand. But I wasn't going away. It took him a while to get it. Once he did, his pace slowed. His shoulders relaxed. He pulled a pack of Marlboro Lights out of his pocket and offered me one. I shook my head, so he turned against the wind to light his, then dropped the match.

We kept on like that for a while, walking next to each other, not talking. He smoked three cigarettes in a row. I watched the water. It was low tide. The sand stretched on forever. Rocks, clumps of seaweed, shells: hairy black mussels, pink mussels, moon snails, mysterious striped bits. I bent down to pick up something brown, with ridges.

"Chocolate clam," he said.

I nodded.

Halfway back up the beach, he finally sat down, his knees hiked up around his chest. I sat down next to him. The sun was strong, but the sand felt cold through my thin dress. We looked out toward the Long Beach skyline, with its tall buildings and billowing smoke.

"She left me for roadkill," he said. "I had to build my life up from scratch after she was done."

"I'm sorry."

"It was a big game to her. Everything was a game. I saw her stick her hand into so many fucking pockets it was ridiculous. She tried to take something from me, that's what started it. I made the mistake of threatening to tell her boyfriend about it, and she paid me back real good."

"You mean Rafe Simic?"

"Old Rafe. You know him?" He smiled as he lit up another cigarette.

"Yes—well, a little."

He inhaled deeply, then blew out smoke rings. We watched them dissolve into nothing. "Rafe Simic was one stupid guy. Never saw things the way they were. Never saw Maren for who she was. That's why she screwed around on him. He thought she was this goddess, but I knew the real her."

He paused, turning the full intensity of his gaze on me. "That's what people want, you know. To be seen the way they really are."

I held his gaze for a minute, shaken in spite of myself. But when he dropped his cigarette, it was over. He was good, though. He'd almost worked me over. Had he worked Maren over? She was only a kid then. Jesus, maybe he *had* raped her. Maybe she'd dropped the charges because she'd gotten scared. But Maren didn't get scared.

"We all saw Maren the way she was," Oscar Nichols said. "It wasn't just me."

"Who's we? The Bay Boys?"

"Yeah. The Bay Boys. She wanted to surf, and she was willing to do what she had to do to hang with us. It didn't seem like a big deal at the time."

Nice.

"She became a hell of a surfer, I've gotta say. She used to talk about going pro. But it was just talk. She didn't have the juice."

"What do you mean?"

"She didn't want it bad enough. She was cold when she should've been hot. Cold as fucking ice."

Myrrh had called her a firecracker. But they say at extreme temperatures, you can't really tell the difference between hot and cold. You get burned either way.

He lit another cigarette and buried the match. "The only time I ever saw her freak was at a funeral."

"A funeral?"

He nodded. "Owen Madden was the guy's name. He was a science teacher at the high school. Everybody loved him. All the nice kids." He said it with a sneer. But I wasn't buying his act.

"What happened?"

He shrugged. "I can't explain it exactly. She just lost it. Totally freaked out. We all thought she'd taken a bad acid trip."

"She must have really cared about him."

He barked out a laugh. "What's your name, by the way?"

"Cece."

"Listen, Cece, the only person that bitch ever cared about was herself. Before she left the funeral that afternoon she walked up to me. I'd just come back after two years away. She knew what she'd done to me. I thought maybe she wanted to tell me, in person, in front of everyone, that she was sorry she'd lied about me. Like an idiot, I was trying to decide if I was going to forgive her or if I was going to tell her to go to hell. She walked right up to me that day and put her mouth close to my ear so that her breath was warm on my cheek, and she whispered one word. Then she walked out to her car."

"What was the word?" I asked.

He told me.

It was the vilest epithet in the English language.

CHAPTER TWENTY

One hour later, while trying to load a microfilm cartridge onto a microfilm machine, I found myself involuntarily uttering that very same epithet.

A sixtyish librarian with a jet-black flip came rushing over, threatening to eject me from the premises. Within minutes I had her cursing, too.

"I keep telling them," she said, wiping the beads of perspiration from her wrinkled upper lip, "that microfilm is at the end of its product life and is not part of the future of information management. Microfilm is far less reliable than digital media. It dries out and gets brittle with age." She shot me a warning glance. "And this machine! Always on the fritz!" She pushed up the sleeves of her cream-colored Qiana blouse and wrestled the film into place, over the black roller and down between the glass plates. "Number seven. I don't know how many times the technician has worked on it."

" 'Film loads from the top,' " I said, reading from the frayed sticker stuck to the side of the machine. " 'Put the reel on the metal spindle. Pull back and lift the take-up roll lever. Slide the film forward and over the black roller.' That's exactly what I did."

"Now the Reset button," she said, grinding her teeth. "It's blue. Automatic. Just push."

I pushed, and the thing started spinning until it stopped dead and we smelled burning.

With a sigh, she directed me to machine number 6.

The Peninsula Center Library had the full run of the *Palos Verdes Peninsula News*. Twice a week, every Thursday and Saturday since 1937, residents of the four cities on the Peninsula (Rolling Hills, Rolling Hills Estates, Palos Verdes Estates, and Rancho Palos Verdes) could turn to the *Peninsula News* to learn which challenger had ousted which incumbent for a seat on the water board; which middle-school vice principal played which Shakespearean villain in which local production; when the next city-council meeting would be held; where the best surf breaks were; who was coaching the Little League.

I sat at machine number 6, looking for Owen Madden.

Oscar Nichols said he had been a popular science teacher at Palos Verdes High. Maybe an article about the science fair? This was a small, close-knit community. Somebody's prizewinning project about how a windmill works, or how to measure the accuracy of meteorological forecasts would definitely constitute local news. And the prizewinning student would, of course, insist on posing for a picture with good old Mr. Madden, who'd always been so supportive.

No such luck.

I made my way through the 1970s. The weeks and months flowed by. People lived. People died.

I finally found a mention of him. Owen Madden was, in fact, a *Dr.* In 1975, he'd received a grant from the National Science Foundation on behalf of a group of his advanced-placement students who were involved in an ambitious oceanography project. They were building a model of the outer three hundred kilometers of the earth, which could be used to develop a better understanding of the principal features of plate tectonics, including seafloor spreading, the pattern of magnetic stripes frozen onto the seafloor through faulting, thrust faulting, subduction, and volcanism.

Unfortunately, there was no picture.

I moved on to the next decade.

Dr. Madden had died around the same time Oscar Nichols had come back to town. Nichols had been arrested in 1978 and had stayed away for two years, which put Dr. Madden's death somewhere around 1980.

Sunday, April 3, 1980, to be precise. A full-page obituary appeared that following Thursday.

Dr. Owen Madden of 562 Pilgrim Lane, age forty-seven, had been a widower. Born in Marblehead, Massachusetts, undergraduate degree from Boston College, Ph.D. in zoology from Harvard University. An amateur bird-watcher. A chess player. He liked to roller-skate. When he failed to get tenure at Connecticut College, he moved out to California to work at Palos Verdes High, where he'd been a beloved teacher for over fifteen years. Several of his former students went on to pursue careers in the sciences, crediting Dr. Madden with inspiring their young minds. He left behind a daughter, age eleven. Her name was May.

The cause of death was suicide.

There was a picture.

Dr. Madden had a prominent nose, bushy eyebrows, and a mustache to match. A halo of brown hair. Kind eyes.

The memorial service was to be held at three P.M. on the following Saturday, at the Wayfarer's Chapel, on Palos Verdes Drive South.

I was at the end of the reel, so I turned the knob to reverse and waited for the machine to finish rewinding the film. Then I slid the cartridge off the spindle and loaded the next one.

It didn't take long to find it. The article was prominently positioned in the society section.

The reporter wasn't the sentimental type. He stuck to the facts.

The school principal gave the eulogy.

The school choir sang hymns.

Over four hundred people came to mourn Owen Madden's passing.

And Maren Levander was among them, just like Oscar Nichols had said.

I read this particular sentence several times: *"'His daughter loved him dearly,' commented baby-sitter Maren Levander, 18, of Palos Verdes Estates, her eyes brimming over with tears. 'May's life will never be the same.'"*

Maren was the baby-sitter. Maren was sad for the kid. No hysterical outburst. No acid trip. No inappropriate behavior. Just the phrase, *"Emotions were running high,"* which is no more and no less than you'd expect.

Had Oscar Nichols made the whole thing up? But why make something like that up?

I was going in circles. Smoke rings. Everything dissolving into nothing.

I heard the hard snap of the microfilm as it finished rewinding.

I was done here—fine. But I was hardly done.

562 PILGRIM LANE.

It was a nice house, not as fancy as the houses along Paseo del Mar, with their picture-postcard views of the ocean, but nice all the same, backed up against a hillside, two stories, ivy-covered brick, with a neatly trimmed front lawn, a bay window, and an attached garage.

This was the house where Owen Madden had lived with his daughter, May. It was a long shot, but maybe May still lived there.

There'd been a girl there that day Maren and Lisa got their tattoos. That's what Barker had said.

Maybe May Madden was that girl.

I walked up the stone pathway. Next to the water hookup, a green garden hose was coiled inside a large, terra-cotta pot. It looked like a snake. The mailbox was stuffed with circulars. Some had fallen onto the welcome mat. I picked one up.

It was addressed to "Resident."

I rang the bell, but there was no answer.

"You won't find anybody there," I heard a voice call out. I turned around. It was the woman next door. She was sitting on her porch with a bottle of beer in her hand.

"You don't look familiar, but I'm not wearing my glasses. You looking to buy?" She took a sip of her drink, then put it down on a metal card table. "Everybody who buys around here tears down these perfectly good houses to build a mansion or some such crazy thing. Perfectly good houses. Poor Phoebe. She must be turning in her grave. Not me. They'll have to drag me out by my bootstraps."

"Phoebe?" I walked across the lawn toward her.

The woman shrugged on a flannel shirt that had been hanging over the back of her chair, taking care to pull out her long, gray ponytail. She separated the ponytail into two parts, then pulled on the ends to tighten it.

"Phoebe Madden was my neighbor," she said. "My friend of twenty-some years."

"I see."

"Don't be shy," she said, patting the chair next to her. "Have a drink with me." She squinted into the sun. The lines around her eyes deepened into furrows. "It's almost cocktail hour, after all."

I smiled. "I'd love some water."

"Join me for a whiskey," she said.

"Lemonade?"

"Whiskey sour."

"How about a beer?"

"Done."

She bent down and opened a small portable fridge at her feet. She handed me a Molson's Golden and an opener.

"Thank you," I said, cracking open the bottle. I sat down on a flimsy rattan chair and took a sip. "I thought this was Owen Madden's house."

"It was Phoebe's house," she said. "Phoebe moved in after her brother died. Raised his daughter all by herself. Lung cancer. She went like that." The woman snapped her fingers. "Two weeks tops. Terrible thing. And the house went even quicker." She laughed. "It sold in maybe a day. So you're out of luck, dear."

"I wasn't looking to buy."

"Were you a friend of Phoebe's?" she asked.

"No," I replied. "I wanted to talk to May, actually. We know some of the same people. I'm worried about them. I thought May might be able to help."

"You just missed her," the woman said, opening another beer. "In and out of town real fast, that girl was. She cleaned out the house, gave away what she didn't want, and left in a whirlwind. She's got a big, important job. Phoebe was so proud. Fund-raising, I think. Philanthropy. Save the whales, something like that. Guess she had to get back to work. Can I get you some cheese, maybe?"

She brought out a tray with a nice, runny Camembert and a hard white cheddar. We ate the cheese and talked for a while— about movies, the economy, local politics. She told me you could learn everything you needed to know about the history of the Palos Verdes Peninsula from its plants: food and drink plants from pre-Columbian times, like the lemonadeberry and the prickly-pear cactus; medicinal plants from the mission days, like horehound and castor bean; hitchhiking plants like tumbleweed; wild oats that arrived with feed grains during the cattle era; landscaping plants like acacia and eucalyptus that escaped from the large estates of the 1900s.

Her name was Diana Muldaur.

We watched the sun go down together.

When it was time for me to go, Diana went into her house with the empty tray and came back with a shawl wrapped around her thin shoulders. She was carrying a stack of brochures.

"May left these behind," she said, handing them to me. "You might want to look through them. Maybe make a donation. She always liked a good cause, May did."

I thumbed through the brochures on my way back to my car.

Pollution, habitat destruction, and overfishing take a serious toll on our oceans, so Oceans Conservancy works to preserve and restore the rich diversity of ocean life and the quality of coastal waters.

May worked for the Oceans Conservancy. A good cause, yes.

I started up the car, then Gambino's phone started to ring. I fumbled around for it in my bag.

"Hello?"

A hang up. Again. This was getting weird. I looked at the register. The call came from a 323 number I didn't recognize. I turned off the engine. I took off my seat belt. I pressed Redial.

It rang once, twice.

A woman's voice answered: "Hello? Peter?"

"Are you looking for Peter Gambino?" I asked sharply. "Who is this?"

She hung up.

My hands shaking, I pressed the button for a full readout on the last fifty incoming calls.

Four were from me.

Two were from Gambino's partner, Tico.

The remaining forty-four were from her.

I stared at the phone in disbelief.

It started to ring. I picked it up. "You better talk to me this—"

It was Gambino.

"You're right. We need to talk," he said in a voice I didn't recognize.

In *The Glass Key,* Janet Henry has a dream. She and her lover, Ned Beaumont, are lost in a forest. They wander for a long time, then come upon a house. They find a glass key under the mat. When they open the door, the key shatters in the lock. Inside, there are hundreds of snakes slithering and hissing on the floor. In despair, the lovers realize they can never lock them in again.

Once you open a door and see what's on the other side, you can't unsee it. The knowledge is yours forever.

I pulled away from the curb.

I knew how to get home, but that didn't mean I wasn't lost.

CHAPTER TWENTY-ONE

I saw Gambino through the shattered glass of the dining room window. He was sitting at the table, staring into his lap.

I let myself in and called out a halfhearted hello.

No answer.

"How'd your meeting with the D.A. go?"

No answer.

It's over, I said to myself. Out loud, I said, "Talk to me."

He was quiet, like he always was when we were fighting. He hated fighting. I hated having to drag the words out of him.

"Is this really how it's going to end, Peter?"

Pause.

"Please. Say something."

"I don't have the energy for this today, Cece."

"For what?"

He closed his eyes, then opened them, like he was just waking up. "I need to show you something."

He took my hand and led me over to the wall opposite the broken window. I was confused.

Gambino looked me in the eye. "Do you know what this is?"

"A small, round hole. Maybe a third of an inch in diameter. So?"

As soon as I'd said it, I knew.

I'd been right the first time.

"That's right," he said angrily, "now you see my problem. I get here a couple of hours ago, see the broken glass, the patched-up window, have a look around, and find this. A fucking bullet hole. Somebody fired a thirty-eight special into this house. Do you understand what I'm saying?"

"Yes," I said in a small voice.

"Were you here when this happened?" He was gripping my shoulders now, hard.

"Yes."

"Jesus! Why the hell didn't you tell me? Are you crazy?"

I pulled away from him. "Why don't you give me a minute to explain?"

"Fine." He yanked out his chair and sat down.

I leaned against the wall, hoping it would swallow me up. "It was this morning, early. I heard a noise. I tried to call 911, but I couldn't find my phone. Your cell phone was out of juice. I waited a long time. I didn't know what to do."

"You could've gotten out of there," he said. "Screamed for help—"

"I wasn't thinking straight," I protested. "When I finally saw the broken window, I thought the paperboy had done it. The newspaper was right outside."

"So you cleaned up the mess. Good-bye, evidence."

"I'm sorry."

"I know you're sorry," he said quickly. "You're always sorry. One day it's going to be too late for sorry. No matter what I say, you just refuse to think, for god's sakes."

"Are you done now?" I asked.

He looked at me like he was trying to make up his mind about something, which didn't exactly make me happy.

I held his gaze.

He keep looking.

"I can beat you at this game," I said, not blinking.

"Come here," he said, holding out his arms. I fell into them. "This isn't about you, Cece."

But it was about me. About me not being able to let things go. About me thinking I was immune to danger.

"I'm scared for you," he said.

I pulled away from him, ashamed.

"And I'm angry at myself," he continued. "Furious, actually. This whole thing is turning out so wrong. I keep making mistake after mistake."

I was confused. Were we talking about the same thing? "What does this have to do with the woman who keeps calling you?" I asked. "Is she one of the mistakes you're talking about?"

Instead of answering, he walked into the kitchen. There was a Baggie on the sink. He picked it up and stuffed it into his pocket.

"What is that?" I asked.

"The slug I took out of the wall." He put on his jacket.

"What about the woman?"

"Look, I can't talk about that now."

I was afraid to ask. But I couldn't go through it again. I couldn't make the same mistake twice. "Are you having an affair with her?" I whispered.

"Of course not."

"Then who is she?"

"She's not your concern."

"What does she have to do with the bullet in my window? Was she shooting at me?"

"Don't be ridiculous. You're not the target, Cece."

That's when it dawned on me. "You're talking about Julio Gonzalez, aren't you?" I followed Gambino to the front door. "But Julio Gonzalez can't be responsible. He's in jail."

"Things are complicated."

"Is she one of those complications?"

"Let it go, Cece. I've got to get to the lab."

"Now? I thought you were going to come with me to Rafe's party."

"I've got more important things to deal with," he said, his hand on the knob. He turned to face me. "I'm trying to keep an innocent woman from getting hurt."

I wondered later if he meant me or her.

CHAPTER
TWENTY-TWO

Nine-thirty on the Venice canals. The Chinese lanterns were lit and the air smelled like jasmine.

Rafe opened the door. Music spilled into the night. He looked like hell—thin, pale, and drunk.

"What do you think?" He had on a vintage smoking jacket, maroon satin with a black medallion motif. "Wardrobe let me borrow it."

Will, resplendent in an oversize Hawaiian shirt, stood by his side. "Why are you opening the door? You're the fucking star, man."

"You're right," said Rafe. "Why don't you make yourself useful and get me another drink?"

Will looked at him for a minute, then walked away.

"I thought you weren't a method actor," I said.

"People change." He lost his balance for a minute. "Fuck." A beautiful redhead wearing peacock-feather earrings grabbed him under the arm. "Sorry," he said, drifting away with her. "Make yourself at home."

Inside, it was smoky and loud and decorator perfect. A single orchid stood in an otherwise empty modular bookcase, which covered one wall like honeycomb. Hothouse-flower-type women leaned against a mirrored console. A fire crackled in the fireplace. Will was sulking by the bar. Oblivious, Rafe poured himself another drink. His forehead was slick with sweat. The redhead was slipping an oyster down her throat.

A cool hand touched my shoulder. I turned. Fredericka, Rafe's assistant. She looked ethereal in a pale blue halter and billowing white silk pants. I must've looked like the grim reaper by comparison in an ankle-length cobweb of black crochet. At least the skirt was tight and semisheer. I could still get arrested in certain Muslim countries.

"Long time no see," I said, smiling. I should've worn my red satin hourglass dress. It was by Philip Hulitar, the house designer for Bergdorf Goodman in the fifties. Philip Hulitar understood that there is no substitute for a long-line bullet bra. It suddenly occurred to me that underwire could save the bat-wing-sleeve sweater. Maybe not. In any case, I didn't have the heart for red after that scene with Gambino.

"Can I get you anything? Champagne?" Fredericka grabbed a glass off a passing tray.

"I've already filled my quota today. I'm a little worried about Rafe, though. Is he okay?"

"Rafe?"

His smoking jacket was hanging open now. He had lemon-yellow board shorts on underneath. He and the redhead were laughing too loudly together. "Yes, Rafe. Your employer. Does he always drink this much?"

"He's got a lot going on, you know?" She took a sip of the champagne.

"I was just asking."

There was a loud crash upstairs. I looked at Fredericka, who downed the rest of her glass without commenting. Nerves of steel.

"I like the way the house looks," I volunteered.

"Will did it. He's got an amazing eye for composition. He sees a frame and knows how to fill it. It's an art, really."

There was another crash from upstairs.

"What was that?" I asked.

"Oh, nothing, I'm sure." She looked over at Will, who was already halfway up the stairs. "Have you met Steve?"

"Steve?"

"Terrell. You really have to meet him. He's the director of the film. The current director, I should say. Will fired the first one, Eleanor Lonner. He said it's always a mistake to work with people you don't know from Adam. Too many surprises there."

That was an understatement.

"Do you like Eleanor's work?" Fredericka asked. "She did that Amelia Earhart movie, in black and white? I thought she had a really provocative vision for *Dash!*, but it's not like my opinion counts for shit around here. Steve!" she called out. A short, dark man with thick black glasses and several days' growth of beard extricated himself from a conversation with a shorter, darker man and came over. He moved in a way that was supposed to denote street cred, but I suspected a round of hip-hop classes.

Steve Terrell kissed Fredericka with more fervor than was necessary. Her girlfriend, Lana, appeared from out of nowhere and wrapped a proprietary arm around the former's tiny waist. Steve Terrell was not fazed. Diamonds glinted in both of his ears. You are the man, said the little voice in his head. A beast.

I introduced myself. He sat down on a large, black leather couch and patted the spot next to him. "B and B Italia. Six thousand euros, with the designer discount. And Rafe's got the bed to match."

He looked at my blank expression.

"Sorry. I'm kind of passionate about design. Brad Pitt and I like to hang out with Frank Gehry."

This seemed to require a response, so I said, "Cool."

He grinned. His teeth were like beacons in the night. They matched his white Nikes. "So. Cece Caruso. I gotta tell you, your book was really intense. I derived a lot of inspiration from it."

Throwing caution to the wind, I sat down next to him. "Thank you."

"No, really, I'm not bullshitting you. When I saw the book was by a woman, I had my doubts. I'm coming clean with you here, okay? But you've got balls."

I crossed my legs primly.

"I said to Will, Will, that girl can talk dirty. She gets the violence of the language, she gets how it's a perfect metaphor for the corruption of society, you know what I'm saying? My work is like that, too. Hard, tough, spare. *Red Harvest,* that's my Hammett. I don't know how many corpses piled up in that one." He laughed. "You kind of lose track after a while, you know what I'm saying? That's what I'm bringing to the film. Violence. Action. Have you seen my movie *Punched*? Will loved it. Rafe, too. About Jack Johnson, the prizefighter? I won a Golden Globe. Two hundred million domestic." He was ready to burst.

I came clean about not having seen *Punched,* and started to point out that Hammett in fact had reduced the level of violence in each of his successive books (there are only four murders in *The Maltese Falcon,* and all occur offscreen), but Steve Terrell wasn't having any of it. He wanted to talk chairs. He'd recently acquired a new Cappellini chair, which cost $3,000 with the designer discount and resembled a bird in flight, and was planning to bid on a set of twenty-four Artifort little tulip chairs, upholstered in black suede, at Sotheby's next Saturday. Steve Terrell studied my legs, then asked if I'd ever actually seen a little tulip chair. When I confessed my ignorance, he invited me to join him for the auction.

Rafe ambled over at that point and practically fell into my lap. "Sorry, Cece. Why am I always apologizing to you?" He pushed his hair out of his face. "Anyway, don't listen to a thing this guy is telling you. He hasn't got a pot to piss in." Steve Terrell looked uncomfortable. On the set, he outranked Rafe, but we weren't on the set now.

I sensed it was a good moment for me to get up. I wandered through the dining room, past a trio of semiclad starlets clustered in front of an Andy Warhol triptych of Rafe, and into the kitchen, which at my parties is always the central hub of activity. Rafe's kitchen was as spotless as a laboratory, and not exactly hopping. Two men in wraparound aprons were covering large, plastic trays of grilled shrimp with tin foil.

An angry-looking woman with a frying pan in her hand stomped through the swinging door. Will's assistant, Kat, followed close upon her heels.

"Would you slow down?" Kat panted.

"Boys!" the woman snapped. "Do not forget the bruschetta!"

"Take pity on me," Kat pleaded, bending down to pick up a yellow file folder that had dropped out of her hand. She pulled up her low-rider jeans and tugged down her tie-dyed wife beater. "Won't you reconsider? We're expecting over a hundred people tonight. You can't just take the food and go!"

"Watch me. Get into the van, now!" the woman directed her helpers. She opened the stainless-steel fridge and removed six bottles of salad dressing, which she placed in an empty wine box.

Kat turned to me. "Cece." She handed me the file. "Can I ask you a huge favor? Can you please run this up to Will's desk? I have to deal with this situation right now."

The swinging door swung open yet again.

"Fredericka! Thank god." Kat grabbed the file back out of my hand and was about to hand it to Fredericka when the latter burst into tears.

"What is it?" Kat asked, concerned.

"Lana's leaving me," Fredericka said, sobbing.

The caterer uncorked a bottle of pinot noir and poured some into a Dixie cup. "For pain and suffering," she said, sucking it down. "Mine, I mean."

"What happened?" asked Kat, on the verge of tears herself.

"It's Will's fault," Fredericka wailed.

"I'll second that," the caterer said.

"Asshole," murmured Kat.

"Weeks and weeks ago, he walked in on something that was nothing," Fredericka said. "I don't know why he told Lana about it. He promised he wouldn't."

Kat hugged the weeping Fredericka with one arm and with the other passed the file back to me.

The caterer poured three more Dixie cups of wine.

"Hey, you!" She handed me one. "For the road."

Perhaps it was time to acknowledge that this experience was not going well. The whole Rafe thing. Not going well at all. I headed up the back staircase and stopped at the top. There was laughter coming from down the hall. I had no idea if it was a man or a woman. Who exactly lived here, anyway? Rafe. He had a chrome-and-black-leather bed. That was definitely too much information. Will's office was somewhere on the premises. Did he bunk here, too? What about Fredericka and/or Lana? Kat and/or Riley? Were they live-in watchdogs, too?

I ducked into the guest bathroom and locked the door behind me. Everything was black and high gloss. The toilet paper was folded neatly at the end, like at a fancy hotel. I swung open the vanity. The shelves were bare except for a pink Daisy razor and a bottle of extra-strength Excedrin. I wrestled with the child-safety lid, then popped two aspirin in my mouth and washed them down with the rest of the wine. I closed the door of the vanity. My hair was holding up surprisingly well. But I was out of this place as soon as I dropped off the file.

I turned off the light on my way out. More laughter down the hallway. The redhead emerged from a bedroom, wearing one peacock-feather earring. The other earring, as well as her dress, had evaporated.

"Excuse me," I said. "Do you know where the office is?"

Her eyes looked huge and glassy. I tried not to look elsewhere. "Right behind you. Tread softly and carry a big stick."

The naked ingenue was quoting Teddy Roosevelt.

The light was on in the office, so I knocked. There wasn't any answer. "Hello? Will? You in there?"

I figured that was enough warning.

The room was empty except for Will's desk, which had been placed front and center, a thick, smudge-free piece of tempered glass balanced on an elaborately carved plywood base. This was not a desk meant for work. No papers, no scripts, no contracts, no bills, no to-do lists. This was a desk meant for show. All that was missing was the cardboard computer monitor.

There was another door at the back of the room. Maybe it led to the real office. No light under that door. I knocked once, then entered. It was dark. I hit the light switch. Nope, this wasn't it, either.

This was, however, the heart of the operation, the epicenter: Rafe's home gym.

Three of the walls were mirrored, the other covered with a huge, flat-screen TV. The sound was off, but there was a golf game going on. I'd never noticed how much the dents in a golf ball resemble cellulite. And talk about stuff: in one corner, a speed bag mounted to a platform, with two pairs of red boxing gloves underneath; opposite, a rowing machine, a treadmill, a stationary bike, an elliptical trainer, and a Pilates machine called a Reformer that looked like it would lend itself to all sorts of things I didn't want to know about. Also, a rolling rack with half a dozen wet suits hanging from it, and a floppy leather bag bearing a logo I recognized from the other day.

O'Neill.

The curling wave.

"Cece?"

I could see Will's reflection in the mirror. I could also see Tiger Woods raising his hands over his head. Two men in white polo shirts were clapping him on the back. Then it was time for a commercial break. Michelob. Everybody looked so happy.

I spun around and gave Will a guilty smile. "Here," I blurted out, handing him the file. "Kat asked me to put this on your desk."

"So, why didn't you?"

"I tried to. But I wasn't sure I'd found the right place."

He led me out of the gym, then hit the lights. "No worries." He took the file out of my hand and tucked it under his arm. He looked thinner than he had the other day. Different. Maybe not thinner. Younger. More relaxed. "We're cool. But this isn't the right place. This is Rafe's office, not mine."

We both looked at the empty desk. In answer to my unspoken question, he explained, "Rafe doesn't do much work in here. You want to see where I work?" I didn't appear to have a choice. He was already halfway down the hall. He turned left and I followed him up a spiral staircase made out of spindly white iron.

"You have your own floor?" I asked.

"Sure do," he answered, walking into his office.

It was a wreck. The furniture was old and cheap. Pock-marked file cabinets were bursting at their metal seams. Cardboard boxes stuffed with papers littered the floor. Trash cans overflowed. There were keys and thumbtacks and wires and zigzagging cords and neon-yellow Post-it notes covering every visible surface. Phones were ringing; monitors were buzzing; faxes were coming through. Will tossed the folder nonchalantly onto his desk and knocked over a plastic champagne glass. Luckily, it was empty.

"You're working in the middle of a party?" I asked.

He sat down and ripped the fax out of the machine. "I'm always working. The media is on a twenty-four-hour cycle. And you've got to feed the beast. I didn't say that, by the way. Pat Riley said that, but I could have."

Will pulled a large checkbook out of the top drawer of his desk.

"What day is today?" he asked.

"The twentieth."

"Right-o. Here you go, Cece."

It was a check for $25,000.

"What's this?" I asked, confused.

"Your money," he said. "You did a great job, so I threw in a bonus."

"A bonus?"

"Richly deserved."

"But it hasn't been two weeks!" I protested. "Rafe and I aren't done."

"I think you are."

"But what about Lillian Hellman, the Communist party, the six months in jail for contempt? I've barely even gotten started with that stuff."

"A: Lillian Hellman was a monster. Every idea she ever had was stolen from Hammett, so who gives a shit about her? B: Hammett never officially became a member of the Communist party. C: When asked how he felt about going to jail, he said, 'I felt like I was going home,' and that's a direct quote. In other words, I can handle it from here."

My cheeks were burning. "If you're such an expert, why'd you hire me in the first place?"

Will sighed. "Cece, you've done an incredible job. But I think Rafe needs some downtime now. He's pretty stressed.

I'm sure even you can see it. I don't want to keep upping the pressure on him. He's going to crack. He's done it before."

"I didn't realize—"

"Look, I've already said too much here. Can we just stop now?"

Downstairs, the party was raging, but I left in a hurry, like the maid who's been dismissed after getting caught stealing the silver.

Only I hadn't stolen any silver.

I'd stolen Rafe's keys off Will's desk.

And nobody had caught me.

CHAPTER TWENTY-THREE

I don't know why I did it, I thought, draping my naked self across the wooden riser. I just saw those keys sitting there, and something came over me.

Bad Cece. Lawbreaker. Underachiever. Impulse shopper.

I closed my eyes and tried to relax, to let the shimmering waves of heat heal my broken mind and body. Unfortunately, neither mind nor body was interested.

I stole those keys because I wasn't finished opening doors.

I bolted upright and pulled my towel out from under me so I could wipe the sweat off my face. I didn't actually do well in saunas. They were too hot.

Bridget twisted her head to look up at me, nearly losing her turban in the process. "Can you please not position your sweaty self directly above me? There's plenty of room in here."

"You were just sitting in the hot spring practically on top of five old ladies."

"Mrs. Park and her friends are extremely clean," she said curtly. "Didn't you see how they were scrubbing each other's backs with nailbrushes?"

"With your short hair, why do you need a turban anyway?"

She smiled. "I like the way the white looks against my black skin."

Lael burped delicately. "That's the last time I eat kimchee before noon."

A ghostly face peered through the filmy glass: Mrs. Park, smeared with cold cream.

"I'm heading into the steam room," I announced, "if anyone wants to join me." But the door to the steam room was covered with yellow hazard tape, so I headed through the grotto and sank back into the hot water instead, right in front of a bubbly jet.

Beverly Hot Springs, located on a narrow side street in Koreatown, was not your typical day spa. The city's only natural mineral thermal spa, it was discovered by some oil wildcatters around the turn of the century, and rediscovered in the thirties, when the well's contents sold for drinking water at ten cents a gallon. They'd fixed it up a little since then, with a man-made rock waterfall and baby grand in the lobby, and complimentary Paul Mitchell shampoo in the showers. But there was definitely room for improvement. I'd start with the robes, which made you feel as if you were at the Ob/Gyn's, waiting for your Pap smear. Still, it was cheap.

Sunday. R & R with the girls. After Beverly Hot Springs, we were getting manicures and pedicures on Larchmont Avenue, a yuppie oasis just to the west.

"Why is there a No Pets sign posted in here?" asked Lael, climbing into the steamy water beside me.

"Good question."

"So, Cece. What's going on in your life? You've been awfully quiet since we got here."

I pointed to the Silence Is Golden sign.

"Please," she said.

I fanned myself with my hand. "Also, I'm a little dizzy."

Lael popped out of the hot water, padded across the concrete floor, and popped into the cold pool, then popped out of
the cold pool and back next to me.

"What are you doing?" I asked.

"It makes the hot feel hotter and the cold feel colder."

That was Lael, an experience junkie. On cue, she shivered
with pleasure and sank down deeper into the water.

"I think the more interesting question is, what's going on in
your life, Lael? How's Officer Murray?"

She went all the way under, then poked her head up. "It's
over."

"Why?"

"He's unadventurous."

"Oh."

"Sexually," she said, taking her time with one of her favorite words.

"I got that."

"Got what?" asked Bridget, climbing in next to us. "Scoot
over, Cece."

I scooted two jets over. "Lael is talking about her sex life."

"What about your sex life, Cece? And when's the wedding?"
Bridget, like my neighbor Butch, was on a mission. In her case,
it was because she'd found me the perfect dress, a diaphanous
Greek goddess number studded with baby pearls and cut down
to there. It was from Chanel's winter 1991 collection. She'd

gotten it for a steal because the runway model who'd worn it had had a thing against antiperspirant. Bridget, however, had sponged the dress with her famous fifty-fifty vinegar and water solution, and it was as good as new. But the way things were going, I wasn't sure I was going to be needing it.

"What wedding?" I asked.

"Cece," warned Lael.

I pulled off a hangnail. "Gambino and I had another fight."

"Oh, no," Bridget said. "What'd you do this time?"

I told them about the phone calls. The woman. Gambino's sort of explanation.

"And you believed that?" Bridget, being typically supportive.

"Of course I did."

"Then, honey, I've got an Elsa Schiaparelli capelet back at my shop I'd like to sell you."

I was astounded. "You got fleeced?"

She smiled ruefully.

"I never thought I'd see the day," I said with satisfaction. "Welcome to the club."

Lael looked at me disapprovingly. "Gambino did not fleece you."

"That's not what I meant." I didn't even know what I meant. "Plus, I got fired."

"Oh, Cece," said Lael, giving me a hug.

One of Mrs. Park's friends was leaning into the fresh, boiling water, which was spilling down from a stone funnel in the center of the pool. She caught my eye, and nodded.

I nodded back.

She floated over.

"Excuse me?" she asked in a tiny, accented voice.

"Yes?"

"Are you the lady in the magazines?"

"No," I said with as much dignity as a person could muster naked.

"Now, don't be modest," said Bridget.

"So sorry, but may I take a Polaroid in the locker room? For my son, Jin? He loves celebrities. And I recognized you right away! You are a famous lady!"

My best friend, Lael, popped back into the cold pool, shaking her head.

My second-best friend, Bridget, laughed so hard her turban fell into the water.

Turned out Mrs. Choi knew her way around a camera. As I was zipping up my gym bag, I asked her if by any chance she did weddings.

The answer was no.

MONDAY MORNING. BANK OF AMERICA, WEST Hollywood branch. I grabbed a complimentary cherry lollipop out of the basket and popped off the cellophane wrapper. There were lines even at this hour. People just loved to chat up the tellers, and vice versa. How's your uncle? Your sister? Your brother? It was probably wrong of me to begrudge them this simple, human pleasure. Still, I never found bank employees to be particularly intriguing. But I was probably asking the wrong questions: Can I order new checks at this window? What's my current balance? Boring.

The man in front of me groaned impatiently, then grabbed three orange lollipops and shoved them in his pocket. Maybe a $25,000 deposit would spark somebody's interest. Easiest money I ever earned—sort of. It was done, at least. Twenty thousand for Annie and Vincent, and the five thousand bonus for me. I'd treated the girls to a day of beauty, and there was a lot left over. Enough to pay for a honeymoon, even.

I was trying to think positive.

That worked until I got back home to discover that I'd brewed a full pot of coffee without putting in the gold filter, which meant the hot, watery grains had spilled down the sides of the carafe instead of into it, dripped onto the counter, and snaked into the open cutlery drawer—all over the serving spoons, rolling pins, and spatulas—before puddling ignominiously on the floor.

Upon surveying the mess, I thought briefly about moving.

I barricaded myself in the bedroom instead. My unmade bed was calling out to me. What else was I going to do? It was high time to get cracking on my new book, but I wasn't ready to face a blank screen. I checked my messages. One from the director Steve Terrell, who was desperate to see me. Give me a break. None from Gambino.

I picked the Rafe Simic scrapbook up from the floor. Time to close that door. I carried it back to the closet where I'd found it, but before putting it away, I flipped it open, to the page with the collaged yearbook photo.

Annie.

My little girl.

I used to call her Moon Pie when she was little—not after the graham-cracker treat, which we both loved, but because of the shape of her face. Her face was perfectly round. No angles anywhere. Her eyes were saucers. Even her curly hair fell into ringlets. Moon Pie wasn't her only nickname. Her Royal Goodness was another one. Most of us have to struggle with it, but goodness came easily to Annie, which was why I was so worried about her. She had no armor. No limits. She'd opened herself up to Alexander, and he'd crawled into her arms. They loved each other now, and love is a big responsibility.

Alexander's mother. I had no words for her. A woman who leaves her child. Gone, without a trace.

Like the dead woman.

The dead woman.

I felt my knees start to give.

Oh, god. Did the dead woman have children?

I sat down on the edge of the bed. I was shaking all over. That possibility had never occurred to me before. I'd thought about her parents, and that was bad enough, their not knowing what had become of her. But this—this was worse. There might be children out there who didn't know what had happened to their mother. Children who dreamed about fires they couldn't put out. Children with no choice but to assume their mother had just up and walked away.

And now I was walking away.

I stood up suddenly, closed the scrapbook, and put it back in the closet, where it belonged. Then I went into the kitchen and spent the next half hour cleaning up the mess I'd made. The floor needed a good mopping anyway. Afterward, I put on another pot of coffee.

My mind was made up.

I'd made many mistakes in my life, but I was not someone who walked away.

CHAPTER
TWENTY-FOUR

A person who lives in a trailer park probably has little use for a set of twenty-four little tulip chairs. But let no one accuse Steve Terrell of being the practical sort.

This was a man who dropped out of the University of Nevada at Las Vegas one semester shy of graduation to be an extra in *Rambo: First Blood, Part II*. A man who stomped off the set of his directorial debut, a music video, when LL Cool J demanded casting approval. A man who turned down a meeting with the chairman of Universal because he was already committed to a foie gras seminar in Sonoma. But by that time, he'd earned the privilege—$200 million in privileges, if you wanted to get technical about it. What did he care if he didn't have room for more chairs? Everyone in L.A. rents a storage space.

Traffic was light today. During the spring rains, Pacific Coast Highway can be impassable. I noted all varous artifacts from treacherous seasons past: sandbags, wire netting, plastic trash bags, concrete drainage channels, wooden barricades— anything to keep the hill from literally sliding into the ocean and taking the road and the houses fronting the beach along with it.

Just past the seedy Topanga Ranch Motel and Cabins, which always struck me as something out of a film noir, I started counting off the canyons: Las Virgenes, Malibu. According to MapQuest, it was another two miles after that. If I hit Corral, I'd gone too far.

Just then I saw the sign, looming high above a cheesy-looking seafood joint: Malibu Hills Trailer Park. There was an arrow pointing right. I followed a green truck (bumper sticker of the day: "If going to church makes you a Christian, does going to the garage make you a car?") up a windy path through a grove of skinny palms and parked in the empty front lot.

The office reminded me of a gift shop in a high-end car wash. I passed on the scented accessories and got a map and visitor's pass to stick on the dashboard. Before heading over to number 31, I surreptitiously checked the rate sheet stashed behind the front counter: $1,209.60 per month for a full hookup with ocean view. You can't beat that with a stick, I thought, walking past the laundry room and pet run, not with the waves cresting just outside your front door and the fluffy cumulus clouds practically falling on your head. The only hitch was the noise from the cars zooming by below, but you could talk yourself into believing it was the roar of the crashing surf.

I tucked the bottom of my pleated Depression-era white blouse into the waistband of my brown bias-cut tweed skirt with the pink satin piping: Faye Dunaway in *Bonnie and Clyde,* only with gold-sequined sandals. It was a vaguely professional look. But what did Steve Terrell want from me, professionally speaking? I knew what I wanted from him. He had answers. All I had to do was ask the right questions. Like why he lived in a recreational vehicle.

I'd never given recreational vehicles much thought before. These appeared to run the gamut, from ratty little Airstreams propped up on concrete blocks, to "Dan and Betty's Den," a camper from Casper, Wyoming, complete with plastic Christmas wreath and barking poodle, to state-of-the-art luxury coaches with landscaping. The front of Steve Terrell's motor home, for example, boasted half a dozen dwarf citrus trees in fancy stone pots: Meyer lemon, Kaffir lime, satsuma tangerine. And herbs galore. This man actually employed a gardener. In a trailer park. I bent down to pluck some cilantro. Just then the crimson-accented door swung open. I saw the white Nikes, and sprang to my feet.

"I'm happy to give you some to take home," said Steve Terrell, "but use scissors, okay?" He wagged a small pair at me. There were sweat stains under the arms of his silky black shirt.

"Sorry."

"Come on in. I'd set up chairs out here, but it's too windy. I've ordered a heat lamp, but it's not here yet. Fucking FedEx, am I right?"

Inside, a sleek blonde was sitting on a sleek built-in couch studying a sleek Palm Pilot. Everything in there was sleek: silver and/or black, like a spaceship. I suddenly experienced a desire to sell all my possessions, in particular anything with folkloric motifs or fringe. He gave me a quick tour, which consisted of swinging various things in and out of various hidden compartments. I was particularly enamored of the tiny galley kitchen. In a space no more than six by six feet, he had all the necessities, including a deep-fat fryer for his Thanksgiving turkey, which descended from the ceiling with the push of a button.

We went back out to the living room.

"Elsa was just leaving to run errands," he announced.

Elsa picked up her silver-mesh handbag and slung it over her bony shoulder. "Double meat, no cheese, right?"

Steve Terrell gave her the thumbs-up and shut the door behind her. Then, he yanked up his droopy jeans.

"Now where were we?" he asked lasciviously. "Just kidding." He patted the spot Elsa had vacated. "I won't bite."

"You had something serious you wanted to talk about?" Let him think my being here was for his benefit.

"Right." He removed his thick, black glasses. "It's Rafe, as you might have guessed. He's fucking up my movie big time."

Now it was Steve Terrell's movie. "How is that?"

"How is that? Look at him!" he exploded. "He's skinny as a fucking rail, his drinking is out of control, he can't remember his fucking lines—where do you want me to start? The nutritionist was the beginning, as far as I'm concerned. He should've been at the gym getting buff, not running scared from frigging cookies! He's supposed to be an action hero, for fuck's sake!"

"Slow down, okay?"

"Okay," he said, manically running his fingers through his hair. "Sorry. I get too excited about this shit. It's bad for me. I've got to de-stress."

"Excellent idea."

"I'm calm now."

"Good," I said. "Listen, Rafe cares about this film. As much as you do—maybe more. But he's done all this work because he wants the character to be complex. A tough guy—"

"Yes!" he broke in hopefully. "That's good! That's perfect!"

"Who is also smart," I continued. "Who lives the life of the mind."

"The life of the fucking mind?" Steve Terrell snatched a Rubik's cube off the table and started fussing with it. "Who are we kidding here? Why the hell would anybody cast Rafe in a role like that?" He bit his lip. "I didn't say that, okay? But you of all people, I thought you'd get it. Blood, guts, violence, remember? I am not doing tortured guy sitting at old-fashioned typewriter. That was Eleanor's take, but she's fucking history because IT'S NOT FUCKING CINEMATIC!" He started whacking the Rubik's cube against the side of the table. "Total, un-fucking-mitigated disaster!"

Eleanor interested me. Someone else Will had fired. "Why didn't Eleanor work out?"

"She's a great gal," he said, taking deep breaths. "I'm serious. Great gal. Gorgeous, too. A real California blonde. Too bad she's a lesbian. For me, I mean." He laughed. "I loved the Amelia Earhart flick. Not my thing, but solid." He attempted a Black Panther salute. "Next up is a film about a cross-dressing pirate. Yo-ho-ho, if you get my drift."

The cheaper the crook, the gaudier the patter.

Sam Spade said that, but I could have.

"Then why did Will fire her?" I asked.

He laughed, then started to cough. "You see? You see? This is making me sick. Don't even get me started on Will. Will's useless. Rafe runs the show, which is the whole fucking problem. He's the one who does the hiring and the firing. And he's the one who needs the talking to, before he winds up doing something stupid again."

"What are you talking about?"

"You have to work on Rafe, Cece. You've got to get him to pull himself together."

"Me?"

"We all have a lot riding on this movie. It's not just my ass that's on the line. People go see my movie, they go buy your book. Nobody goes to see my movie, we're both fried."

"I hate to break it to you, but I have nothing riding on this movie. I barely even have a career. And I certainly don't have any influence with Rafe."

"The hell you don't."

"I am so out of the loop it's pathetic. I don't even know what you're talking about when you say he did something stupid." It was worth a try.

He cocked his head, which I think was his way of denoting disbelief. "Yeah, right." He walked over to the sink and washed his hands, which didn't look dirty. In fact, they were beautifully manicured.

"It's true," I said, following him.

"Well," he said, stretching the word out as long as he could. "I really don't like to gossip." His face started to light up, like the Hollywood sign after dark.

"Of course not."

"Anyway, it's public knowledge." He turned off the water and reached for a towel.

"What is?" I asked.

He leaned in close, speaking in a delirious whisper. "Rafe's crazy. You ever see him go nuts?"

"Not exactly," I said hesitantly.

"Why do you think he does yoga?" Steve Terrell waited a
beat, grinning from ear to ear. "Mandated by the court. Anger
management. After the ten weeks in county lockup."

"What?"

"You heard me. It was a while ago. Right after the filming
of his first movie. He punched out a photographer, really
messed the guy up. He was getting in Rafe's face, that part was
true, literally, even did a little damage, but come on. Did Tom
Hanks ever serve time? Tom Cruise? I don't think so. The poor
guy wound up needing surgery. I think it was his spleen.
Whatever it was, it was bad. He was near death or something.
The family sued. They settled out of court. Will fixed it so it
wouldn't wind up in the tabs, but everybody knows. Still, you
didn't hear it from me, okay?"

I thought of that first day on the canals. I'd been frightened
to go into Rafe's house with him alone. "Is this why you want
me to talk to him? Are you scared of Rafe?"

Steve Terrell shook his head passionately. "That's not who I
am. No fucking way." He puffed up his chest like a pigeon. A
pigeon wearing diamond-stud earrings. "It's just that you have
a pleasant way about you. I thought you could be more effec-
tive getting the message across. I get upset, I start schvitzing, it
gets ugly, you know what I'm saying?"

"You're saying you want me to do your dirty work."

"I'm awesome in the sack," he murmured.

"Excuse me?"

He made a sort of kissy face. "Just thought I'd sweeten the
deal."

Steve Terrell was not the stuff dreams are made of.

"Kidding! I'm kidding, Cece!"

Once he dispensed with the kissy face, I agreed to talk to

Rafe. It was, of course, the perfect excuse for keeping this thing going. I needed an excuse now that my services had been terminated.

"And all I want from you in return," I said, heading for the door, where Elsa was just coming in with lunch, "are some Kaffir limes." I had a recipe I'd ripped out of the paper for an aromatic tom yum kai soup.

Steve Terrell took the bags from Elsa, emptied them onto the counter, grabbed the one most liberally stained with secret sauce, and headed outside with his scissors.

"This is a big sacrifice, Cece." He started snipping limes off the tree and dropping them into the greasy bag. "Do you know why I planted these? The Thais believe the juice prevents your hair from falling out. Not that I have that problem at this point in time, but it's good to plan ahead. This is Hollywood. Don't forget that. They'll kill you for less."

No doubt.

CHAPTER
TWENTY-FIVE

There was one place I wanted to stop on my way home. Then I'd save Rafe's film, Rafe's soul, maybe the world.

17575 Pacific Coast Highway. The former site of Thelma Todd's Sidewalk Café.

Thelma Todd was a wisecracking bombshell best known for acting opposite the Marx Brothers in films like *Horse Feathers* and *Monkey Business*. But she also starred in the first film adaptation of *The Maltese Falcon,* which was why I was interested in her.

It was Thelma Todd—as the faithless Iva Archer, lover of Sam Spade and wife of Spade's murdered partner—who'd uttered the line that had so incensed the Hays Office they'd denied the film a second release (which, ironically, paved the way for John Huston to later remake the film).

Upon seeing Spade's new lover in his bedroom, she'd whined, "Who's that dame in my kimono?"

It sounds so innocuous now.

Poor woman.

On the morning of December 16, 1935, Thelma Todd was found slumped over in the front seat of her car, dead of carbon monoxide poisoning.

That was the other reason I was interested in her.

The car was a chocolate-colored Lincoln Phaeton convertible, brand new; the garage belonged to the swank apartment the dead woman shared with her married lover, Roland West, just above the café; she was wearing a silver evening gown and mink wrap, having spent the earlier part of the evening at a party in her honor at the Trocadero nightclub on Sunset Boulevard.

Aside from that, nobody knew anything about anything.

For years, I'd noticed the place, a sprawling three-tiered Spanish-style ruin with Moorish arches, smashed up against the hillside opposite the ocean. But I'd never known its significance, not until it was put up for sale, and the write-ups all recounted the lurid history of its former proprietress.

She'd been a small-town beauty queen from Lawrence, Massachusetts, who'd come out to Hollywood to be a star. She ate men for sport, drank like a fish, and specialized in drunken car crashes.

"Hot Toddy" was the nickname she'd picked for herself.

I turned onto Porto Marina. This was the Castellamare section of Pacific Palisades: ocean views and permit parking only. The street was narrow and windy, with houses climbing along the north side, and to the south, a vertiginous drop to PCH and the ocean beyond. A man in a New York Mets cap polishing a blue Lexus pulled off his headphones long enough to tell me I could find a legal space farther up the road.

I squeezed my car in between a pool man and a roofer, then headed down the hill, hugging the side so as not to get run over. The yuccas fanned out over my head. The hibiscus glowed hot pink. The cattails brushed against my legs. Sometimes I forgot how beautiful it was here in Southern California. Today it struck me anew. Even the lines extending from telephone pole to telephone phone looked as perfect as if they'd been drawn with a compass.

It must have been beautiful like this on the day Thelma Todd's maid found her lifeless body.

The building looked less decrepit up close. It had been bought by a movie-production company. I buzzed a couple of times without getting an answer, then peered through the stained-glass window and saw a grand staircase with a tiled fountain, framed by a pair of potted palms. I knocked on the glass, hoping someone could let me in, maybe show me an old menu or something, with gin fizzes and milk punch and lime rickeys for forty-five cents a pop. I was certain Hammett had frequented the place. He was in Hollywood in 1934, living off and on in the forty-four-room Harold Lloyd mansion, which was in Beverly Hills, not far when your chauffeur's behind the wheel. And Hammett wasn't a person who ever said no to a gin fizz or some milk punch or a lime rickey.

Nobody answered, though.

The garage was next.

There was a steep flight of outdoor stairs that led up behind the building. It was dark and shady back there, with low concrete walls on either side. I started up the steps, shivering ever so slightly. The ground was littered with dead leaves and bougainvillea, like confetti from a long-ago party. Halfway to the top, I turned around and looked back. I could see all the way across the pedestrian bridge that led to the ocean on the other side of the highway. The shadows of the rails fell on the concrete, like zebra stripes. They reminded me of a beautiful, geometric-patterned swimsuit Thelma Todd had on in an old picture I'd seen of her somewhere. I wondered if she'd liked swimming. The water was so cold this time of the year, though. People never realized just how cold it was.

When I got to the top, I turned left. This had to be the garage. It had a huge padlock, and as if that weren't disincentive enough, twisty, spiky vines growing across the door.

Keep out. Haunted house. Death trap.

The grand jury made a ruling of suicide, but that didn't hold water with those who knew Todd well. They insisted she must have turned on the motor to keep warm, and then fallen asleep. Or they pointed a finger at Lucky Luciano, who'd tried unsuccessfully to coerce her into allowing gambling at her café, which she'd said would happen over her dead body. Or they suspected her lover, frustrated with her drunken carousing, of locking her in the garage to keep her from slipping out yet again. That latter theory, however, failed to account for the key found in her handbag. It would've allowed her to escape. But she hadn't escaped. And her body had been cremated.

Case closed. Suicide. Pity. End of story.

Of course, stories are arbitrary. As a biographer, I knew this better than most.

I looked down at my watch. And that was when I felt a hand grasp the back of my neck.

Jesus Christ. What was this?

Then, the hand jerked me around.

I was face-to-face with a hulking man in a blue uniform. "Private property," he said in a dull monotone. "Keep it moving."

"How dare you touch me?" I asked, more unnerved than outraged, but determined not to show it.

"You should calm down now," he said.

"What kind of psycho security guard are you?" I asked, readjusting my blouse.

He didn't smile. "It's my job to make sure people don't go where they aren't supposed to."

"I could report you." I scanned his uniform for the name of his company, but there didn't seem to be any name.

"Sorry, miss," he said, pulling his walkie-talkie from his belt.

Sorry, miss, my ass. I started down the stairs. Overzealous nutcase. Speaking of, it was time to go home and call Rafe.

In the car, I tried to shake off the feeling of doom hanging over me. One phone call. That was all. A way back in. I pulled away from the curb and drove farther up the hill, looking for a space wide enough to make a U-turn. I suppose I could have gone straight, and eventually found my way out onto Sunset Boulevard, but I was suddenly in a hurry to get this whole thing over with.

At Lecco Lane, I swung my wheel to the left.

The rest, even now, is a blur.

My phone started to ring; the radio news went to a traffic report (jackknifed truck on the Grapevine); something green flashed in my rearview mirror; my neck snapped back; my hands flew off the wheel; and flesh hit metal as my Camry crashed through a retaining wall, plunging down the embankment toward the thousands of drivers speeding along Pacific Coast Highway, totally oblivious to what had or had not just happened to me.

CHAPTER
TWENTY-SIX

t'll take a miracle," I heard someone say.

It was a man's voice.

Twangy. Kentucky, maybe. Or Texas. Tennessee? I had no idea. My eyelids fluttered open. He was wearing a blue-and-red-striped shirt with a patch over his heart that said, "Hi, I'm Nate."

"Nate?" My tongue felt thick.

"Yes, ma'am." He walked over and took my hand. "Like I was saying before, it don't look good." His eyebrows were knitted together in concern.

"Please do everything you can. That Camry means a lot to me."

"Good to see you up again," said someone else. It was the man in the baseball cap who'd been polishing the Lexus earlier.

I looked around, confused. I seemed to be lying on a piece of expensive pool furniture that had been wheeled out into the middle of the street. I needed water. My mouth felt dry.

"The paramedics left half an hour ago. They said you were fine. No concussion, nothing. Just a nasty cut. Clean bill of health. Do you remember?"

"Yes."

"Then you just sort of keeled over. I thought maybe you needed to lie on the chaise longue another minute. Take it easy. Nate here, from D.J.'s, concurred."

I saw the D.J.'s Garage tow truck. It looked like a monster with something silvery clenched between its jaws. That would be the remains of my car.

"I'm fine now," I said, trying to sit up. My head felt like it was being pummeled with a meat tenderizer. I reached up and felt a huge bandage on my forehead. I couldn't afford a new car. I didn't want a new car.

"Anybody you need to call?"

"My purse." I needed to call Gambino.

Nate said, "We got it out of the front seat. That, and a bunch of papers. Right here when you're ready."

"Do you know how lucky you are?" The man in the baseball cap shook his head. "If it weren't for those yuccas—"

I closed my eyes and massaged my temples. Nate handed me a bottle of water. I took a slug, then felt like I had to throw up.

"I'm going to be sick," I said.

The man with the cap looked stricken. "Put your head between your knees and take deep breaths."

I could feel him watching me. "You okay?"

I raised my head tentatively. "I think it's passed."

"You know, I've seen cars come back from worse accidents than this one," said Nate cheerfully. "It's the alignment that usually suffers, but that's my specialty. I think your car's gonna make it." He smiled. "But, if you don't mind my saying, you

should've known better than to make a turn like that. Didn't
you see the sign?" He pointed to the No U-Turn sign directly
above my head.

Of course I'd seen the sign. But I'd thought I knew better.
I sighed deeply. If only I'd continued up the road. But, no. I
was too lazy. I didn't want to have to figure out the way back. I
wanted to go the way I knew. Stupid, stupid, stupid.

The guy in the baseball cap said, "I've been telling the people I work for, they need a guardrail up here."

"Rich folks." Nate wiped his hands on his pants. "I could
tell you stories."

I struggled to my feet and ran over to the side of the road
and vomited into a pile of dead leaves. Then I sat down on the
curb and wiped my mouth on the back of my sleeve. Something was very wrong here. I tried to remember what had happened, but it was all so hazy. I'd had both hands on the wheel.
I'd started to turn left, hand over hand, just like my father had
taught me, and all of a sudden I was hurtling down the hill.

I remember seeing black. Black smoke.

And blue. Blue sky.

And green. Something green. In my rearview mirror. The
reflection of my ring? I looked down at the emerald on my left
hand. Couldn't be. I'd seen it just before I'd felt the wheel spin
out of my hands. If I didn't know better—but no, it was im-
possible. Nate, the guy in the baseball hat, the paramedics,
who'd already come and gone—somebody would've said
something by now. You couldn't do something like that and
have nobody notice.

Or could you?

"Nate?" I asked.

"At your service." He sat down on the curb next to me.

"Did anything about the rear of the car strike you as odd?"

"How do you mean?"

I went over to my Camry, and pointed toward the general vicinity of the trunk. "Around here, I mean. Any strange dents or marks or anything?"

He followed me over. "Try to remember what happened, miss. You rammed the front of your car into the trees. Why would I see anything strange back here?" He ran his hand over the rear fender. His veins were thick and ropy. "No," he said. "Absolutely nothing out of the ordinary."

I started stabbing at the car with my finger. "What about this?" I stopped stabbing.

Nate looked at me with genuine concern. "It's called a scratch, miss. And I think the paint job is the least of your troubles at this moment in time."

"That scratch wasn't there before." I was sure it wasn't there before. Ninety-seven percent sure. Eighty percent sure. Shoot.

"So you're saying?"

I spoke in a whisper. "Could somebody have given me a little bitty push?"

He looked at me like I was a little bitty crazy. "People don't go around doing stuff like that. You better lie back down, miss."

I got my purse and sat down on the chaise longue to call Gambino. He wasn't answering. I tried Annie next, but she was out, too, and didn't have a cell phone. Looked like I was going to have to hitch a ride back to the garage with Nate. I thanked the guy in the cap for all his help, gathered together my things, and climbed into the cab of the tow truck.

What about the green Toyota truck at the trailer park? Lisa Lapelt Scofield had a green car, a Honda Odyssey. What color car did Oscar Nichols drive? What about the psycho security guard? How many people in Los Angeles drove green cars?

According to scientists, the human eye is more sensitive to the color green than to any other.

My phone started to ring.

It was Rafe. He was on the 10 heading west from downtown, which, given his history, could mean anything: that he was on the 405 heading east, that he was around the corner, that he was in Athens, Georgia. He said he had to see me. I said I'd be at D.J.'s Garage in the Palisades in half an hour.

While Nate was rooting through his glove compartment for a pen, I suddenly remembered that Rafe had a green car, too.

CHAPTER
TWENTY-SEVEN

But it was a black Land Rover that hopped the curb at D.J.'s, music blaring. Rafe stepped out and caused the usual commotion. Customers stopped filling their gas tanks. Mechanics emerged from the shadows, wiping their dirty hands on their coveralls. The cashier, wearing a beautiful gold-and-blue sari, came running outside, waving a small camera phone in his face: "You are at this moment looking at Rafe Simic. Please say hello to my sister in New Delhi, Rafe Simic!"

Rafe was sweet as pie, for a while.

"You see that?" he asked with a grimace, indicating two men on the other side of the street. Their telephoto lenses were pointing in our direction. Instinctively, I crossed my arms over my chest. "The fat guy in the motorcycle jacket? I've got a re-straining order out on him. Asshole can't come within a hundred feet of me."

"Let's go inside," I suggested.

We went into the minimart. Rafe bought a tin of cinnamon Altoids and signed some autographs while I finished filling out the paperwork.

"Would you mind spelling your name for me?" Rafe asked, pen poised over paper.

The cashier nodded her head. "D-E-V-I J-A-Y-A-S-H-R-I. My American friends call me D.J."

"It's really a shame," Rafe said, handing D.J. the slip of paper with a smile. "What happened to you earlier, I mean. Is your insurance going to handle the rental?"

"Don't you worry about me." I returned D.J.'s clipboard. She tore off the top sheet and handed it back. "Seven to ten days, minimum." She addressed me in clipped tones. "We will telephone you. Do not telephone us. We are very busy." They were so much friendlier at Hollywood Toyota. I felt like a turncoat.

"You're lucky you weren't hurt," Rafe said, staring at my bandage. "I don't think that cut's going to leave a scar, do you?"

"Where's the sports car, Rafe?"

He jangled his keys in his pocket. "In the shop. Where those things usually are. I've got Will's car today. It's decent enough, but I think I'm going to get something sensible next. Maybe a Camry, like you."

Yeah, right. "You should get an electric car. There are long waiting lists, but Will could fix that, I'm sure. It'd be good for your image."

"You think my image needs work?" he asked.

It might.

"Do you, Cece?"

"Is there someplace around here to get a good cup of coffee?" I asked D.J.

She ignored me.

"Excuse me," Rafe asked in honeyed tones, "can you recommend a place to get some coffee?"

D.J. indicated the cappuccino cart in the corner. "Low fat, nonfat, regular fat. All are available. For you." She blushed prettily.

"On second thought, I think we could use some fresh air." Rafe took me by the arm. "C'mon."

Once we were back outside, the photographer in the motorcycle jacket started yelling. "Miss, look over here! Rafe! Over here! Give me a break, wouldja? I gotta earn a living!"

"Can you believe this shit? This place looks fine," Rafe pulled me into the doughnut shop next door. We took the back booth. I ripped a few napkins from the dispenser and wiped off the table. The window was already decorated for Christmas, or else that was powdered sugar. Rafe went to the counter to order.

"What do you want?" he called over.

I was suddenly starving. I told him two old-fashioneds and a coffee. Black. Normally, I liked it with cream and sugar, but not with sweets.

Rafe came back with two black coffees and two old-fashioneds.

"You're not having any doughnuts?" I asked.

"Nah."

"You do know that you look awful."

"Thank you. This jacket cost four thousand dollars. And you've looked better yourself, since you brought it up."

"I'm not talking about the jacket." It was suede, the color of bittersweet chocolate. "You've gotten way too thin." He actually looked better than he had the night of his party, but that was probably because it was still too early in the day to have started drinking.

"All this crazy dieting isn't good for you," I continued, Steve Terrell's voice in my ear. "You need to calm down and to remember that your job is to entertain people." Why was I helping Steve Terrell exactly? I'd forgotten. My head was throbbing. I grabbed one of the doughnuts and stuffed it in my mouth. Nothing could kill my appetite, unfortunately. "It's not going to help anybody," I said, "if you go overboard."

Rafe looked at me curiously. "Since when do you tell me I shouldn't take my work seriously?" He stretched out his arms and clasped them behind his head.

He was still talking, but I couldn't hear what he was saying. In addition to the pounding in my head, there was now a roaring in my ears.

Everything had changed.

Guns do that.

I saw a gun.

When Rafe stretched out his arms and his jacket pulled away from his chest, I saw a gun.

"Cece," Rafe said. "I asked you a question."

"Why did you need to see me, Rafe?" My voice was quavering. My mind was racing in a million directions. "You said it was important, so here we are."

"Will told me what he did to you."

"What *he* did to me?" What *you* did to me. Someone shot at my window. Gambino was sure it was one of Julio Gonzalez's thugs, but sometimes even Gambino got it wrong.

I saw a gun.

I didn't know what to do, what to think. Then, something from Hammett's story "The Gutting of Couffignal" came to me. It was something the Op said to the Princess Zhukovski. She was wrong, he said, in thinking that because he was a man and she was a woman she was safe. He wasn't a man and she wasn't a woman; he was a hunter, and she was the thing running in front of him.

Rafe looked confused. "Will fired you, of course. Without asking me, which was not cool."

A hunter does what hunters do.

A detective does what detectives do.

The Op shoots the princess.

Ready, aim, fire.

"Will didn't fire me, Rafe," I said. "We came to the end of our work."

"I don't think so. This isn't the end. What I mean is, I want you on set with me. It's important that you say yes."

I didn't answer.

"As a kind of coach, I'm talking. You know," he said, "help me with motivation, focus. You're good at that."

Did he want me on the set to keep an eye on me? To make sure I stopped making trouble for him? I could see the door from my seat. All I had to do was get up and walk out. But he wasn't going to shoot me. This was crazy. He wasn't going to shoot me here. He wasn't going to shoot me anywhere. He wasn't a hunter. He wasn't the Op.

"Look, don't say no right away," he pleaded. "Will and I, we're going out of town for the rest of the week. We'll be back on Sunday. You're right, of course. I'm a little tightly wound." He laughed. "See, I'm admitting it. We're going to go out to the desert. I've got a house out there. We're going to do some hiking, look at the stars, then we'll be ready to go first thing next Monday morning. That's when the shoot starts, bright and early. Just think about it, okay? Think about being there with me. You can give me a call on my cell when you've made up your mind. No pressure."

No pressure.

"I saw the gun," I blurted out.

"Fuck." He opened his mouth, then closed it.

"And now I magically understand what I'm supposed to do, like you understood what you were supposed to do when you got Maren's letter. Is that how it works?" I asked.

He looked at me, then started to shake his head. "You've got it all wrong, Cece. This has nothing to do with you. Or with Maren. I can't believe—well, since you saw the fucking thing, here it is: Will gave it to me, okay? It's his gun. I've got some kind of crazy stalker, been writing all kinds of notes, threatening ones, lunatic stuff. Calling, too. Will's got her on tape, of course. But he's worried for me. He told me it made sense for me to carry this thing, for protection."

I had no idea if what he was saying was true or not. After a while, I wasn't even listening. I was staring at the scar on his cheek, which stayed white even though the rest of his face had turned bright red.

CHAPTER TWENTY-EIGHT

Gambino came over sometime after midnight. He held me close, massaged my sore back, changed my bandage, gave me Advil, and didn't say much, all of which I appreciated.

I wasn't ready to talk.

I don't think he was either.

I slept like a log. When I woke up, it was close to eleven. He was gone and the house felt empty. I went into the kitchen to make coffee and saw that the pets had been fed, which was the only reason I'd been able to sleep in unassaulted. I was duly impressed—and that was before I glimpsed the croissants. They were arranged on a plate, next to a bouquet of dahlias. There was also a note, the contents of which are private. But I smiled as I read it.

The glass company called back around noon. Gus would be over later. They apologized for the delay, but they were really up to their ears. It was a seasonal thing. September to December were good months. Crime was up. Holiday season and all. The weight of family obligations, personal demons, existential angst—lots of bad cheer. January to April: those are the slow months. That's when I should get in touch. They've got nothing but time then.

After my shower, I telephoned Annie. I had an important question to ask her. Unfortunately, she didn't know the answer. She did mention that Alexander was doing better. He'd made a friend in the neighborhood, a little girl. They were over at her place today, playing. I was happy to hear that. As for my question, she recommended I consult her Rafe Simic scrapbook, which I did. But that turned out to be no help either, so I walked to the video store on La Cienega, rented every Rafe Simic film they had on the shelves, and invited Bridget and Lael over for movie night.

Though both led busy and exciting lives, they were available.

BRIDGET ARRIVED AT SIX ON THE NOSE. SHE was decked out in a silver-and-maroon Thea Porter caftan, influenced in equal parts by Art Deco, Chekhov, and the designer's native Israel. Or so she said, sashaying through the entry hall. She might have sashayed more gracefully had she not been juggling, in addition to her small dog, Helmut, an obscene profusion of movie snacks: Red Vines, Hot Tamales, Junior Mints, peanut M&M's, Cool Ranch Doritos, and microwave popcorn.

The caftan was probably a wise choice, considering.

After the grand entrance, she tossed the snacks and Helmut onto my green velvet couch, agitating Buster and sending

Mimi skittering down the hall to one of her many hiding places. Thus unencumbered, Bridget headed into the kitchen, where she appraised the dirty dishes with a raised eyebrow and tore open the cellophane-wrapped popcorn envelope with her small, white teeth. She handed it to me and I shoved it in the microwave. Before long, the smell of Butter Light was wafting through the room.

Bridget immediately reached into her pocket for a pillbox. "Does this stuff give you a headache? I don't know why I buy it. It gives me a headache. And when I get a headache, it lasts four entire days."

I still had a wicked headache from the accident, but I'd maxed out on Advil. Even the sound of my own voice made me nauseous. Good thing Bridget didn't consider conversation a give-and-take proposition.

"Do you know I practically stole this caftan from a dowager in West Palm Beach? It was very satisfying." She popped two aspirin into her mouth and swallowed them without water. Impressive. I ate three Red Vines simultaneously, which was also a talent of sorts.

"No luck at the video store, by the way. Sorry, Cece. People keep the ones they like. Pretend they're lost. I've done it myself."

I'd asked Bridget to check for copies of Rafe's first three movies, *Tahoe Nights, Uptown Boy, and Margaritaville,* in which he played, successively, an amorous ski instructor, an amorous masseur, and an amorous bartender. Having seen *Margaritaville* when it'd first come out, I knew for a fact that nobody had kept that one because they liked it. I suspected Will of having personally destroyed all copies. Unbelievably, they'd made a *Margaritaville 2,* which I'd also had the misfortune of seeing, on a blind date. I had no particular memory of Rafe in it, but the Turks and Caicos setting was indelible. Picturesque grass huts. White sand beaches. Gratuitous nudity in picturesque grass huts and on white sand beaches. It'd been an awkward evening.

No copies of the early films, then. So much for my plan. Well, I was happy to have the company. Gambino wouldn't be back until late. I'd have to tell him about the gun, of course. And that would be the end of that. Then I'd have to tell him everything. And what would that mean for Maren?

"Did you hear me? I'm persona non grata at Blockbuster," Bridget said.

"Officially?"

"She speaks. I dropped a one-pound Hershey bar and they tried to make me buy it, but I refused to pay for a broken candy bar."

"But you broke it," I said.

"And how precisely might that be relevant?"

Lael's arrival saved me from having to debate moral philosophy with the essentially amoral Bridget. Lael made a big to-do over the cut on my forehead, which Bridget had not even noticed. She also brought homemade lemon squares and a copy of *He Loves Me Not,* Rafe's only big-budget flop. After the runaway success of *Dead Ahead,* the studio had decided to try him in a light romance, but screwball comedy is harder than it looks.

"Let's watch this one first," said Lael, who loved romance even when it was a disaster. "Is that okay with you, Cece?" she asked, squeezing in next to me. She patted my knee. "Bridget, make yourself useful here!"

Bridget turned down the lights.

The movie opens with Rafe seated at a drafting table. He

takes off his glasses and rubs his eyes, then leaps up to hurl a cardboard model of an office park across the room. He takes a weathered wooden oar down from the wall and strokes it longingly. A secretary rushes in to sweep up the mess and hands Rafe a message from his mother in Maine: that run-down oceanfront property, by old Doc Sweeney's place, is up for sale again.

Rafe leaves and hits the local Chili's. He orders a big fried onion and a double scotch at the bar. The bartender is a woman, busty, with great hair. She wants to open up her own seafood restaurant someday. She hates big cities. Her dead father was a fisherman. Did I mention she was busty? It's clear where this is going.

I bit into a Junior Mint, then remembered I don't like mints. "What I want to know is why the leading man is always an architect."

"The dad in *The Brady Bunch* was an architect," said Lael. "I think it's supposed to be macho."

"He was gay," Bridget said. "I met him several times." She fed Helmut some Hot Tamales because chocolate is bad for dogs.

Rafe didn't look all that great in a suit. Good thing he stripped it off fifteen minutes into the movie. Several close-ups of him and the bartender exchanging loving, postcoital looks followed. I saw Rafe's scar and pointed it out to Lael and Bridget, who likewise had never noticed it before.

By mutual agreement, we moved on to *Lords of Venice*, which was Rafe's breakthrough film. He played a cop in the seventies who goes undercover as a skate punk in Venice Beach to quell gang violence. I wouldn't call it a nuanced performance. Nobody had ever accused Rafe of being much of an actor. But he had an amazing physicality. He filled the screen.

You couldn't take your eyes off him. It was actually sort of uncanny.

We watched that one all the way through. Lael cried at the end, when Rafe's girlfriend took a bullet meant for her man, but the dry-eyed Bridget was more interested in the girlfriend's trampy seventies attire. I was interested in Rafe's scar. The makeup and lighting couldn't hide it, once you knew it was there.

We fast-forwarded through most of *The Cut of the Sword*. None of us was particularly enamored of all-male movies. No one to identify with. Well, Bridget sort of identified with the relentless samurai master. He would strike his students with a wooden sword at random times of the day and night until they learned never to let down their guard. Rafe was good wielding the deadly, curved katana. This was the movie that cemented his reputation as a Zen mystic, which is what the media, when they're being generous, call Californians who practice yoga and drink green tea.

Blue Sky in the Dark had been a huge hit. Lael hadn't much liked it. She said, without elaborating further, that she'd known a confidence man or two in her time, and Rafe was no confidence man. Bridget, not about to be outdone, said she, too, had been around the block, thank you very much, and Rafe was absolutely the type. Then it was my turn, but since I had no experience whatsoever with flimflam men, unless you counted my ex-husband, I really didn't know. There was one scene, however, that chilled me to the bone.

Rafe, playing a con artist named Joe Allan, is ten months into a long scam where he's pretending to be a car-parts sales-man named Al Joseph. Al is telling a story to a guy he meets in a bar. The story is about his mother, who hanged herself in the bathroom when he was eight years old. The story is long and involved and painful. After it's done, the con man looks up, dazed, and you realize that not only do you, the audience, have no idea exactly whose memory has just been recounted—the con man's or that of his alter ego, Al—he doesn't know either.

Liars lie, even to themselves.

Joy Popping had come out last year. We'd all seen it. Rafe plays a rock climber and recreational drug user who has to re-build his life after his girlfriend plunges to her death during a climbing expedition somewhere in Cambodia.

We skipped to *Hollywood and Vine*, Rafe's most recent film, the one that didn't get him the Golden Globe nomination everyone thought he deserved. We watched the last half hour, which included the pivotal scene where Rafe the hustler con-fronts Gordy the pimp, now dying of AIDS. We then fast-forwarded to the kiss, which fueled rumors for months on end that Rafe and his male costar were romantically involved.

By that point, we'd finished off the candy and both pizzas (sausage and green peppers followed by pepperoni and olive), which meant it was time for dessert. After the lemon squares, we were exhausted. I walked Bridget and Lael out to their cars. They made a big fuss over my rental, which was a newer, cleaner version of my own car, still at D.J.'s. The people at the rental place had tried to give me a red Ford Escort that smelled of disinfectant, but once I spied the white, late-model Camry on the lot, that was that.

As a parting gift, Helmut threw up on my lawn.

I was about to close the front door when Lael screeched to a stop halfway to Santa Monica Boulevard and backed up at what had to be fifty miles per hour.

"Sorry, Cece!" she yelled. "I forgot all about this."

I walked out to the middle of the street in my slippers and took a videotape out of her hands.

Tahoe Nights.

Rafe's first movie.

"I found it in the back of Tommy's closet. You know boys," she said, smiling. "Yucky."

I went back inside and settled down on the couch.

It smelled low budget from the opening credits, a cheap James Bond rip-off with ski bunnies in silhouette performing unseemly tricks with ski poles. Perhaps in some alternate universe people did ski double-diamond runs in lingerie, drink pink champagne in hot tubs, have sex in pro shops, outrun police cars, only to return to their Ivy League colleges to pursue degrees in kinesiology and special education. I was obviously not getting out enough.

Rafe was the kinesiologist-to-be.

Buster and Mimi joined me for the penultimate scene, in which Rafe valiantly rescues the beautiful townie girl (the special-ed teacher-to-be) from an avalanche, realizing only at that moment that she—not the vacationing debutante he's been bedding for most of the film—is the one for him. Just before they make love in the pine trees, there is a close-up on Rafe's face, a smile slowly spreading across it.

I froze the frame for a minute, rewound for a couple of seconds, then froze it again.

Caught.

CHAPTER
TWENTY-NINE

There was no scar on Rafe's cheek. Not a trace of one. Which meant there had been no surfing accident in high school. The scar came later, a gift from a photographer, whom Rafe had practically killed by way of thank you. Steve Terrell had as much as told me.

I fell asleep thinking about Rafe. His lies, his temper, his gun.

Bang.

Bang.

Bang.

I woke up to the sound of rain pounding on my windows. And to the realization that the other side of the bed hadn't been slept in. I called Gambino at his apartment, but there was no answer. I got up to go to the bathroom and saw that I'd left a window open. There were tiny drops all over the sink before I'd even turned the faucet on.

I closed the window, washed my face, and brushed my

teeth. Then I headed into the living room. *Tahoe Nights* was still in the machine. I hadn't made it to the end.

Not on an empty stomach.

I put a pot of coffee on and grabbed a calcium-rich chocolate pudding from the fridge, then sat down on the couch and hit Play.

Cut from Rafe's unscarred face to the beautiful townie girl's undimpled thighs, back to Rafe's muscular chest, then to the beautiful townie girl's flat stomach.

I looked down at the half-eaten pudding in my hands, set it on the floor for Mimi, who loves pudding, and got myself a hard-boiled egg instead. While I was tossing the yolk in the sink, I heard the music swell climactically. By the time I was back, the screen had gone black, then it was Bob Seger and the Silver Bullet Band. *Night Moves.* Oh, well. I should've hit Pause. Now I'd never know how it ended. I curled up on the couch with my egg white and let the closing credits scroll by.

Actors, producers, executive producers, assistant directors, set designers, production designers, best boys, key grips, Foley artists, gaffers. Man, it takes a lot of people to make a movie. No wonder you can never find a parking space in this city. I glanced down. Mimi hadn't touched the pudding. Might as well finish it off. I scraped up the last bits with my spoon.

And then I dropped my spoon.

What the hell was this?

I fumbled for the remote, sending cushions flying.

"Stop right there! Stop! Stop!" I yelled at my TV, frantically pointing the remote at the screen. The credits froze in place.

It couldn't be.

But it was.

It takes a lot of people to make a movie, even a piece of schlock like *Tahoe Nights*.

But who'd have believed three wardrobe assistants with the unlikely names of Maren Levander, Lisa Lapelt, and Eleanor Lonner?

ELEANOR LONNER'S NUMBER WAS LISTED, WHICH made sense. People in the entertainment industry like to make themselves available. Unless they're as big as Rafe. Then they don't need to be available. In fact, the less available, the better. But Eleanor Lonner was not as big as Rafe. She wasn't even as big as Steve Terrell. Despite that, she lived on Rossmore Avenue, which is what Vine (as in Hollywood and Vine) turns into south of Melrose—a step up from a trailer park, if you asked me. There were lots of beautiful, old Art Deco apartments on Rossmore, like the El Royale, with its glamorous rooftop neon sign, and the Ravenswood, where Mae West holed up for half a century and eventually died.

The message on Eleanor's machine was curt: "Please contact the Ron Stencil Agency for Eleanor Lonner." No number was given. Happily, the Ron Stencil Agency was listed as well. A secretary who sounded like there was a clothespin on her nose answered. I asked for Ron Stencil, which elicited a death-defying laugh. I think I was supposed to know there was no Ron Stencil. The secretary put me through to Miriam Halevy, who did, apparently, exist. Miriam Halevy had her doubts about me at first. I may have been a bit eager. But after hearing that I was a colleague of Steve Terrell's (which I was, in a manner of speaking) and that I was involved in *Dash!* (which I definitely was, or had been, and might still be), she informed me that Eleanor was in India, doing research, and unreachable. I said it was really important that I speak with her. Miriam said if it was that important, I could fly into New Delhi and take an elephant ride to Eleanor's encampment by the Goa River, in the middle of frigging nowhere. I didn't appreciate the sarcasm, not to mention that this is not how an agent is supposed to operate. Might be some personal stuff there. It was just as well.

I'd always been curious about what those old apartment buildings on Rossmore looked like on the inside.

CHAPTER THIRTY

Eleanor Lonner didn't live in the El Royale or in the Ravenswood, but in a blisteringly white Streamline Moderne building that curved back gracefully from the street. Shaded by arching palms, it reminded me of a luxury liner that had docked on a tropical island.

Her apartment number was 4A or 4F. I couldn't tell because the plastic letter in question was dangling illegibly. Didn't matter either way right now. First I had to get inside, out of the rain. I tried the old buzzer trick that'd worked so brilliantly at Hammett's apartment building on Post, but nobody went for it. Next, I tried to hitch a ride with a UPS guy carrying a stack of boxes, but that was similarly a no-go. Then I remembered a scam I'd read about recently in a novel about a burglar. It had impressed me. The burglar, however, had devoted several days to pulling it off, something I did not have the patience for. And was that kind of advance work really necessary? I wasn't planning to steal anything, after all. I just wanted to have a look around.

Denise Manovich. Number 6D. Massage therapist.

I buzzed.

"Yes?" Thick Russian accent.

"Denise? I got your name from—" I sneezed loudly. "I was in the area and thought I'd take a chance, see if you were in. My body is a wreck." It was no lie.

She buzzed me in. I shook myself off. I was soaked. An older gentleman in a Burberry raincoat reached into his pocket and offered me a hankie, which I politely declined. I didn't want to get makeup on it. I dripped rainbow colors onto my own coat instead. The lobby was elegant and spare: a bouquet of white lilies; a crystal chandelier; shiny black-and-white tile floors. The elevator, however, was in serious need of rehab.

I remembered to look pained when Denise Manovich opened her door. It took a while. There was a lot of clicking and sliding, which meant padlocks and bolts. Then some cursing in Russian, which I assumed meant they were ancient. The padlock and bolt part, not the cursing, did not bode well in terms of Eleanor's apartment, 4A or 4F, two floors down.

"Hello! Hello!" Denise said. "Please, darling, come in!" A middle-aged woman, she looked ready for a night of boogying in a skintight black Lycra jumpsuit, a thick gold-studded belt, and matching gold-studded mules. Her feet were tiny. Everything about the woman was tiny, in fact, except for her hair and teeth, which were enormous.

"You are no wreck!" Denise said, peering at me through pink-tinted granny glasses, the same shade as her lipstick. "Just soggy a bit. And the head, of course." She did some mother hen–type clucks at my bandage. "But is no problem for me.

You should see most of my customers! They cannot stand straight. But when I am done with them, they walk proud, like kings and queens!"

Denise relieved me of my hat and coat and had me bend over while she ran her hands up and down my spine. Then she karate-chopped me from my neck to my waist and then back up to my neck, after which she put her ear to my back. I could feel her starchy blond hair through my silk blouse.

"Aha! Nobody home! What I am listening for is infection. General White Cell, I am pleased to report, is not in the house. But you are distorted." She nodded gravely. "I will fix you with my techniques. Do you know I have patents?"

That was when she sent me into the bedroom to strip.

The bedroom featured brocade. Headboard, bedspread, curtains, slipper chairs. Gold and pink brocade. I started sweating. As I remembered, the burglar pulled this scam on a podiatrist and wound up with orthotics for his running shoes. I walked out of the bedroom, fully clothed.

"I forgot to put money in the meter," I told Denise, taking back my coat and hat. "Also, I have to pick up my twins from school. I was hoping this would be a sort of consultation."

"Tomorrow, then? Around ten? You shouldn't wait too much longer," she added ominously.

I nodded, which she may have interpreted as a yes, but in fact was me trying to get the feeling back in my neck.

I walked toward the elevator, waiting to hear Denise's door shut. When I heard that, along with the clicking and the sliding and the cursing, I headed for the exit sign at the end of the hall and went down two floors.

Number 4B it was. Eleanor Lonner's name was on the plate. It was near the stairwell, which helped. If the need arose,

I could escape quickly. I looked both ways. No one seemed to be around, which didn't mean the elevator doors couldn't open any second and Eleanor's neighbor couldn't get out, her hands full of groceries, and wonder about the strange woman at Eleanor's door. Which is exactly what happened, except for the groceries.

"Eleanor's in India," said the woman, who was tall and gaunt and the type not to suffer fools gladly, which was too bad for me.

"Yes, I know," I said.

"Can I be of some service to you?"

"Indeed you can." She waited for me to go on. "I work at the Ron Stencil Agency. We represent Eleanor."

"The Amelia Earhart movie was simply marvelous. Kudos." She bent down to pick some lint from her welcome mat.

"Thank you." I blushed. "I don't usually boast, but I helped negotiate the deal."

"Kudos," she repeated, straightening up.

"Yes, well, Eleanor is away, as you know."

"Yes. I believe we've established that."

Perhaps a pet Eleanor had forgotten she owned that we needed to rescue from starving to death?

Ridiculous.

A fern drooping inconsolably?

"How are you?" I asked desperately.

"Fine."

So how exactly was I supposed to get into this apartment? I eyed the lock, not that I had the slightest idea of how to pick it.

"And you?" she asked dutifully, pointing at my forehead.

"Oh, this?" I asked, touching my bandage. "It's nothing. I'm kind of accident-prone."

"Look, is it the package that came last week?" the woman asked impatiently. "It was downstairs in the lobby for a couple of days. I was afraid someone would steal it, so I let myself in and put it away."

Bells went off in my addled head. "You let yourself in?"

"Yes, I did."

I laughed as if this were the pinnacle of hilarity. "That is such a coincidence! Because that package you put inside when you let yourself in is the whole reason I'm here! I really need to get that package back."

"And why is that?"

"It has some scripts in it that we need to go over before Eleanor's return?" It was supposed to be a statement, not a question. "It was a mistake that they were sent here," I said with greater conviction.

"Let's get them, then. I'll be right back with the key."

She shook out her umbrella, opened the door to her apartment, and went inside. I had a small window. I could make a run for it, or I could continue to stand here, taking life lessons from a burglar in a mystery novel whose name I could not remember.

"Here we are," the woman said, closing the door behind her.

The window had closed.

She stuck the key in Eleanor's lock and opened the door.

It smelled musty, the way apartments do when you return from a long trip. I took a quick look around. Eleanor was a minimalist who didn't abide clutter, or else she'd cleaned up furiously before her departure. There was a beige tweed couch in the living room, accented with two red pillows placed at rakish angles, and a rattan coffee table, accented with two issues of *Film Quarterly,* also placed at rakish angles. In the dining area, there was a glass table with four metal chairs. The mail was on the table, in piles placed at rakish angles, but probably that was my imagination. I cast my eye over the return addresses: American Express, Comcast, Department of Water and Power. Big whoop.

Then I saw a skinny green envelope.

From In the Green Room.

Will and Rafe's production company.

The woman crouched down to retrieve a smallish cardboard box from under the table.

"Here you go," she said, just as I was frantically shoving the envelope from In the Green Room into the pocket of my coat.

I took the box out of her hands and stood there, sort of paralyzed.

"I think I hear my phone ringing," the woman said. Her phone was not ringing, but she clearly wanted to be rid of me.

"I have to wash my hands," I said suddenly, starting down the hall.

"You can do it at my place," she shouted after me.

"What?" I asked, closing the bathroom door behind me.

I turned on the water, grabbed the envelope out of my pocket, and slit it open furiously with my nail.

"Dear Eleanor," it began.

"Yours, Rafe," it ended.

That was as far as I got. Then there was a loud pounding on the door. "I'm expecting an important call. Can you hurry up, please?"

I turned off the water, folded up the letter, and shoved it back in my pocket.

"All done," I said, smiling brightly. "Oh, look how pretty Eleanor looks here." I pointed out a picture in a gold frame of Eleanor shaking hands with Clint Eastwood.

The woman shepherded me out, making sure I didn't forget the package. She stood next to me, like an armed sentry, as I waited for the elevator. She was still standing there when the elevator doors closed.

When they opened, I stepped out, tucked my hair into my hat, tucked the package under my arm, and walked down the front steps into the falling rain, feeling exactly like the burglar I wasn't.

That would be two times, in less than one week.

CHAPTER
THIRTY-ONE

The defogger in my rental worked brilliantly, which surprised me, as climate control was not a big Camry selling
point. The letter surprised me, too. I read it once outside
Eleanor's building, a second time parked in my driveway.

Dear Eleanor,

*First, let me apologize for Will. You of all people know
how he can be. He thinks he's doing the right thing, loyalty is his number one priority, but he gets a little carried
away sometimes. Sorry if he said hurtful things. I really
mean that.*

*I hope this gets to you before you take off for India.
That is so cool. Hope you have a productive trip, and that
you'll show me pictures when you get back. If we're still
friends, ha, ha.*

I also wanted to remind you about our conversation

regarding the Oceans Conservancy. They do really impor-
tant work, and given your interests, it's a natural fit for
you. Tell anybody you want to. All donations are appreci-
ated, no matter how small. They're tax deductible.
   Take care of yourself, Eleanor.
   Steve Terrell is a dick, did I say that already?

Yours,
Rafe

I went inside to do some thinking. Then I did some pacing,
the latter with a cup of coffee in my hand, which I now know is
not a good idea unless you happen to be preternaturally graceful.

It was like those games in kids' magazines: find ten things
wrong with this picture.

Rafe and Eleanor obviously knew each other well, so why
wasn't this letter handwritten? Stranger yet, it was printed on
the computer with perfect margins and no typos—in short,
nothing Rafe could have managed on his own. Fredericka must
have typed it for him. Or maybe even Kat. But it didn't make
sense. Could he really have wanted either of them to know his
true thoughts about Will? Not that Will was the one with the
temper. Will had fired me as calmly and as matter-of-factly as
I'd ever been fired. I'd never seen Will get carried away. No,
Rafe was the one who got carried away. Rafe was the hothead.

Just how well did Eleanor and Rafe know each other? They
went back at least as far as *Tahoe Nights.* Was Eleanor another
high school pal, another gorgeous blonde from Palos Verdes?
That wouldn't be hard to find out.

And what was that bit about the Oceans Conservancy?
Why would Rafe Simic be working on behalf of a conservation

organization, much less one that May Madden worked for? The daughter of his high school science teacher? He was a surfer, yes, meaning he probably cared more than your average person about the state of the environment, but something here wasn't ringing true.

I went into the bedroom and dug around for the stack of brochures Owen Madden's old neighbor Diana had given me, the ones that May had left behind. Then I peeled off my wet shoes and soggy clothes and slipped under the covers to read.

Pollution, habitat destruction, and overfishing take a serious toll on our oceans, so Oceans Conservancy works to preserve and restore the rich diversity of ocean life and the quality of coastal waters.

A good cause.

Our widely covered beach-pollution research has prompted many states to clean up their beaches.

I flipped through and found a report from the field: they'd been extremely successful at the Malibu Lagoon.

We work to stop destructive fishing methods, end overfishing, rebuild fish populations, and reduce the tonnage of fish caught accidentally and thrown away dead. We helped create networks of fully protected marine reserves off the California and Florida coasts, and are pressing for more elsewhere. Finally, we work to ban offshore drilling in coastal areas, while promoting sound coastal-zone management.

How was the Oceans Conservancy paying for all this?

I found the section that tells who ponied up in the previous calendar year. There were big donors, in the $500,000 and up category, mostly large corporations; small donors, in the under $250 category, individuals, mostly; and a lot of folks in between.

Like In the Green Room.

In the Green Room had given the Oceans Conservancy two hundred and fifty thousand dollars.

A quarter of a million smackeroos.

Now why would Will and Rafe have done that?

The rain stopped.

I went for a run, because there went that excuse.

The good news is, I lasted four miles. The bad news is, my Walkman ran out of battery power after five minutes, so I had no choice but to listen to the voices in my head, which were having a field day. I tried to sing show tunes to drown them out, but it's a problem when you don't remember the words.

Gambino called while I was out. He sounded elated. The judge in the Gonzalez case had ruled the evidence admissible, despite the iffy circumstances. He said the twenty seconds Gambino and Tico had waited before forcibly entering Gonzalez's apartment had been more than sufficient, given their reasonable concern about the destruction of evidence. And further to the fact, because Gonzalez was in the shower at the time they approached the apartment and did not hear them knock and announce themselves, additional delay before entry would have made no difference in how subsequent events unfolded. Gambino and Tico were still up for disciplinary review, but given the judge's findings, it was pretty much a slam dunk. All anybody wanted, Gambino said, was to see the son of a bitch go down for a long time.

It made me happy to hear him so happy. How could I lay my garbage on him when he was feeling so happy?

He was going out with Tico to have a celebratory drink, then to his apartment for a while. He'd see me at my place, late, around eleven.

My story could wait until at least then.

In the meantime, I needed to talk to May Madden. I went out to the office to find the Oceans Conservancy online. There was an 800 number on their Web site, but I don't trust 800 numbers, so I called them directly in Washington, D.C. It was two in the afternoon L.A. time, which meant almost closing time for them. I hoped someone would still be in the office.

Someone was. Unfortunately, May Madden proved more elusive. She was out in the field, on a research expedition in Woods Hole. The man on the other end of the line said he'd be happy to leave a message for her and that she'd get back to me when she returned.

I left my information, then got back online to look up Woods Hole, which turned out to be the Woods Hole Oceano-graphic Institution, pronounced "whooey," an international center of oceanographic studies located on Cape Cod. The guy who answered talked to me for a long time about scuba diving, which was interesting up to a point. He, however, turned out to be an intern, subbing for the regular receptionist, who was out until Monday, and he had no idea how to access the guest/

visitor database, which meant that unless I had specific information about May's research area, he wasn't sure he'd be able to track her down.

This didn't seem possible to me.

He let out a sigh. In the applied ocean physics and engineering department alone, he explained, there was the advanced engineering laboratory, the air-sea interaction group, the coastal and ocean fluid dynamics laboratory, the deep submergence laboratory, the ocean acoustics lab, and the ocean systems laboratory. And that was just one department.

Couldn't he find her in the cafeteria at breakfast time? I asked.

Apparently not.

I hung up after leaving my name and number, and called the Oceans Conservancy back. Someone there would be able to tell me May's research area at least. But they'd all gone home for the day. I even tried the 800 number, but it was only in service from nine to five, eastern standard time.

Useless, just as I'd suspected.

I took my shower and walked around the corner to the mailbox store, where I mailed Eleanor Lonner the package I had borrowed from her, which turned out to have contained two Egyptian cotton sheets, one fitted, one flat, ivory with sage trim, four hundred thread count. They would've looked great on my bed, but I'm not that far gone yet.

Then, for lack of a better idea, I decided to surprise my fiancé.

CHAPTER
THIRTY-TWO

In point of fact, I was the reason Gambino no longer lived in Simi Valley, the bedroom community consistently rated by the FBI as one of the country's safest places to live. Six months ago he'd sold his two-bedroom house in a perfectly nice development favored by what seemed to be half the officers in the LAPD on the understanding that he and I were moving in together, which had sounded like a great idea until the Bekins Moving and Storage truck pulled up outside my front door.

It had been a bit of an inconvenience for him at first—being homeless, I mean—but as it turned out, Annie's brother-in-law (Vincent's brother) had a great apartment in the Villa Gina, a courtyard building on Los Feliz Boulevard, that he needed to sublet for a while. He was going to Anchorage to work in talk radio, and who knew how long that would last. That apartment had been our silver lining. Even Gambino saw it that way eventually. At which point I cried, if memory serves me right. But you can't have it both ways.

Los Feliz Boulevard is a broad, tree-lined residential street that runs along the southern border of Griffith Park, an urban oasis of hiking paths, horse trails, golf courses, tennis courts, and other diversions for athletic types. Griffith Park was named for Colonel Griffith J. Griffith, a corpulent businessman who was not, himself, the athletic type, and despite his name, never, in fact, served in the armed forces. In 1882, he acquired the bulk of Rancho Los Feliz, including the entirety of the Los Angeles River, which made him the grand poobah of water rights, much to the dismay of city officials who'd never had to pay for the privilege of draining the river before. A decade or so later, at Christmastime, he went soft on them, and donated over three thousand acres of rolling hills, oak groves, and manzanita for use as a municipal park.

The colonel was one of those colorful characters who probably should've avoided alcohol. Or perhaps he suffered from the infamous Los Feliz curse, uttered on the site of the original adobe by Antonio Feliz's disinherited niece, Petronilla. In either case, one balmy summer evening, he accused his long-suffering wife of plotting with the pope to poison him, and shot her in the head. She leapt off the balcony of the hotel they were staying at, broke a leg, and lost the use of one eye. Griffith was convicted of assault and served one year at San Quentin. Upon his release, he tried donating more land, but nobody would touch it until after his death, when the Greek Theatre and Griffith Observatory were both erected on his dime.

You could walk to the Greek Theatre from Gambino's sublet in the Villa Gina, though we hadn't done it yet, and likewise the observatory, though the latter was closed right now for

renovations. It was still a great location, though. I skipped up
the path toward the colorful outdoor staircase that led to the
second floor. Maybe after Gambino came home, we could
stroll down Vermont to that French place we liked. Or com-
mandeer a white leather booth at the Dresden Room and listen
to Marty and Elayne, who came on at nine. We could do all
sorts of things once I cleared the air.

Clearing the air is what grown-ups do.

The gardeners had obviously just been there. The bottom
of the stairs was one huge puddle. Villa Gina's resident cat, the
morbidly obese Coco, started to meow at my feet. She was ker-
flummoxed as to how to get to her napping spot without wet-
ting her massive paws.

I scooped her up in my arms, scratched a little behind her
ears, and deposited her with a thud underneath the chipped
plaster birdbath in the courtyard.

I usually didn't get as far as the courtyard. It really needed
a paint job. There were rust stains everywhere. For some un-
known reason, I was estimating how much it would cost to
paint an entire apartment complex when I heard a door open. I
glanced up to the second-floor landing and saw a young
woman with long black hair coming out of the apartment in
the far corner.

That would be apartment number 16.

Gambino's apartment.

She didn't look like the building manager. The building
manager had gray hair. And a walker.

The woman shut the door and started down the hallway.

I ran back to the entryway and ducked behind a pillar. If
she wasn't the building manager, who was she?

That was pretty obvious.

I heard her heels clicking down the short staircase. Then the clicking stopped. She was outside the building. I waited a couple of seconds, then crept into the alcove and peered down the sidewalk. She was heading east on Los Feliz, toward Vermont. I stared at her narrow white jeans and red poncho. I had a red poncho, but hers was nicer. Her brown leather shoulder bag wasn't as exciting, but she was holding on to it like her life depended on it.

That was it! She was a burglar! She'd taken something from Gambino's apartment and was hiding it in her purse! I was going to scream. If I screamed, someone would stop her. She'd start running, but someone would catch her.

Except that she wasn't a burglar.

And I wasn't an operative.

Not that that was going to stop me.

I started down Los Feliz Boulevard after her, maintaining a brisk pace. I was wearing earth tones, which seemed a plus, camouflage wise. I considered, then rejected, tucking dead leaves in my hair. Too much.

So far, so good. She didn't see me—wait, she was turning around. Oh, my god. I leapt behind a bus bench near the corner of Vermont and froze in a sort of militaristic crouch, hands on hips. No, she wasn't turning around, she was just reaching into her purse for her cell phone. She started talking animatedly. My fiancé, no doubt. The nerve. Did Tico know about her? Gambino was with Tico, celebrating. At least that's what he'd said. Maybe he wasn't with Tico at all.

I tried not to get carried away here. Gambino was not my ex-husband. But our relationship had been on again, off again since the beginning. I thought we were on again, but maybe my on was his off. Even in a paranoid frenzy, I didn't believe that. But a person should finish what she starts.

I emerged from my hiding place as she took a right on Vermont. I sprinted toward the corner, but a huge flatbed truck carrying a fleet of new cars was crossing the intersection, so I couldn't exactly dash across.

Once the truck passed, I turned the corner and caught sight of her on the other side of the street. She was still chattering away on the phone, keeping up a good pace, but so was I, though it was hard to maneuver downhill in stilettoes. I kept feeling like I was going to topple over. I was going to break my neck, on top of everything else.

In these situations, there are standard protocols. You don't wear stilettoes, for one thing. The Op didn't have to worry about that. He did, however, adhere religiously to the four tenets of shadowing: stay behind your man as much as possible; do not ever try to hide from him; act naturally, regardless of what happens; and never look him in the eye.

Who would be dumb enough to look the person in the eye?

There was a church coming up on her left, Our Mother of Good Counsel. She stopped—feeling guilty, no doubt. I knelt behind a black Dodge Ram parked at the curb. It had tribal detailing and was for sale by owner for $2,650. Seemed like a good deal, but the guys at D.J.'s were going to save my Camry.

Nope, she didn't feel guilty. She'd stopped to put her cell phone back in her purse. Then she walked on, past the Gurdwara Vermont, a fortresslike Sikh temple with gold onionskin domes poking out of the top. I managed to keep an eye on her while sidestepping a pile of dog poop.

She took off her poncho and draped it over one arm.

I took off my sweater, and tied it around my waist.

She picked up her pace.

I picked up my pace.

She put her poncho back on.

I refused to put my sweater back on. It was hot.

One time, when Hammett was working as a Pinkerton, he trailed a suspect for six entire weeks, riding trains, passing through half a dozen small towns. I could barely keep this up for six minutes.

I scurried past an old woman in a gray overcoat banging on the door at 1955 1/2. "Open up," she was yelling. "Open up!" She turned around for a second and I made the mistake of smiling in what I thought was a noncommittal way.

"Excuse me, miss? Young lady?"

I pretended not to hear her.

"Would you be so kind as to help me?" She knew full well I could hear her. "I'm locked out. My nephew is inside." I glanced across the street. I could still see her, red poncho swinging. "At least he's supposed to be. He may be indisposed."

I started banging on the door before the old woman could elaborate further. "Your aunt is stuck out here! Open the door! Are you in there"—I turned to her and asked her nephew's name—"are you in there, Sid? Sid?"

The door opened.

"Thank you for your help, dear," the woman said, grabbing Sid by the collar and shutting the door.

I hadn't lost her. She was in front of a low, brick building now, with a huge parking lot behind it. As I got closer, I read the sign: MASONIC ELYSIAN TEMPLE. My father had been a Shriner, and all Shriners are Masons, but not all Masons are Shriners. Maybe somebody could explain that to me one day.

There was a banner out front saying they rented the place out for movie shoots. Good to know.

Hammett said shadowing was a kind of compulsion. I could see that, actually. I was noticing all kinds of things I'd never noticed before. Like the fact that Vermont goes downhill. That it's got all these houses of worship. That people drop all sorts of things on the ground, not just garbage. I'd seen a Chinese jump rope, a spelling test, dice, a pair of lavender mittens. Maybe I could keep this up for six weeks. How did you change clothes, though? Eat? But my cover was blown across the street from the 7-Eleven on the corner of Vermont and Franklin when, running for the light, I tripped on the plastic top of a Pringles can, twisting my ankle and causing a VW bug making a right turn on red to slam on his brakes so as not to kill me.

The guy didn't have to yell.

She looked up at the commotion. Maybe she knew who I was, and maybe she didn't, but either way, she didn't like what she saw. In the blink of an eye, she'd disappeared behind a huge Metro bus.

So much for the Op's rule number four.

When the light changed, she was gone.

I sat down on the bus bench and took off my shoe. My ankle had started to swell. Great. I tugged on my sweater and waved away a downtown bus that was preparing to stop for me.

This experience struck me as somehow symbolic: a symbolic failure. I squeezed my fat foot back into my shoe, and for a brief moment thought about getting on the next bus. I could see it already, the big crosstown bus. I could just hop on and keep going, to the end of the line. I could stay wherever I wound up. Build a whole new life.

No, I was going back to Gambino's to surprise him, as planned.

To clear the air, as planned.

To ask a simple question about the attractive young lady with the not-fat foot I'd seen coming out of his apartment, which was the part that wasn't planned. After that part, of course, I'd have to clear the air again.

I was trudging back, thinking about what all this said about me—and none of it was good—when I saw a dress hanging in the window of a vintage clothing store kitty-corner from the ill-fated 7-Eleven.

A slip of a dress, poison-green satin, with peacock-feather trim at the bottom.

Something like that could really change a person's mood.

Plus, it looked like my size.

In my current state, I was unlikely to be prudent, but I didn't care. A salesgirl wearing a leopard-skin pillbox hat told me to have a look around, she'd be right back, then zipped into the back and came out with another salesgirl, wearing a beret, who started nodding and smiling, and eventually burst out with how much better I looked in person.

I said thank you because it seemed easier.

They were thrilled but not surprised that I liked the green dress. It had been worn by Jean Harlow. Now it was my turn to nod and smile. I'd heard that line about every thirties dress cut on the bias I'd ever come across. Not that I particularly cared either way. When it comes to vintage clothing, all that matters is whether it fits or not, and this dress fit like a dream. They made me come out and show them. Then they put a hat with a black veil on my head, which I promptly removed. Then they made me stand by the window, where the light was better, so I could see how fabulous the color was with my hair and eyes.

And that was when I saw her, the girl in the red poncho, on her way into the House of Pies.

"Hello! You!" I screamed, banging on the window, not that she could hear me.

"Is everything all right?" asked the salesgirl in the beret.

I ran back into the dressing room, grabbed up all my stuff, and made a frantic dash for the front door. How could she eat pie at a time like this?

"Stop!" yelled the beret. "You haven't paid!"

"I am so sick of fucking celebrities!" yelled the pillbox hat. "They want everything for free!"

I reached into my purse, threw a couple of twenties at them (which was more than the dress was worth because Jean Harlow was maybe half my weight and height, and everybody knows platinum blondes don't wear green), and flew across the street.

I was hoping for an explanation, but I got a hell of a lot more.

CHAPTER
THIRTY-THREE

B anana cream, Bavarian cream, Dutch apple, black cherry, pecan, pumpkin, fresh strawberry: around and around they spun, glistening under the hot lights of the display case. Under normal circumstances, it would've been hard to resist, but these were not normal circumstances. At least my shoes were on.

"Table for one?" asked the hostess, pulling a laminated menu from the rack.

"Actually, I'm looking for a friend." I scanned the room. It was filled with teenagers eating French fries, old people eating boiled eggs, and nobody eating pie.

Maybe she was in the bathroom.

"Restrooms and telephones to the left, in the rear," the hostess responded to my question. "Nice dress."

"Thanks."

I marched down the aisle, and pushed open the freshly

painted door marked LADIES. There were two stalls inside, both occupied. I squatted down to check the respective footwear. One pair of navy-blue pumps, and one pair of brown leather mules. I hadn't noticed her shoes, but I was betting on the mules.

A toilet flushed. Navy-blue pumps came out and left without washing her hands.

One down, one to go.

I waited. I studied the faux-wood grain on the doors. I checked my face in the mirror, and wiped off the mascara collecting under my eyes. Then I was done waiting.

"Time to face the music," I said out loud.

She didn't answer.

"I know you can hear me. When you come out, I expect you to say something."

I heard a flush, then the door swung open and a hefty, middle-aged woman with flame-colored hair and delicate ankles stepped out. She was wearing a pink ruffled apron.

"Is there a problem, miss?" She turned on the hot water and lathered up. "Because if not, when I'm through here, I'd like to get back to my shift."

I smiled sheepishly. "Just wanted a recommendation on the pie."

"Anything but the coconut cream. Nice dress."

"Nice mules." I pointed to the sink. "I'll be washing my hands then."

"Pardon me," she said, passing somebody on her way out.

I looked up into the mirror.

It was the woman in the red poncho. And she wasn't empty-handed. She was carrying a gun. Which seemed to be pointing at me.

"Hello," I said in a small voice.

With her free hand, she reached around behind her and locked the bathroom door. "Don't turn around."

"Okay."

"I know that Julio sent you," she said, "and I'm not afraid of you or of him. Not anymore."

"Julio? I don't think—" was as far as I got.

"Yeah, it's better when you don't think, isn't it? He hits you when you think too much," she said, looking at my bandage.

"You don't—"

"I'm glad you're here, actually, because you can give him a message for me." Her mouth was quavering now. "You can tell him to go fuck himself."

"Please, stop for a minute," I said, starting to turn around.

"Excuse me?" she asked sharply. "Did you not hear me? I'm thinking you did not hear me."

"Sorry." I looked at her face in the mirror. "If you'll just listen to me, I can explain." She wasn't listening, but I kept talking. "Julio Gonzalez didn't send me. You're totally off the mark. I've never even laid eyes on Julio Gonzalez."

"Don't lie to me. Why else were you following me?"

I started to get a very bad feeling.

"Answer me!"

When I didn't, she asked, "Are you sleeping with Julio? Because, take it from me, that's a very bad idea."

"Why, are you sleeping with Gambino?" I was taking a chance, going on the offensive. But the defensive was working so poorly.

"Detective Gambino?"

"That's right."

"Detective Peter Gambino?"

"That's him."

All the fight went out of her. Her shoulders fell, everything fell. "You know him?"

"I'm his fiancée," I said. "I think we've spoken on the phone."

"You're Cece?" she asked incredulously.

"Yes."

She buried her face in her hands and started to weep. This was now officially surreal. "Can I please turn around?"

She nodded and put the gun back in her purse.

"You're going to keep that in there, right?"

She nodded again, wiping her eyes on her sleeve.

"So who exactly are you?" I asked.

"Tina Aguilar."

I handed her a paper towel.

"Julio's girlfriend," she continued. "Ex-girlfriend, I should say. Your fiancé saved my life. And now I'm fucking up his."

"Don't worry," I said. "I'm taking care of that all by myself."

She burst out laughing, then resumed crying.

Half an hour and two slices of boysenberry pie later, it started to make sense.

Gambino and Tico had been trying to nail Julio Gonzalez for years. It wasn't happening. He was too connected, had eyes and ears everywhere. Tina had been trying to run away from him for years, too, but he'd always bring her back and make her pay the price for crossing him.

They realized there might be a way they could help each other.

On May 17, at eight o'clock in the morning, Julio dropped his shorts to the floor and stepped into the shower. Every single morning he took a long shower—sometimes he'd stay in there an entire hour. But Tina knew, even if he didn't, that you can't wash away that much dirt.

That was when Gambino and Tico arrived. Tina was expecting them. They banged on the door, just like the three of them had planned, loud enough for the neighbors to hear, but not so loud that Julio could hear over the running water. Tina stood to the side as they broke down the door, and when they came in, she made her move. She escaped, safe in the knowledge that—at least for a while—Julio Gonzalez would be unable to get to her.

They'd planned it for weeks. She'd lie low while he was in custody, hanging around long enough to make sure the charges were going to stick. And then she'd leave. Then everybody would have what they needed and she could go home to Jalisco.

But there were complications.

Gonzalez's brother had his suspicions about the arrest, in particular Tina's role in it. He'd already contacted Tina's mother, telling her in very graphic terms exactly what he was going to do to her daughter when she showed up at her mother's house.

"Detective Gambino has been great," Tina said. "He's a wonderful person. You're really lucky. But this is getting out of hand. I don't know how much more I can ask of him."

"What about the witness-protection program?" I asked.

She shook her head. "That isn't an option for me. I'm not testifying, remember? That was something Detective Gambino and I agreed on from the beginning. He tried to talk me into it, but you don't testify against Julio Gonzalez and live to tell about it. Nobody in your family lives to tell about it. I won't do that to my mother."

"Come on," I said. "That can't be true."

She fiddled in her bag and pulled out a packet of cigarettes, then remembered you couldn't smoke in the House of Pies. Her cold coffee was meager compensation, but she sucked it down anyway. "Ask Peter. He'll tell you about Julio. Things you'll wish you didn't know. He killed his own cousin. He looked the other way when his sister was raped because it was good for business. That's the kind of man he is. He trusted me, and I betrayed him. How do you think he's going to repay me?"

"So how come you're walking around like this, out in the open? Shouldn't you be hiding somewhere?"

"I'm sick of hiding. I've been afraid for too long. I'm done with that." She glanced down at her purse. "If that man or anybody he knows comes near me—"

"Tina, please. Stop talking that way. You're going to get yourself in trouble."

"I'm already in trouble."

"Worse trouble."

"What else do you suggest?" she asked. "I don't have a whole lot of choices. My mother and I, we're stuck. What we need to do is disappear. We need to start over somewhere else. But I don't see how it's possible. Not if I won't testify. Detective Gambino can only do so much."

Something clicked. I pulled my cell phone out of my purse and dialed a number in San Pedro.

"Hi, it's Cece Caruso. How've you been?" We exchanged pleasantries for a minute. "Listen, I don't have a lot of time right now. Is she in?"

She was. I explained the situation, and she was full of excellent ideas, as always.

I put my hand over the receiver. "I hate to be vulgar, but do you have any money?"

Tina nodded. "That's not a problem."

I passed the phone over to her. "Then say hello to the Mayor. Trust me on this one. She's going to fix you up. You and your mother both."

CHAPTER
THIRTY-FOUR

At eleven-thirty, I heard Gambino's key in the lock.

I greeted him au naturel, with a strawberry cream pie in my hands.

At one o'clock, I put his strawberry-smeared shirt in the washing machine, so he'd have it in the morning.

At two o'clock, I bolted upright. I couldn't sleep. I felt guilty. I hadn't told Gambino about Rafe and the gun. Nor about my little visit to the Villa Gina. I'd do it over breakfast, I thought sleepily, laying my head back down on the pillow. Breakfast is a good time for true confessions. I turned the pillow over to the cool side.

At four-thirty, Gambino woke me up, not that I'm complaining.

At five-thirty, he said "Eggs Benedict" as he was falling back asleep.

At six, the delivery guy whacked the papers against the front door. Good thing I hadn't reported him to his superior. I glanced over at Gambino. Still sleeping. Buster, however, was wide awake and wanted to be let out. I opened the French doors for him, then went into the kitchen to put on a pot of coffee.

The bread box creaked, like everything else in this creaky house. No English muffins. Can you make eggs Benedict on wheat toast? I didn't see why not. I peeled back the plastic and squeezed the remains of the loaf. Still soft, after more than a week. I didn't want to think about the chemicals that made that possible. For hollandaise, you beat egg yolks and stir in melted butter. I had eggs and butter in the fridge. I needed a lemon. I went out the side door and plucked a nice fat one from the neighbor's tree, which spread over the wooden fence, spilling complimentary fruit into my yard. We had an arrangement.

I took a deep breath. It was so clear this morning. What a relief after all that rain.

Rain made me think of water; water reminded me of the ocean; the ocean reminded me of May Madden.

I brought my lemon inside and looked over at the clock. Six-twenty, which meant nine-twenty in Washington, D.C. I went out to my office to try the Oceans Conservancy again.

One of these days I had to really clean the place up. You could no longer see the desk, which had been buried under an avalanche of papers. No one but me even knew the desk was Lucite. Luckily, the May Madden pile was still near the top, just beneath an empty green file folder I'd labeled "Critical Responses to *The Dain Curse*," which didn't mean there were no critical responses to *The Dain Curse*, but that I'd most likely filed them in a folder labeled "Critical Responses to *Red Harvest.*"

Good thing that book was done.

I found the number on the glossy back cover of the latest annual report.

No one there.

I left a message asking for a specific description of May's research area.

Then I called Woods Hole and got the intern again, who had nothing for me, unfortunately.

I pulled together the Oceans Conservancy papers to take them back into the house.

As I shuffled them into a pile, something slipped to the floor.

Curious, I bent down to pick it up.

It was a Polaroid of two people in bed.

What was this doing in May's things?

I brought the photograph up close to my face so I could see the two people more clearly.

A young blonde in sexy lingerie, with an hourglass tattoo on her shoulder.

A man with a prominent nose, bushy eyebrows, and a mustache to match.

Maren Levander and Owen Madden.

May's father and May's baby-sitter. Jesus. Were they lovers?

I looked at the picture again. They were leaning against the headboard, their bodies entangled in a blue blanket. You could see their bare arms touching, but still, they seemed less like lovers than strangers.

Owen was sad. You could see it in his eyes.

And Maren? No, Maren wasn't sad.

Maren was laughing.

Beams falling, over and over again.

I GOT DRESSED QUIETLY, SO AS NOT TO WAKE Gambino.

I threw the whole wheat bread away. I needed English muffins. That's what I told myself, anyway. I was just taking a slight detour, then it was straight to Gelson's.

There was nobody on the road all the way to Palos Verdes.

Diana was sitting on her porch when I got there. She was wearing her flannel shirt and looking up at the sky. "Sun's up so early this time of year. Makes the days too long, don't you think?"

"You don't seem surprised to see me," I said.

"What happened?" she asked, looking at my bandage.

"I walked into a door. I'm fine." Though I'd been feeling kind of dizzy the whole drive down. I needed more Advil.

"Good." She took a sip of coffee, then got up, pulling a red chenille blanket off her lap. "Mine's cold. I'm going in for a fresh one. Can I get you anything?"

I shook my head. "No, thanks." While she was gone, I sat down and glanced at the crumpled newspaper on the table. Sports pages. Browns sign star to 5-year, $11M deal; Vikings DE braves shoulder surgery. I looked at the date. Three months old.

Diana came back out with two mugs, the steam hovering over them like storm clouds. She set one down in front of me and held the other between her small, gnarled hands. "Can't seem to get going in the morning without drinking the whole damn pot. Good thing I don't have to rush off anywhere. I've got all the time in the world, which is too much time, if you ask me."

"You still haven't answered my question," I said gently.

"You know the answer."

"You've been waiting for me."

She bent her head over her coffee, drinking in the steam.

"Waiting for me to find the picture," I went on.

"You certainly took your time." Diana sat back down and draped the red blanket over her legs. She was wearing a thin housedress under the flannel shirt and beige lace-up shoes with no socks. No wonder she was cold. It was clear but windy. The newspapers were starting to blow around.

"Look at this mess!" she suddenly cried. "For god's sake! I can't keep up with it anymore."

I took the picture out of my purse and handed it to her. "Where did it come from?"

She didn't touch the picture. She didn't even want to look at it. She cocked her head at me instead. "Are you sure you're asking the right question, Cece?"

"What is the right question?"

"Have some coffee before it gets cold." I took a sip. It was thick and strong. "What's the right question, Diana?"

"Do you know who that man is, in the picture? That's not the question, by the way. I'm just wondering."

"Owen Madden," I said.

"Owen Madden lived next door to me for fifteen years. Then his sister moved in, lived there for more than twenty. Phoebe Madden. But those are just names to you. You never knew these people."

"No."

"Let me tell you something about Owen Madden. He was a good man, a good father, a good brother. He wasn't the person you see in this picture." She started to shake her head. "Can you imagine what it would be like if somebody showed you a picture of yourself that coincided not one whit with the person you knew you were? Can't imagine it myself. At least you'd know it was a lie. But what if that person showed the picture to someone you loved? Would she know it was a lie? Or would it change how she felt about you forever?"

"Is that the question?" I asked.

"Owen was scared," she answered. "Phoebe told me that. Just before he died. Phoebe couldn't imagine what could scare a good man like her brother so much. His daughter was safe, happy, he'd seen to that. So what on god's earth could shake him enough to make him throw himself off a cliff? Once I saw this picture, I understood."

I thought I did, too. But I had to be sure. "You say he was a good man. But good men can make mistakes. He was lonely. His wife was dead."

"You're way off track, my dear. He didn't care for this girl. He wasn't a predator. No, it wasn't anything like that."

"How can you know that?"

"Cece. Just look at her face."

"You can't know what she's thinking."

"Can't I?"

"All I see here are two people in bed," I said, "one of whom is underage. Maybe Owen threw himself off a cliff because he didn't want to go to jail."

"I didn't know the girl," Diana said, sighing. "I didn't pay much attention to her. Probably should have. I heard talk she was trouble. But talk is usually just talk." She didn't believe that for a second, and neither did I.

"What did you hear exactly?" I asked.

"Nothing much."

"Diana, please."

She looked down. "Another friend of mine, her husband sold insurance. Nice people. This girl baby-sat for them, too. But the husband caught her strung out on drugs while the kids were still up. At least that's what he told his wife when he fired the girl. Does she look like an addict to you, Cece?"

She looked like she was in the pink of health.

"I think she might've worked for other families, too. For a short while, at least. Until the husbands put a stop to it."

There were more pictures. That's what she was telling me. More men.

"Did May go away because she found this?" I held up the picture again.

"I don't know why she went away. But she left it behind. She wanted me to see it, the way I wanted you to see it. I'm an old woman, Cece. There's not much I can do about this now. Not from here."

"You underestimate yourself, Diana."

"That I do not. But maybe you're speaking from experience."

"Just what is it you expect me to do?" I asked.

"Whatever you've been doing. Whatever it is that brought you here."

My coffee was cold, but I finished it anyway. Diana held out her arms to give me a hug good-bye. As I hugged her back, she whispered, "Who took the picture? That's the question, Cece."

CHAPTER THIRTY-FIVE

Even if she'd been expecting me, I don't think Lisa Lapelt would've baked a cake. More likely, hired armed guards. But I knew better than to give her any warning.

She was halfway down her driveway when I squealed to a stop, perpendicular to her minivan. Good tires, I thought, for a rental. I cut the engine and walked around to her driver's-side window. It was tinted, but Lisa knew exactly who'd come calling.

The window went down. "Morning," she said, attempting a smile. "I've got to get my kids to school."

"You look tired," I said.

She rubbed the sleep out of her eyes. "Is there a problem?"

"I'd say so." I waved to the kids in the backseat. A boy and a girl. They waved back. "We need to talk."

"We're done talking." The window started to go up.

I held up the Polaroid of Maren and Owen Madden in bed. "I don't think so."

The window stopped midway, then reversed course. Lisa Lapelt was wide awake now.

"Where did you get that photograph?" she asked.

"That's not important."

"I have a meeting at the school at nine."

"You should cancel it."

The kids were bickering. She spun around to quiet them, then turned back to me.

"I'll meet you back here in half an hour."

"Nope," I said. "I'll follow you to the school and we'll go from there."

"I don't want you anywhere near my children's school," she said, her chin trembling.

"I'm not a threat to your children."

"Yes, you are." Tears started to appear. "I won't let you fuck around with my kids."

"Look, I'm sorry to show up like this, but you haven't been honest with me."

"Oh, you're a fine one to talk about honesty."

"This has gone far enough, hasn't it?"

"I hate you!" yelled Lisa's daughter.

"I hate you more!" her brother yelled back.

"Topsail Elementary, on the corner of Randall and Matilija," she said, drying her eyes on her sleeve.

"Thank you."

"Shut up already," she said. "Shut the hell up!"

I hoped she was talking to me.

The school was about a ten-minute drive away. I stuck to Lisa's rear bumper like glue, which was a good plan in principle, except that it required running a red light, which I would've gotten away with if not for that pesky surveillance camera. I could see myself in the picture already. I don't take a good picture. The hair tends to dominate. There'd be bags under my eyes. My apricot-colored mohair coat would look like shit. I'd protest, of course: those red-light cameras are housed in bullet-resistant cabinets, which means the people installing them clearly expect them to be shot at, and isn't it irresponsible to place unnecessary equipment in a populated area when you expect it to attract gunfire? Not that that was going to fly.

Drop-off at Topsail Elementary was a labyrinthine process. Lisa pulled the minivan into a driveway behind a long line of other minivans, SUVs, and at least one Hummer. I did the same, though I stuck out like a sore thumb. We inched forward, following the directions of a man wielding a walkie-talkie, through the parking lot, then out onto the street, where another person, a woman, also wielding a walkie-talkie, directed us to turn right and into a second driveway, this one located in front of the school, where cheerful teachers were in the process of helping cheerful children out of their cars and bidding them good day.

When she arrived at the designated spot, the side panel of Lisa's minivan slid open and her comparatively uncheerful children emerged, dragging backpacks bigger than they were. Once Lisa's door slid closed and her children were safely inside, a teacher in a Garfield T-shirt I swear I used to own started to approach my back door, but I put down the window, muttered, "Private security," and sped off behind my quarry.

She pulled out onto Torrance Boulevard. Within seconds, she'd cut off a pickup with screen doors poking out of the rear to get over to the far lane. Was she was trying to lose me? I cut off the truck, too, which I felt bad about, but I needed to stay behind her. Two blocks later, she signaled left and pulled into a car wash.

She had to be kidding.

I stomped out of the car, furious. "What are we doing here, Lisa?"

"Getting our cars washed. I want you to do a really good job on the interior," she said to the attendant who was writing up the ticket. "My daughter threw up in the backseat a couple of days ago."

"Carpets? Upholstery? Scented shampoo? That'll run you an extra forty-five. And it takes a good twenty minutes."

"No problem," Lisa said, smiling. In her grungy sweats, her teeth unbrushed, she'd made a fool of me. Her diamond ring sparkled triumphantly. But seeing her like that, I thought of something.

Maybe the girl in the photograph wasn't Maren.

Maybe it was her.

"How about you, ma'am?" the guy said to me, his pen poised over the next ticket. "Carpets, upholstery, scented shampoo, too?"

Like I was going to shell out a penny on a rental. "No, thank you."

"Just the regular?"

"No, nothing."

"Then what are you in line for?" he asked.

I gave a sigh, then went to move my car, keeping my eye on Lisa, who'd meandered over to the waiting area, where she peeled off her sweatshirt, revealing her hourglass tattoo and figure. The pink of health. The guys with the rags were staring openly at her. She knew it, and she liked it.

"You think you're so smart," she said to me as I took the seat next to hers, "but you're not smart at all. Smart people don't think they have all the answers. They don't expect to be able to tie things up in neat little packages. Life is messy, Cece. You try to clean it up, but it just gets messy again."

"Spare me the banalities, Lisa. I want to know about Owen Madden. What did he mean to you?"

"Maren baby-sat for his daughter, May."

"And?"

"And nothing." She pursed her lips determinedly.

"And nothing?" I asked, holding up the picture. "Who do you think you're kidding? This isn't the only one of these, is it? There are more of these photographs, aren't there? More photographs, with different men."

She looked down at her lap. She was thinking about how to spin it, but there wasn't any way to spin it. It was what it was.

"Say something," I demanded.

She put on her sunglasses. "Rafe is a really perceptive person. Nobody ever gives him credit for that, but he can read people. It's kind of scary. Like you, for instance. Do you want to know what he thinks about you, Cece?"

"I couldn't care less what Rafe Simic thinks of me."

"He thinks you're arrogant. And vain." She took in my apricot mohair coat, which must've looked puce through her blue-tinted lenses. "And I have to say I agree."

"Want to hear what I think of you?" I asked, not waiting for an answer. "I think you're a person who made some terrible mistakes when she was young. I think you and Maren toyed with people's lives because you were looking for kicks. Maybe because you wanted money, maybe just because you could. But then it got out of hand." I couldn't see her eyes behind her glasses, but there were beads of sweat on her upper lip. "Maybe you were sorry," I continued. "Maybe not. But you counted on people forgetting. You didn't count on Owen Madden saving this picture. This picture that shamed him so badly he killed himself. You didn't count on me finding it. Or May."

"May?" she asked in surprise.

"Yes, May."

"May has nothing to do with any of this."

"Poor kid, getting dragged along to a tattoo parlor with you and Maren. Sounds like you put on quite a show for her. She grew up and found this picture of her father, and now she's gone."

"Gone?"

"Gone," I repeated. "As far away as she could get from this picture."

"It wasn't supposed to happen like that," Lisa said, but I didn't hear anything close to regret in her voice. "We never meant for May to see it."

"Life is messy, remember?"

"It was her fault. Maren's." She spat out the name of her best friend, her soul mate, like it was poison. "It was always Maren's fault. From the day I met her, she was always showing off. I was so naive. I just wanted to be cool. Live on the edge, you know, like she did. Oh, she had this great double life. Knew exactly how to work it." She shook her head. "Always so sure of herself. So sure of how far we could push things. There was nothing to worry about, she assured me. Expecially with him. She knew exactly how he'd react. I could kill her, she got it so wrong."

I should've wondered why Lisa was telling me all this. She didn't need to. I wasn't holding a gun to her head. If I had thought about it, just slowed down, taken a breath, I might have been able to stop things from going the way they did. But I felt like I was on a moving train, and the only thing that mattered was getting to the end of the line.

"So did you kill her?" I asked.

"Who?"

I didn't know who. That was the problem.

"Do you mean Maren?" she asked.

"Yes, Maren." Did she really still think the dead woman was Maren, or was she trying to trap me like I was trying to trap her?

"Are you crazy?" she asked. "Of course I didn't kill Maren."

"You told me she never could have killed herself. That she wasn't the type. What happened to her then?"

"I don't know what happened to her. She wrote me to say good-bye and told me not to worry about her, not that I ever did."

Maren wrote Rafe. Maren wrote Lisa. "Do you still have the note?" I asked. If I could just see that note, maybe I could figure it out.

But that was when I blew it. If only I hadn't mentioned the note. If only I'd put away the photograph.

"I tore that note to pieces," Lisa said, "and I put it in the trash."

As the words spilled from her lips, a lightbulb went off over her head.

She grabbed the photograph out of my hand and tore it to pieces, too.

It took a moment for Lisa to realize what she'd done. But I knew instantly what I'd done: I'd let Lisa Lapelt destroy a piece of evidence. And before I knew exactly what it was evidence of.

"We're finished now," Lisa said, standing up.

"Nothing's changed," I said. "What happened all those years ago hasn't changed."

"Right," she said, getting into her freshly washed car.

Of course it had changed. Everything had changed. Now I'd never know if it was Lisa or Maren in the picture. Now I'd never know where Maren ended and Lisa began.

"Tell me one thing," I said, leaning my head into her window. "Since it doesn't matter anyway." There was something else I'd never know, unless I came out and asked her.

She waited a moment before starting the car.

"Who took the picture?"

She looked at me defiantly. "Rafe did."

CHAPTER
THIRTY-SIX

Maybe.
Maybe not.

But if Rafe did take that picture, he had everything to lose.

They all did—Rafe, Will, Lisa. Only Maren had nothing to lose.

She'd lost everything already.

I left my rental behind and walked south on Torrance Boulevard, out toward the Redondo Beach Pier.

The ocean looked cold and gray and inhospitable. I wound my way around the horseshoe-shaped pier until I came to one of those old viewing machines, facing out to sea. I dropped a quarter into the slot, and peered through the lens, but even after adjusting the focus knob, I couldn't see a thing.

They all had everything to lose. And only Maren could take it from them.

Maybe the dead body really was hers.

The only thing I had to tell me otherwise was a theory about a tattoo—that, and Rafe's word. And I already knew what that was worth.

Back by the parking garage, I watched a girl in an old T-shirt and baggy shorts skateboard over to a bronze statue bust. She took a flowered lei from around her neck and draped it over the statue, then stood around for a minute, head bowed.

After she skated away, I went to have a look.

George Freeth (1883–1919)

He was a Hawaiian-Irish athlete who was hired by legendary land baron Henry Huntington to hang out in front of the old Hotel Redondo and demonstrate the ancient Polynesian art of surfing to day-trippers. The idea was to get them to marvel at the man who could walk on water, on a solid wood board that weighed two hundred pounds. Well, that wasn't the real idea. The real idea was to get them to stick around, buy a soda pop, a postcard, some property, maybe. They don't call them land barons for nothing.

I stopped to try on some sunglasses on the way back to the car. Classic aviator, cat's-eyes with glitter, oversize Elton John, police, mirrored, all plastic, all $8.99.

"You surf?"

I turned around. The skater girl was back, chugging on a can of Pepsi.

I shook my head. "I know some surfers, though."

"Don't trust 'em," she said, deadpan. Then she smiled. "I like the glasses you've got on."

They were superhero frames with flames on the temples and

spiderwebs etched onto the lenses. She picked up the same pair and tried them on.

"No good, right?" I asked. "You can't see a thing."

"Doesn't matter," she said, tucking a strand of hair behind her ear. "I live inside my head most of the time, anyway."

"What's up with George Freeth?"

"He was the father of surfing in the United States. But Duke Kahanamoku gets all the credit. You've heard of *him,* right?"

"Not really. Does he have a memorial somewhere around here, too?" I took off the glasses and put them back on the rack.

"You should buy," said the woman who owned the stand. She was all covered up, like a beekeeper.

"Used to be one at the base of Huntington Pier," the girl answered. "But there's statues of Duke all over. Restaurants named after him, stuff like that. You can eat a Dukeburger for lunch at a dozen places around here. Nobody remembers George, though. Not enough flash." She put her glasses back, too. "I can find them cheaper someplace else."

"Hey," I said. "Can I ask you a surfing question?"

"Shoot." She tucked the same strand of hair behind her ear. Fine gold hoops ran all the way around the lobe, like a spiral-bound notebook.

"What does 'in the green room' mean exactly?"

Her face went serious. "I've never gotten there. I'm still a beginner. It means you've powered the cut perfectly, the wave's dropped over you, you're inside it, and all you see around you is water. It's like being inside a cocoon. No past, no future, only the moment."

"Sounds addictive."

"Better than sex, I hear," she said, grinning.

"Aren't you too young?"

She laughed. "One mother is about all I can handle."

And one daughter was more than enough for me.

I called Annie on my way home. I'd barely said hello when she cut me off.

"It's Roxana, Mom!" She was hysterical. "She's coming back for him! In three days! Mom, we're going to lose Alexander!"

UNLIKE THE REST OF US, ANNIE DIDN'T SELF-medicate with chocolate. So instead of heading straight to See's Candies, I went to a chain bookstore in Redondo Beach, where I spent a lonely hour navigating the self-help section (it wasn't like I was going to ask for help).

The titles all sounded like country-and-western songs. Was Annie a woman who loved too much? Yes. Who needed to heal a broken heart? Yes. A giver, not a taker? Absolutely. I plucked them all from the shelves and dumped them into my basket. Poems for grieving. Good. Meditations on loss. Good. When hope can kill. There was a gruesome thought. Doors close, doors open: better.

I knew she wasn't going to read any of them, but maybe she'd find the fact that I'd bought them amusing. Maybe she could throw them at Roxana when she showed up. That would certainly be $119.50 well spent.

Nobody answered when I knocked, so I went around to the kitchen door, which was always unlatched, and I let myself in.

"Hello? Anybody home? Annie? Vincent? Alexander?"

The kitchen was clean as a whistle, shiny copper pots hanging on a rack over the stove, colorful dishcloths folded by the sink, a bowl of fresh fruit on the counter. You'd never know we were related.

"In here, Mom," Annie called from the back of the house. She sounded angry, which was better than hysterical. "Everybody else is out."

I found her in her closet, furiously grabbing clothes off hangers.

"It's too early for spring cleaning," I said. "What's up?" Then I saw the open suitcase on the bed.

"Don't start," she said, without turning around.

"Annie." There was a jumble of shoes on the floor, and a cardboard box by the side of the bed, half-filled with CDs and tapes.

She tossed the sweaters in her hands onto the bed and actually looked at me for the first time since I'd gotten there. "Oh, my god, your head!"

"It's nothing. The bandage is coming off tomorrow."

"What happened to you?" she asked.

"A little car accident."

"A little car accident? Why didn't you tell me?"

"It was days ago. It was nothing. I'm perfectly fine."

"Really?"

"Yes," I said. "But you're not fine."

"I can't do this right now, Mom."

"Do what?"

"You know what." She pulled open a drawer and started riffling through Vincent's socks. They weren't organized into pairs, so she yanked the drawer out and dumped the entire contents into the suitcase.

"Aren't you getting ahead of yourself here?" I asked.

"Sorry to break it to you, Mom, but you don't know what you're talking about."

I was waiting for the "as usual," but I think the sight of the bandage prevented her from going at me with full guns.

"This is only going to lead to more heartache," I said.

"This is what I'm talking about. You. Your well-meaning advice. You're butting in where you aren't needed, as usual."

Wrong again.

"Vincent and Alexander and I are leaving. End of discussion." She went back into the closet and started in on the jeans.

"You can't just run away, Annie."

"We're not running away. We're taking a trip."

"Annie, please." I pushed the suitcase over and sat down on the bed. The quilt was handmade, a present from Vincent's grandmother. The pattern was a star, with a mosaic of little diamonds radiating from its center. "I brought you some books. They're in the car. I'll get them later, okay? Maybe after we've had some tea. I'm going to make tea."

"Mom, listen to what I'm saying. That woman is not taking Alexander away from us. Not now. Not ever."

"No one is going to take Alexander away from you, honey."

Annie came out of the closet and knelt at my feet. She took my hands in hers. "You don't know Roxana. She isn't like you or me. This is a person who waited two entire years before telling Vincent he had a son. Don't you get it? She wanted him all to herself. Then, boom, all of a sudden, her love life heats up and she's done with him, just leaves him behind. No notes, no calls, no nothing. Now that *that* hasn't worked out, she thinks she's going to waltz right in and take him back, like he's some . . . some *thing*. Like he's a piece of furniture we've been keeping for her. No," she said, holding back the tears, "I won't let that happen."

"You can't bend the situation to your will," I said gently.

"The hell I can't."

"You're not in control here."

"I can't believe what you're saying to me," she said. "Don't you want me to fight for what's right?"

"That's what the law is for," I protested. "To see to it that Alexander's best interests are served. To protect Vincent's rights as his father."

"You don't understand," she said, shaking her head. "Roxana's not going to wait around to hear what some judge says. She's going to take him and just disappear."

"So you're going to take him first?"

"What choice do I have?" She pulled her fingers through her long, curly hair. She looked so young to me at that moment.

"You have plenty of choice. What about Roxana?"

"Don't go defending her, please." Annie zipped up the suitcase and heaved it onto the floor. "I'm doing Alexander's room next."

"I'm not defending her, but she's his mother."

"By accident of birth."

"That isn't all there is to it. She made a mistake. One mistake. A horrible one, I agree. But a person doesn't lose everything because of one mistake."

"It's not just one mistake."

"Her child needs her, Annie."

"He has me," she said in a tiny voice.

Oh, my poor angel. "He needs you both."

Doors close, doors open.

I took her in my arms, and we cried, the two of us, for what seemed like a very long time.

CHAPTER
THIRTY-SEVEN

Later that evening, after Gambino had fallen asleep, I wrapped myself in my bathrobe and slipped out to my office. Maybe if I could restore order there, I could restore order elsewhere. Homeostasis. The maintenance of external balances facilitates the maintenance of internal balances.

It's a scientific principle.

After an hour of filing, however—followed by fifteen solid minutes of dusting, and several of sneezing, which I wouldn't have had to endure if I'd dusted more regularly—I'd concluded that the whole thing was a crock. Still, I'd done one thing right: I'd waited until Vincent came home, and I'd helped him talk Annie down from the state she'd worked herself into. While Alexander watched cartoons, and the two of them went out for a walk, I'd put the house back together and started dinner (no yeast). When they came home, arms locked tightly around each other's waist, they announced they were going to fight for joint custody. Roxana had a long way to go, but Annie was no longer going to write her off as a lost cause. Not for her sake, but for Alexander's.

Two things right: I'd finally talked to Gambino, who'd realized at some point during the day that he never had gotten his eggs Benedict. There were fireworks, as I'd expected. Words like *gun* had made a definite impact (Rafe's gun, not Tina's; I still hadn't broached the whole issue of Tina). Gambino didn't know Captain Donaldson, but he was familiar with Detective Smarinsky. After a dinner of Indian takeout, Gambino got him on the phone. They talked for a while. Both had meetings all day tomorrow—Friday—but Smarinsky agreed to a sit-down at the end of the day, with the caveat that it was shabbat, and his wife was baking fresh challah, so the clock would be ticking.

After they hung up, and because Gambino asked so nicely, I swore on the latest issue of *People* (I was boycotting the rest of them) that I was going to stay out of it from there on in. I had every intention of sticking to my word. But in my defense, I'd eaten so much garlic naan I couldn't think straight.

That was hours ago, of course. Now I sat at my Lucite desk, which I could actually see for the first time in years, wide awake at two o'clock in the morning. It was too late to call anybody. I could wake up Gambino, but he had a busy day ahead of him. So I walked over to the bookshelf and pulled out the Hammett biography I'd written all those years ago.

It was my second book, and the one that still meant the most to me, probably because I admired Hammett so much, both for his personal integrity and the beauty of his language. I ran my fingers over the shiny white dust jacket with the stark black Roman letters. I'd struggled with the title for a long time. Nothing had seemed right. For a while, I'd wanted to call it *Ink Is a Stain,* which was the first line of a poem Hammett had written early in his career. But I'd finally decided on *The Man Who Wasn't There,* after a verse he used to recite to his younger daughter, Jo:

> *Yesterday, upon the stair*
> *I saw a man who wasn't there.*
> *He wasn't there again today.*
> *Oh, how I wish he'd go away.*

The man who wasn't there. That was how I saw Hammett— not as the thin man, who was so insubstantial he had to stand in the same place twice to throw a shadow, but as someone far more elusive: drinking at the Clover Club when he should have been in his office at MGM; with his lover when he should have been with his wife; in the army when he should have been in the hospital; in jail when he should have been at his typewriter. As a close friend of his, a screenwriter named Nunnally Johnson, once said, you could only live that way if you didn't expect to be around much past Thursday. But Hammett lived to sixty-six. He spent his whole life dodging a bullet that was coming at him in slow motion.

My editor, Sally, had wanted a little-known black-and-white photo of him for the cover. It was taken in San Francisco circa 1921, up on the roof of 620 Eddy Street, where he'd lived while working for the Pinkerton office, when he was first married. But I'd disliked that photograph, with Hammett looking off into the distance, a pipe in his mouth, a large, black drainpipe leaning perilously close. It was so portentous, somehow. Her second choice was a charcoal sketch of a bottle being borne along the waves. She'd taken the idea from one of the early biographers, who'd likened Hammett's first stories for *Black Mask* to letters in a bottle, set adrift in the hope they'd be found by like-minded souls. I'd disliked that idea, too, disliked the whole romantic mythology of Hammett as a tortured hero.

Hammett could've kept writing, that was the thing, penned dozens of Sam Spade rehashes, kept himself busy, out of trouble. But he didn't want to. He'd mastered the form: why repeat himself? Over the years, pressured by his publisher, he'd announced titles of forthcoming novels, serious novels this time: *There Was a Young Man, The Hunting Boy, The Valley Sheep Are Fatter*. But none ever materialized. I flipped to the last chapter of my book, and found a quote from the fragmentary *Tulip*, which Hammett left behind at his death: "If you are tired, you ought to rest, I think, and not try to fool yourself and your customers with colored bubbles."

You miss the story when you get caught up in the myth. The myth is the story's engine, not its conclusion. How well Hammett knew this. Consider the legendary Maltese falcon: when the thief, Caspar Gutman, finally gets his hands on it, he turns the bird upside down and scrapes an edge of its base with his knife: "Black enamel came off in tiny curls, exposing blackened metal beneath. Gutman's knife-blade bit into the metal, turning back a thin curved shaving. The inside of the shaving, and the narrow plane its removal had left, had the soft gray sheen of lead."

It was a fake, a ruse—a myth.

A myth takes you only so far, and not always in the direction of the truth. The truth is right there in front of you. That's what Captain Donaldson had said. But you have to be ready to confront it.

I was ready, I suddenly realized.

All I had to do was open one more door.

CHAPTER THIRTY-EIGHT

It wasn't made of glass, but when I slipped the key into the lock, I half-expected it to shatter. Such are the perils of the literary imagination. It was actually anticlimactic. No shattered glass, no lightning bolt from on high, no little voice in my head asking what the hell I was doing, which would have been a fine thing to ask at four in the afternoon on this unusually bright day in early fall.

I kissed the Playboy bunny for luck, slipped the key ring back into my pocket, and opened the door to Rafe Simic's house.

No one was at home.

I knew that already, having called five times at five-minute intervals, letting it ring until the machine picked up. I'd used a prepaid, throwaway cell phone so the number couldn't be traced back to me, and remembered to pay in cash. Afterward, the phone went into a Dumpster on the corner of Venice and

Lincoln with thirty unused minutes, but what the hell. A find like that would make somebody's day, and god knows I could use the karmic payback. Yes, I'd thought of everything.

"Hey!" someone called out. "Don't shut that door!"

Make that almost everything.

I spun around slowly, giving myself enough time to wipe the look of terror off my face.

"You're Rafe's friend, right?" It was the guy in the Rolling Stones T-shirt from the other day. He was carrying two grocery bags. "Remember me? I'm Sam the neighbor."

"Hey, Sam the neighbor," I said, doing my best to radiate inner peace.

"Rafe went to the desert, didn't he?"

"That's right! In the desert for three more days!" Which is why it was going to be no problem whatsoever getting into his house. I peeled off my sweater. I was starting to perspire.

"Too bad. He borrowed something I need. Well, I guess I don't really need it. You know how that goes."

"Sure."

"Man, I'd love to get out of town. Some guys have all the luck."

I started to play with my wooden bangles. Most people take this sort of thing as a hint, but not Sam.

"No such luck for me," he continued. "I'm stuck here. Editing the movie from hell."

He waited for me to ask for details. I didn't want to ask for details. I rocked back and forth on my heels. I played with my bangles some more.

"Director's a first-timer. Doesn't know anything. So it's all on me. I just spent nineteen hours straight in the editing suite. I could sure use a beer."

Go home then.

He waited expectantly.

I smiled innocuously.

He smiled back, but innocuous wasn't his thing. Exactly the opposite. His smile showed intent. His smile showed teeth. His smile said wouldn't it be great to have a beer in the movie star's house with the movie star's girlfriend and then sleep with her in the movie star's bed while the movie star was out of town? I really didn't have time for this. Sam stroked his five-o'clock shadow, which was one hour early. "Aren't you going to invite me in? I'm a thirsty guy."

"It's just that—"

"C'mon. You look like you could use one, too," he said.

"I'm—"

"Rafe is always so hospitable."

"Oh, fine," I said, taking his arm.

That's when the flashbulbs started popping.

There were three, no four, no five of them. It was like a bad joke, these overweight guys in their safari jackets: man the hunter stalks his prey, finds the perfect moment to strike. I could see the headlines already: "Buxom Brunette Beauty Cheats on Rafe!" "Rafe's Faithless Girlfriend Caught in the Act!" Only I wasn't Rafe's girlfriend, nor would I cheat on him with Sam, of all people, if I were.

Oh, god: what was I wearing? None of the coral beads had fallen off the bangles. The shoes were wood-grain print plat-forms with ankle straps, from the forties and in perfect condition. But my chocolate ballet dress with the spaghetti straps? What a pity I'd taken off my sweater. My arms were going to look like ham hocks.

"Over here!"

"Look this way!"

"Smile for Daddy!"

"Give us a wave!"

Sam started to wave.

"Are you out of your mind?" I yelled, slapping his hand down.

"Sorry, reflex."

I dragged him inside Rafe's house and slammed the door shut.

"Should we call someone?" Sam asked, making himself comfortable on the sofa.

Good idea. The police could just take me away now. "Who'd you have in mind, Sam?"

"Oh, I don't know. How about that beer?"

I went into the kitchen and opened the stainless-steel fridge. There was extra-firm tofu, soy milk, something horrible-looking that bore a slight resemblance to bacon, a vat of sour cream, a six-pack of Diet Coke, and beer, two kinds: Chimay, from Belgium, and Budweiser. A Bud for Sam.

Speak of the devil, the door to the kitchen swung open and there he was, proffering a tub of sweating ice cream as if it were a dozen red roses.

"I'm lactose intolerant," I said.

"Too bad. It's vanilla bean." He maneuvered himself behind me—which would have been desirable only if I'd been choking and he were performing the Heimlich—then started shimmying down to open the freezer. "Don't want it to melt," he murmured, "but as for you . . ." I feinted left, then dodged the bullet by sliding sideways out of his embrace.

"Beer in the living room!" I cried gaily.

I choked once, on onion soup gratinée. It was in the kitchen of the faculty club at the University of Chicago, where I worked as a hostess while my ex-husband went up for tenure.

But instead of Heimliching me, the chef put down the chops he was Frenching and stuck his hand down my throat to remove the offending cheese. Gruyère.

Sam found his spot on the couch. "So." He took a slug of his beer.

"So," I replied, perching myself on the arm of a leather chair that looked like it could take it.

"You're awfully far away," he said.

"I'm comfortable, thanks." Of course, I wasn't, so I sort of slid into the chair proper, landing with a thud. He didn't care.

"How long have you known Rafe?"

"It seems like forever. Another Bud?" Maybe he'd pass out, and I could go about my business undisturbed.

"I'm fine." He got up to look out the window. "Looks like the photographers are gone."

"Oh, good," I said.

"Rafe's got problems I can't even imagine."

"So true."

He shook his head. "Paparazzi."

I nodded.

"They'll eat you alive," he said authoritatively.

"Tear your flesh off in chunks."

"Shall I put on some music?" he asked, changing the subject.

"No, I have a bit of a headache."

But he was already fiddling with the stereo. Marvin Gaye. *Sexual Healing.* Subtlety was not Sam's middle name.

"Dance?" He started swaying in my direction.

I got out of the chair and turned off the music. "I'm so sorry if this sounds rude, but I really need to lie down. I had a head injury recently, so I'm prone to migraines. Dizziness. I throw up. It's a nightmare, really. You don't want to be here for that."

Sam began to pale. Vomit is not an aphrodisiac.

"The night before last, I threw up for four hours straight," I added, just to be on the safe side.

"Sounds like you'd rather be alone, so I'll just get my ice cream," he said, picking up the two grocery bags, "and be on my way."

"Really, I'm sorry," I called after him.

After he was gone, I went into the kitchen to get myself a Diet Coke, which I richly deserved. Just as I was about to pop the top, I heard the front door open. My first thought was, Had this man really not given up? My second thought was, I *know* I locked the door. Before I could get to my third thought, which wasn't a pleasant one, I heard laughing. A woman. Then a man. Who was here? Will and Rafe were in the desert until Sunday. This was only Friday. Then the distinct sound of a zipper being unzipped. Metal teeth biting metal teeth. Then some other biting-type sounds, shoes clattering to the floor, muffled laughter. Oh, my god.

I backed against the Viking range, then heard the hiss of a burner going on. I flipped around and turned it off.

I shouldn't have kissed that Playboy bunny. Pheromone overload.

"Do you want a beer?" The girl.

"Sounds perfect." The guy.

I dashed over to the other side of the room, pressed myself flat against the wall, and mouthed a prayer to St. Jude, patron saint of lost causes.

The door swung open, missing me by an inch. I grabbed on to it before it could swing closed and pulled it back toward me until the hinge clicked into place. Then I held my breath.

"It's freezing in here," the girl called out.

That's because you have no clothes on.

The door to the fridge opened with a sucking sound.

"Bud or an import?" she yelled.

"Bud."

I heard two bottles clinking against each other, then the refrigerator closing.

As the girl pulled the door closed behind her, I caught a glimpse of telltale tie-dye.

Kat, Will's assistant, and Riley, the boyfriend.

It's so hard to get good help these days.

"You are so hot," Riley said from the living room, loud enough for me to hear it. "Take off that thong."

"Baby," murmured Kat. At least I thought it was "baby."

I hunkered down for round two, hoping for brevity, but they didn't get very far.

"Riley," Kat said breathlessly, "I think somebody else is here."

I looked down, panicked. No, I had my purse with me. My sweater, too. The keys were in my pocket. How did they know?

"We're in deep shit," Riley said. "I thought he only drank the imported stuff."

Sam's beer. I'd forgotten to toss it. Lucky for me. But it wasn't over yet.

Metal teeth biting back into metal teeth.

Scrambling sounds.

The pattering of feet.

"Hurry up," Kat said impatiently.

Hopping. Hopping?

Finally, the front door slammed shut.

I gave it a minute or two, then started to feel the tension leave my body. My face relaxed. My arms. My legs. But my headache was back now, for real. I emerged from my hiding place and walked upstairs with my Diet Coke. In the guest bathroom, I nabbed two more extra-strength Excedrin, which must rank near the top of the list of man's greatest achievements. Better than Advil.

I headed left down the hall.

Then the phone rang. I froze in place.

One ring.

Two rings.

Three rings, then the machine picked up.

Will's voice, then the beep.

"Hello, Mr. Simic, this is Mrs. Meloni from Joshua Tree Elementary. We just wanted to thank you again for hosting the auction while you were out here. It was a huge success: we raised close to thirty thousand dollars for the library fund! Thanks again. You were wonderful. So handsome, too! I guess I'm a little overexcited, I'm going on and on here. Well, good-bye."

Rafe went to the desert to see the stars. But I suppose there's no escaping being the star. At least it was a good cause.

I was surrounded by good causes.

I went up the spiral staircase that led to Will's office on the third floor.

I hit the switch.

Looked like the same mess it had been the night of Rafe's party.

I squinted at the pockmarked file cabinet against the far wall.

The same drawer was open—the middle one—with the same papers poking out at the same odd angles.

Strange.

My gaze traveled around the room.

The trash can was filled to the top, as if it hadn't been emptied all week. And in the middle of Will's desk, on top of the Post-it notes, and the tangle of thumbtacks and wires and papers, was the plastic champagne glass he'd overturned when he'd tossed the file Kat had given me onto the desk.

This didn't look like the same mess, this *was* the same mess.

Exactly the same mess.

Which would seem to indicate that it wasn't a mess at all, just a clever facsimile of one.

The thumbtacks.

The wires.

The papers.

The champagne glass.

The file.

All props.

It was a stage set.

Like Rafe's office, I suddenly realized.

Rafe's office was as serene as this one was frenzied, as pristine as this one was chaotic.

I cast my eye over Will's desk again.

The yellow file.

It wasn't just a prop.

I'd seen it before.

Not the night of the party, but before.

I'd seen it in Captain Donaldson's office. He'd started fingering it absentmindedly when our talk had turned to Maren.

I moved the champagne glass out of the way and slid the file toward me. Without pausing for so much as a breath, I opened it. There was a note inside, typed on a small sheet of white paper.

Dear Rafe,

This is good-bye. I need to disappear. I've made mistakes before, but these are ones I can't undo. Say a prayer for me, and be happy. We will always belong to one another. You have always been there for me. Remember, nothing on this earth is final.

No signature.

This must be Maren's "suicide" note to Rafe. What was Will doing with it? Had he stolen it from Captain Donaldson's office?

I put the note back and was about to close the file when I saw the Post-it notes that had been affixed to the other side.

Dozens of them.

You will get what you deserve.

Don't take things that don't belong to you.

Stop interfering with other people's lives.

What you are doing, young lady, is very, very wrong.

I'm talking to you.

Oh, my god.

He was talking to me.

I leapt out of the chair and ran out of the room, down the hall, down to the second floor, down the main staircase, out the front door. The sun was still shining. My car was close by, just across the second bridge. I flew over the first bridge without so much as looking right or left. The ducks were squawking wildly. I was headed toward the second bridge, already thinking of what I had to do next—and, for the first time since Captain Donaldson showed us that dead body with that white, white skin, I knew, I absolutely knew—when I saw him coming toward me, Maren's brother, Will, a smile on his face.

CHAPTER
THIRTY-NINE

ey, Cece," he said. "Fancy meeting you here! What're you doing in our neck of the woods?"

"Where's Rafe?" I asked, trying to catch my breath. The latter's sports car was parked on the tree-lined street just beyond the bridge. Freshly washed. Impeccable. Green.

Will's eyes followed my gaze. "Oh, the car. I borrowed it for a couple of hours. I think Rafe's at home. Maybe not. I don't really know. Are you okay? You look kind of messed up."

Rafe was nowhere in sight. All I could see was a couple of kids on roller skates and a young woman pushing a stroller. It was a beautiful day for a walk, but there was a chill in the air. The woman bent down and tucked the blanket tighter around her baby, who reached up to tug on her long hair. She laughed.

Out here, in the open air, there was nothing to be afraid of.

I returned Will's smile. "Come on. You know everything Rafe does. You help him do it, as a matter of fact."

He tipped his cap. "I live to serve."

"How was the desert?"

"Hot."

"You're back early," I said.

"Yeah. Last night. We got bored."

"It wouldn't do to let Rafe get bored."

He wrinkled his brow. "I don't get you, Cece, but I never did, to be honest."

I looked down at my hand and saw the Playboy-bunny key ring at precisely the same moment he did. Shit.

Will scratched his head. "Those are Rafe's keys, aren't they? How'd you wind up with them?"

"He forgot them. I was hoping to return them. That's why I'm here."

"You're heading in the wrong direction then."

"These canals," I said. "I keep getting turned around."

He held up his surf bag. "Here. Stick 'em inside."

O'Neill.

The curling wave.

"I would do it," he went on, "but I'm kind of loaded down here." He indicated the other bag he was holding. "Stan's Liquors. My home away from home."

I dropped Rafe's keys into the worn leather bag.

"Cece," he blurted out.

"Yes?"

"Did you take those keys from my desk?" His voice turned low, conspiratorial. "Because if you did, I could understand that. I could totally understand that."

"You could?"

"Yes."

"And why is that?" I asked.

"Somebody like Rafe, well, people get kind of excited being around him. Sometimes they take things. They want to have them as keepsakes. Or as an excuse to come back, you know, you left these at my place kind of thing. I would understand something like that, I really would. No need to be ashamed of yourself. It's not like you caused real harm. Like you hurt anybody or anything."

"You think I'm a fan?" I asked.

"I'm a fan, too—and damn proud of it. People like us, we keep the wheels turning. We make it all happen. We're invisible, sure, but there's no industry without us. It's nothing to feel bad about. It's the way it is. Not everybody gets to be the star."

He was so good. He could've been the star. Maybe he should have been the star. But the show was over. I knew what I had to do. "I know about Owen Madden."

The roller skaters were gone. The woman with the stroller was gone. The wind was picking up.

"Owen Madden." He staggered backward in mock surprise. "Whoa. I guess you got me." He laughed. "Owen Madden. That's a name I haven't heard in a long time. Everybody loved that guy. Things didn't work out too well for him, unfortunately."

"No, they didn't," I said.

"Suicide is so hard on the family. What a legacy."

I couldn't bring myself to respond.

"What?" Will asked. "Do you not like that I said that? Something wrong with what I said?"

I choked back my anger. "It's time to own up to what happened, Will."

"You are absolutely right," he said, his head bobbing up and down. "This is about me firing you, right? Not that I did fire you, but I should have known you'd see it that way. I understand how pissed you are. So you're venting on me. But if I can say something here, you really need to get your emotions in check, Cece. Don't let them carry you away. You may find yourself doing things you don't mean to." When he saw the look on my face, he added, "I'm telling you this for your own good. As a friend."

"You're not my friend. You're Rafe's friend. That's the sum total of who you are. It must get pretty frustrating."

"Just doing my job," he said with a grin.

"I was on the subject of Owen Madden," I said.

"You're all over the map actually. Maybe it's the accident. Rafe told me. He said your forehead looks fine. But those things leave psychological scars, you know?"

I pushed the hair out of my face. I didn't care about the mark on my forehead. I wanted him to see my eyes.

"You blackmailed Owen Madden," I said. "And he wasn't the only one. Maren and Lisa, they got these good men like Owen Madden into bed, then you took their pictures. Both of you." Rafe didn't make a move without Will. And Will was the one who had a way with composition. Like Fredericka said, he was a real artist.

"And her imagination is undimmed! I love it!" Will stamped his feet for emphasis. "I'm telling you, Cece, you're in the wrong business. You should be writing scripts. I'm dying to know what happened next. Don't keep me in suspense here."

Asshole. "I'm sure you didn't expect Dr. Madden to kill himself. You were just four kids having fun, right? But you miscalculated. That's why Maren freaked out that day, at the funeral. It wasn't a game anymore. You agreed to forget about it, all of you. Pretend it never happened. Go about your business, lead good lives, blah, blah, blah. But you felt guilty. God, at least you felt guilty. That's why you and Rafe donated a quarter of a million dollars to the Oceans Conservancy. Blood money."

"Nice rhetorical flourish, but we don't have time for that shit in showbiz." Will looked at his watch. "Time is money. And I'm dying to get home. Put up my feet. Crack open a beer. It's cold out here." He shivered. "Why don't you get to the point?"

"Owen Madden saved that picture: that's the point. He should've torn it up. Anybody in his right mind would have torn it up. But some strange compulsion must have come over him. It was as if he wanted somebody to find it. His daughter, May, was the one. She was cleaning out her house after her aunt died. And there it was. And she wanted an explanation."

"I remember May," Will said, closing his eyes for a minute. "Sweet little kid. Cute. Blond hair. She had one of those bowl cuts. A real dreamer." His eyes blinked open. "Maren used to baby-sit for her. She liked the kid, but Dr. Madden, I gotta say, he was one cheap son of a bitch. I mean, four-fifty an hour and no rounding up, come on. What the fuck is that?"

"May would've talked," I said. "You knew that. She would've ruined everything you worked so hard for."

I was swimming against the current now, and I had to keep pushing. Harder and faster, or I'd drown—like May. "She would have destroyed Rafe's whole career," I said. "You had to stop her. You had to take care of things. That's what you do. You take care of things. Keep the wheels turning. What's that look, Will?" I asked. "Those were your words, not mine."

He'd started to say something but stopped himself.

"Your sister, Maren," I pressed on, "your beloved sister,

Maren—her reputation, well, that was already shot. But she was in trouble again. Maybe it was more serious this time. So you figured you'd kill two birds with one stone. You'd get rid of May and make everybody think it was Maren who had died."

I'd received a call earlier in the morning from the people at Woods Hole. May Madden had never arrived. That confirmed any lingering doubts I'd had. Diana Muldaur—her neighbor, her friend, her father's friend, her aunt's—was the last person who'd seen her alive.

No, Will Levander was.

A smile made its way across his face, but I saw his eyes. The light had gone out. They were dead. "You're on a roll, Cece. Please. Don't stop for my benefit."

Oh, I wasn't doing anything for his benefit. "You couldn't identify the body yourself, because then there'd be nobody to corroborate the story. So what did you do? You dug up an old picture of the four of you from high school. Maren, Rafe, Will, and Lisa. The four of you were unstoppable, remember? You tore the picture down the middle, and after you pushed May off the cliff, you planted the half showing Rafe and Maren on May's dead body. You knew it would lead the police straight to Rafe."

Rafe, who never saw Maren for who she was. Who saw her forever as the girl he'd met on his first day of high school, the girl with the devil-may-care attitude, the girl who'd whispered in his ear.

"Rafe was always such a sucker for your sister. You knew he'd be in a panic after receiving that note from her. The perfect state of mind. For half his life, he'd played the sap for her, and he was hardly going to stop now. You knew that he'd

identify the body as hers. You knew he'd do just about anything to save her."

But Will hadn't planned on Rafe's asking me to come along
to the coroner's office. I was an unseen complication. No wonder he wanted to get rid of me. The bullet through my window. The car running me off the road.

"It was a great plan, Will. The beauty of it was, Rafe would
never have to know any more. Okay, maybe he and the rest of
you were the reason Owen Madden had died, but at least Rafe
would think he'd done the right thing by Maren. You handed
him his redemption. You were a true friend. You gave him
everything he needed to get back to the business of making
money. Not just for him, of course. For the both of you."

Will shifted his weight from one foot to the other, then
stated the obvious: "It's a good story. But that's all it is."

And there was the hitch.

I had nothing.

Not a single shred of evidence.

I'd had the Polaroid of Dr. Madden with one of the hourglass blondes, but, like a fool, I'd let Lisa tear it up.

A car went over the bridge behind us. Its lights were on.
I looked up at the sky. The sun was going down. It would be
dark soon.

"Of course, if you'd been able to find the supposed missing
half of the supposed picture," Will said suddenly, "the one you
mentioned earlier, of Maren and Rafe and me and Lisa, I suppose that would be something else entirely."

"What are you talking about?" I asked slowly. I brought my
hand up to the cut on my forehead. It had formed a scab, but
I could still feel a bump under the skin. I was starting to feel

dizzy. All that running. I needed to sit down. Lie down. I was supposed to be taking it easy.

Will put down his things, opened up his surf bag, and pulled something out. "I've got half of a picture here," he said, straightening up.

It was black and white.

It had a ragged edge.

"This isn't the picture you mentioned earlier, of course," he said. "This picture right here"—he was waving it in front of my face now—"man, it's something special. It got torn somewhere along the way, but I still have what's left, all these years later. I really loved it." He looked at it and smiled. "It was a picture of Rafe and his high school gal pals, Maren and Lisa. All three of them so young and beautiful. It was taken, oh, I don't know, I guess it would be senior year. We were out surfing, the four of us. Having the time of our lives. My old, beat-up camera was in my surf bag. I wanted to be in the picture, but somebody had to take it, right?" He grinned. "Good old Will. I never minded being invisible. Anyway, I could really fill a frame."

I closed my eyes for a minute and saw rainbow colors shimmering behind my eyelids, spinning in circles.

"But like I said," Will continued, "this picture isn't the picture you were talking about. This isn't a picture anybody wants anymore. All that's left is Lisa. Rafe and Maren are long gone."

Then white started to crowd out the colors. I grabbed on to a post at the water's edge to steady myself. "Will, stop—"

He brushed past me, and—like a flash, pop, pow—he threw the picture into the canal. I saw Lisa's pretty face hover on the surface of the water for a second, then disappear.

"Sorry, it's not bread, dudes," Will said to the quacking ducks, "but feeding you violates a local ordinance."

I blinked a few times, let the white recede to the edges of my vision, let the world come back into focus. Then I let go of the post and skidded down the embankment, nearly losing my balance in the process, but I was too late.

It was gone.

Two pictures gone.

"You okay, Cece?" Will asked. "You look pale. You should sit down. You shouldn't take chances with head injuries."

"You're not in your right mind," I shouted. "Why'd you show that picture to me if you were just going to destroy it?"

"Aha. That's where you're wrong. Unlike the esteemed Dr. Madden, I'm completely in my right mind. Anyway," he said, "I have another story for you."

He was staring out at the water. It was dark now. The little Christmas lights were lit. There were people coming home from work. Home to their husbands and wives and children. But not May. She wasn't going home to anyone.

"I think my story works a little better than yours," he said. "You tell me. Start with May Madden—you were right about her, at least in part. That was her body you saw at the coroner's office. But May wasn't a dreamy little girl anymore. She was a dangerous young lady."

"You're lying."

"You don't know shit, I'm sorry to say. Why don't you listen to me before you decide what is and isn't true? May Madden was after Rafe. She was a stalker."

"Liar," I said, massaging my temples.

"Well, at least that's what I thought at the time. Like I was saying before, someone as famous as Rafe is, people get obsessed. I blame the media. They throw this celebrity shit in people's faces, it makes sense that some of them are going to blow. This May was one of those people—at least that's what I assumed. And I wasn't so off base to assume it. I mean, she was walking around with this half-ripped picture in her pocket, of Rafe and his first love, Maren. It's creepy, right? She must've taken it from our house or Maren's purse or whatever, all those years ago, thinking she resembled Maren or something. The blond hair, the brown eyes. She was obsessed, I guess."

No, he was the one who was obsessed. Obsessed with Rafe. Obsessed with Maren. And where was Maren? Was she alive or dead? I'd thought she'd be the one to lead me to May, but I'd found May, and still, Maren eluded me. Maybe, like the Maltese falcon, Maren wasn't real. Maybe she was a dream Will and Rafe and Lisa and whoever else had once shared.

Not a dream.

A nightmare.

"Crazy, huh, my stalker theory? Well, now I see it was," Will went on. "May was harmless, of course. Blameless. She thought she was catching up with old friends. But at the time I was scared. Crazy May—that's what I thought. Stupid, right? But she wasn't helping any. She called time and time again. She insisted on seeing Rafe, on seeing me, hell, I even thought that the people Maren was involved with, these no-good criminals, had sent her to come after us. I was at my wit's end, composing responses to May on Post-its."

You will get what you deserve.

Don't take things that don't belong to you.

Stop interfering with other people's lives.

What you are doing, young lady, is very, very wrong.

I'm talking to you.

"I had so lost my mind over this chick," he said with impressive conviction, "that I thought I had to give Rafe my gun.

For protection. Thank god he didn't use it. But I probably should have loaned it to you."

"To me?"

"Look what happened to you! Somebody tried to kill you that day in your car, somebody shot a gun at your house."

"That was you, Will, not May." Not the bad guys. Not Julio Gonzalez.

"I know it wasn't May. I told you, May was a victim. Unfortunately, I didn't see that until it was too late. But this is bigger than May. This is about the culture we live in. This affects even you now. You're Rafe's girlfriend, babe—well, at least everybody thinks you are. And thanks to those piece-of-shit tabloids people buy for whatever the hell reason, you've become one more target."

"Stop it. You can't turn this around, Will."

"I'm not turning anything around. Don't you want to hear the rest?"

He knew I wanted to hear the rest. He could tell a story better than anyone I'd ever known.

"One day, when May called, I agreed to meet her. I thought I'd get it over with. We met out on the cliffs over Lunada. I see now that I wasn't thinking straight. I misinterpreted her. Anyway, I thought she was getting belligerent, threatening Rafe again, threatening me, so I lost it. I pushed her." He shrugged his shoulders. "I thought I was doing my job. That's the long and the short of it. I shouldn't have done it. It was my fault entirely. A tragedy. May died for nothing."

"What about Rafe?" I asked. "Rafe identified the body. Rafe has to take some responsibility."

"He made a mistake." Will tapped at his temple. "He doesn't have much upstairs, Cece. Everybody knows that."

A man whose head was as empty as his desk.

Yes, Will had covered all the bases.

"Who's going to believe what you're saying, Will?"

"Detective Smarinsky is," he said, reaching into his pocket for his cell phone.

"What are you doing?" I asked.

"I'm turning myself in. I committed a crime. I'll take whatever punishment is coming to me."

It was unbelievable. Out of some perverse sense of duty, Will was going to take the fall for Rafe, for all of them. So the truth would never have to come out. So Rafe could go on with his life. So Maren would be safe from the bad guys, if there ever had been any bad guys. So Lisa could keep her house, her ring, her husband, her children.

I didn't understand people at all.

After talking for a few minutes to Smarinsky, Will put his cell phone back in his pocket and shifted the cap on his head. That's when I noticed it was Rafe's lucky cap.

"You're going to jail, Will, for a very long time," I said.

"Speak up, Cece. I can barely hear you."

"You're going to jail, Will," I repeated. "Do you understand that? How does that make you feel?"

He smiled, this time, for real. "Like I'm going home."

That was exactly what Hammett had said.

The sirens were the last thing I remember hearing before I passed out.

CHAPTER
FORTY

That was Friday.

Saturday, I spent in bed.

Sunday, I ate matzo ball soup sent over by Smarinsky's wife.

Monday, production on *Dash!* was shut down permanently.

Tuesday, Roxana was supposed to show up, but didn't.

Wednesday, my speeding ticket arrived in the mail. Two hundred and fifty bucks, but at least my hair looked decent in the picture.

Thursday, the tabloids were full of Will's arrest for second-degree murder. And I got my car back from D.J.'s. Garage. Nate was a virtuoso. Good-bye forever, Hollywood Toyota.

Friday was the day Vincent and Annie filed for sole custody of Alexander. And turned down my $20,000, which I donated to the Oceans Conservancy, in May Madden's name.

Lisa Lapelt called me that day, too, but I haven't called her back. I don't think I will.

Saturday was the day Rafe announced he was going into semiretirement.

Sunday was the big day.

Sunday, I took my first surfing lesson.

I showed up at dawn. There was heavy cloud cover, but that was par for the course. According to KABC-TV, the sun would be blazing by noon. Hog, still wearing his "I Love Soccer Moms" T-shirt, met me in the parking lot where Temescal Canyon meets Pacific Coast Highway, with one of Oscar Nichols's custom boards strapped to the top of his VW van. The thing must've been twelve feet long. Hog said he didn't mean to hurt my feelings, but I was a big girl and its hugeosity (his word, unfortunately apropos) was my only hope.

In the backseat of my car, I slipped out of my sweats and pulled on my new full-body wet suit over my old Dolce and Gabbana bikini. I emerged, hoping for a sort of *Barbarella* effect, but judging by Hog's reaction, I fell a bit short of the mark. I proceeded to slather zinc oxide all over my face, which probably didn't help.

By the time I was ready, maybe a dozen other surfers had joined us in the parking lot. Others were already heading down to the water. The waves looked dark and foreboding, but Hog assured me that Will Rogers State Beach hadn't seen a real wave since the storm of '77, which was before he was even born.

Age, I told myself, is just a number.

Rabbit arrived a couple of minutes later in a blue Impala. He got out, tossed his Taco Bell bag into the trash, took one look at me, and said we had stuff to do first, so I'd better peel down the top of my wet suit unless I wanted to fry like a chimichanga.

Hog doubled over laughing. I told him what I really thought of his T-shirt, which silenced him temporarily. He got his and

Rabbit's boards off the Impala and carried them down to the sand. Rabbit carried mine, proving chivalry was not dead.

Waxing the boards was hard work.

"Rub it on, nose to tail, rail to rail," Rabbit said solemnly. "There's already a base coat down."

The process was time-consuming, but I liked the smell of the wax on my fingers. It reminded me of summer. Rabbit and Hog, who had short boards, were done in about five minutes, and spent the next ten rolling joints in the shadow of the public bathroom, which I pretended not to notice.

Rabbit was a good teacher. He taught me the pop-up, which he claimed was more a matter of resolve than power, and how to hold the board, perpendicular to the body. Then we were ready. It wasn't hard to maneuver through the gentle swells. I could see a bunch of surfers in the distance, already lined up, waiting for something to happen. Once we were waist deep, we hopped up onto our boards and started paddling out. Almost immediately, my arms began to ache.

"How are you doing?" Rabbit asked.

"I'm not cold," I said stoically. I wiped my nose on the shoulder of my wet suit and kept going. We paddled maybe ten more yards. I was exhausted.

"Sit up," Hog instructed.

I did, my legs straddling the board.

"Now wait."

The sea was calm. We were barely moving, barely drifting, just floating in place. My breathing returned to normal. Minutes passed.

I smelled the salt air, listened to the gulls.

Nobody was talking. It was like being in a state of suspended animation.

So calm.

So calm.

Was it calm like this the day Will pushed May Madden to her death? I shut my eyes, tried to put the whole scene out of my mind, but I couldn't. May must have had a moment when she realized what was happening to her. She must have been scared. Had she begged Will to spare her life? Had he hesitated, for even a moment, or had he known what he was going to do to her long before the two of them stood there on that rocky outcropping?

I'd never know the answers to those questions. What I did know was that Will was going to be tried for May's murder, that he was going to be found guilty, that he was going to go to prison.

I think it was the Op who said it. The detective's job is to write stories. We use the bits and pieces we have. Sometimes we write stories that save the people who need saving. Sometimes, no matter how clever the story, those people can't be saved. The best stories, however, are the ones that help punish the guilty. Whether they're true or not is irrelevant.

"Look alive, Cece," Rabbit said. "Anticipate what's coming."

That day at the car wash, I'd anticipated what was coming. That's why I'd brought Rafe's mini-microphone with me, so I could record whatever Lisa Lapelt might let slip. She hadn't admitted anything outright about the blackmail, but she'd wound up implicating all of them—herself, Maren, Rafe, and Will—and with Diana's testimony, it might have been enough.

But in the end, I'd tossed the tape I'd made that day into a Dumpster.

The story needed rewriting. The ending was wrong. The right people didn't get saved.

I don't mean Lisa. I wasn't sure she was worth saving. But she had children who needed her. They were worth saving. Which meant she wasn't worth destroying.

And Rafe?

And Maren?

They were destroyed already.

Rabbit called out my name. A set of waves was coming our way. Quickly, he helped me turn my board around so I was facing the shore. He held it firmly in place as the first wave flowed under us.

"You're going to get this next one, okay? It's coming," Hog said. "This is it! Go! Now!"

Rabbit gave me a serious shove, and as I felt the wave start to carry me along, I pushed myself up with my arms. When the wave began to curl, I jumped into a halfhearted crouch.

"What the fuck is that? Pop the fuck up!" a voice commanded me.

I was scared. I felt it everywhere—in my stomach, in my legs, in my chest. Then I stopped being scared, and that's when it happened. I stood up, catching the wave for a maybe a second, maybe two. Then, just as quickly, the nose of the board was caught by the wave's front end and hitting the point of no return, hurled me into the churning foam. As the water rushed over my head, the roaring sound obliterated any sense of time or place. I covered my head, praying my board wouldn't whack me. I had no sense of where its 144 inches and extremely sharp fin were in relation to my body.

When I surfaced, the board was floating in front of me, well out of the concussion zone.

"Wa-hoo!" Hog yelled, giving me a high five.

Rabbit grinned, then blew his nose into his fingers.

We surfed for the next few hours. I had Rafe Simic to thank for that, but I never saw him again. Our lives had intersected for a time, but that time was over. He lived in Fiji for several years, and when he returned, he became a face on a screen again, a picture in a magazine. Which was exactly as it was supposed to be. Real life didn't suit him.

Afterward, Gambino was waiting for me on the sand. We had a breakfast date.

"How'd she do?" he asked Hog.

"She sucked, like all groms. Maybe a little less."

Rabbit spit out saltwater. "She don't give up easy."

"Out of the mouths of babes," Gambino said.

He helped me out of my wet suit and grabbed a towel out of my bag. "I got a postcard from Caracas, Venezuela, of all places, today," he said, drying off my back.

"Oh, yeah?" I asked, looking over my shoulder.

"Yeah. Turns out we have a friend in common. Someone who says she'll be eternally grateful to you." He turned me around by the thin straps of my bikini. "Her mother, too."

I looked into his eyes, and for the second time that day stopped being scared. "Maybe we can visit them on our honeymoon."

"There has to be a wedding first," he said.

"I've got the dress," I said. "I'm ready."

Hog piped up, "Tonight's gonna be a full moon."

Then he and Rabbit slapped each other on the butt and made those low, growling noises. But I wasn't paying attention. I was already somewhere else, far away, rewriting the ending of my own story.